The Otherling

Heather M. Walker

ISBN 978-1-936556-04-5

Published 2016
Printed by Black Velvet Seductions Publishing
A division of Savage Publications

Visit us at:
www.blackvelvetseductions.com

Acknowledgements

First and foremost, I would like to thank my mother, Linda Walker, for all her help during the time I was writing this book. She was my first ever fan, and encouraged me to complete this book. Thank you for supporting me, and for all the advice you gave me chapter by chapter. Thanks so much to my husband, Billy Watts, for being a wonderful partner, for loving me and believing in me, and giving me the time and space to write. Thank you for being my best friend, my confidant, and for always having my back, especially when it comes to my writing. I thank you for being a wonderful partner and for supporting me every step of the way. To Jennifer Walker, for helping me with the pacing of the story, and for inspiring me to come up with Bubo the owl. Thanks to my sweet daughter, Makaylah, for knowing when it was time to do edits and giving me the time to do them. I know it was hard not to talk or play with me so I could work. You are a good girl and have always been supportive and excited to see me as a published author. To my friend and fellow writer, the tech guru David Schowalter, for helping me with edits and for the endless reformatting you helped me with in the creation of this book. Thank you for sharing your deeply felt, amazingly written poetry in High School, it has always helped to inspire me. To Lisa Gatzen, my first editor, thank you. Your criticism, encouragement, and eye for detail helped my writing become better, and I learned a lot from you in the process. To Laurie Sanders, my wonderful and patient editor from Black Velvet Seductions, I give you my deepest respect and appreciation. Your intense interactions with me to work towards polishing my work and making it blossom into its best form was a lot of fun, even though it was hard work. You've opened up a world within the story as we worked together to make it something deeper, and I have learned so much about editing, revision and story crafting through you. I simply couldn't have made it into what it has become without you. To my friend, Colette Barrett, for never letting me give up, and for believing in my dream of writing this book, and for always cheering me on, thank you! Many thanks to my publisher, Richard Savage, for his vision and passion for my story, and for the help in creating my cover art, and the professional and friendly support with the publication process. I couldn't have done it without you guys!!

For Makaylah

I would also like to dedicate this book to anyone who has been ridiculed, or made to feel lesser than they are, due to bullying. Being torn down by others for your religion, sexuality, race, culture, appearance or for any reason at all, is not okay, and it is not your fault. Don't ever be ashamed of the special, unique person you are, no matter what others say. It takes courage to show your true self while others are trying to put out your light. Never try to please others who try to make you conform to whatever they think you should be. You are the only one in the world who can ever be you, so do it with all your heart, and sing the song only you can sing. Don't let anyone else write your story, because you are special, and you are sacred. Shine on, beautiful souls!

Prologue

Deep in the infernal glow of Hell's belly, the Old Ones began to stir. Called forth out of a dreamless slumber by a growing sense of tension, where they had remained undisturbed for millennia, they awakened. Languidly they spread their scarred, battered wings and stretched their crooked limbs as their ancient eyes began to open. A growing sense of tension and unease began as a subtle stirring in the air and rose until it permeated Hell, down to the chambers in which they had slept undisturbed for millennia. Anger at being disturbed rose like bile in their throats. Ancient mouths filled with rows of hooked fangs yawned and snarled. Yet the Wise Ones knew, it had been no creature of Hell that had summoned them, no foolish mortal in the land of the Above that had recited age old incantations of beckoning. Things in the land of the Above were changing, shifting the balance of Good and Evil towards the powers of the Light. Narrowing newly opened eyes, the daemons concentrated and followed the signature of energy to its source in the world of mortals. The hideous ones smelled this change with flared nostrils, letting it fill their rotten lungs until it burst forth into their minds with a certain knowing.

A woman, innocent and naive, young and beautiful, unaware of the part she would play in the war to come. She would be easy enough prey, as the pure ones always were. There was no true need to worry; what match would she be for beings such as they?

She was enough of a threat to have awakened them, the oldest beings of diabolical renown, granted reprieve from the sufferings and tedious happenings of Hell. How this could be was unknown, and caused a commotion of growls as the Old Ones ascended from their sulfurous tombs. With growing blood lust, the need to destroy and devour filled them with powerful, hateful energy, filling their bones and sinews with the raw need to spill blood and ravage souls.

Having been newly born from the encrusted pits of Hell, they rose to their full heights, and shook off the filth in which they had slept for millennia. The sense of urgency washed over them, filling them with the need to act now before the powers of Good became absolute.

A figure stood among them, guiding them in the awakening. His long red hair spilled past his shoulders in a wave of crimson, flowing out around him as though it were dancing in some unseen tide of water. His wings were huge and mighty, far larger and more magnificent than any of the beings which stood before him.

"Rise my children," He spoke, his eyes on fire, his voice both beautiful and terrible. "Your time to awaken has come. In the land of the Above, she grows in her powers, she can no longer be ignored. Destroy her and the one who will protect her, in any manner which you deem fit. For if you do not, the powers of the Darkness will lose its foothold on the mortal world, perhaps irrevocably. Arise and go forth, unleash your fury!"

With war cries, screams and growls they answered him, heads thrown back on terrible necks, great, clawed hands beating on scaled and rotted chests. One by one they opened the great expanses of their leathery wings, ready to burst forth from Hell and contaminate the world of the Above.

Smiling, the figure stood proudly in the chamber of Hell which had held the oldest, most monstrous of his children.

It was time for war.

Chapter One

Catharsis, The journal of Professor Sebastian James Bainbridge

Friday, August 5th

Today is the kind of day that slowly eats me alive. One of those where irritations gnaw at my nerves like parasites, with vicious smiles and blinking, glittering eyes that peer straight into my soul and see every sin I have ever committed. The kind of day where I am once again reminded of the circle of nothingness I tread in, living the same day over and over without respite, without change, without fail. On days like this, I get stuck in my own head, trapped in the morbidity that breeds there, like some stinking, rotting macabre thing, repulsive and yet endlessly fascinating. Thoughts spin and twirl and dance in the shadows of my consciousness, flitting about as if trying to dart out of my direct line of sight, teasing me with flailing limbs and gnashing teeth that sit in mouths speaking words I can't even begin to fathom. Thoughts that lure me in, daring me to dance with them, to become lost in their world and partake of things which would stain me inextricably, should I be so haphazard in my judgment. I have seen where these dances lead; to the corners of my sanity. These morbid, hateful thoughts lick the gashes inflicted by this morose mental ballet, and then reopen the lips of my wounds, for no other reason than to see the blood run again.

Today, I am reminded again that I am not like others and never will be. Not that I would want to be so dense, so lost in my own flesh that I could never see the spirit and sparks of divinity, both dark and light, which dwell within. Yet, some days I wish I did not know such things; that I was not privy to my own past and the things I've learned, most by outright suffering. There are days when I wish I could be bathed clean of the darkness that hides inside me, allowing me to forget the things I've done, things I've been forced to do, before finally walking away. No, that's not entirely correct. I can't walk away from this thing, any more than I could outrun my own shadow. It is part of me, though I hide it well. Not that I have to hide the darkness from these silly, flesh beasts that call themselves human. They tend to reason away what they don't understand, as if logic alone, however unlikely, is some sort of sacred balm to the inexplicable. I could make my eyes burn in their sockets and melt down my cheeks, and they would shake their heads and clear their throats nervously and say, "It's the heat you know; what I saw simply cannot be." Turning back to me they would smile uncertainly, silently begging me to agree with them, and then that would be that, the whole thing never to be thought of again. How easy, how simple, to think in such a way. Self-delusion, I suppose, is preferable to opening the mind and pontificating upon such things.

I digress. Suffice to say it was one of those days I am not fond of, when the dark, inky questions that reside in my secret places rear themselves for contemplation. I am not given to deep wells of emotion, but the anger that ignited in my chest today was slow to burn out and haunted me quite thoroughly. Not that anyone noticed and not that I was about to share this fact. What would be the point? Those that don't already outright fear me, regard me as something of an anomaly anyway, so why give them more fodder for gossip and self-indulgent, meaningless ruminations? That I even walk among them is something I've been questioning, more and more, as of late. I am not ready to get into that, however; not just yet.

I am not altogether certain why I am even penning this, other than for some form of catharsis to exercise this demon of anger burning in me. I have kept this inside me for far too long. Everyone, even those like me (and I am not the only one, oh no, not by far!), need some form of release, and so here I am, black and gold Waterman pen pressed to parchment, trying to get the ghosts out of my head.

My name is Professor Sebastian James Bainbridge. At least it has been my name for long enough that it doesn't sound foreign to me any longer. As to my name before that, well, we'll get to that, won't we?

I work at the University of Doltree, Georgia, teaching World Religions and philosophical musings to undergraduate students who, more often than not, are wayward souls that don't seem to care about or understand anything I am trying to teach them. It is far more likely that they're more concerned with sex, parties, and other irrelevant drivel that, ten years from now, won't matter one iota. Ah, youth. Perhaps I only envy them, yes? I wonder what it's like to be so carefree; to just simply not know. Sometimes I want to shake them; to burn sense into them with the sheer force of my will alone. It has been many years since I have had a remarkable pupil. Someone with the courage to question me, to argue some sort of point or another, or to care, even remotely about the polytheistic principals of Hinduism or the Five Pillars of Islam. I am resigned to this fact, realizing that most students see my course as some form of extracurricular escape and not something to be taken seriously.

Though previously I bemoaned my life's redundancy, I did not mean my teachings and my classroom. I was speaking more of the way I live my life among these…people. Trying to be like them, or at least convince them (or myself) that I am more like them. It is tiring. I do find comfort in my classroom, in the feel and smell of ink on old pages, of words written long ago from the voices of men and women that were the finest minds of their time, of any time. I find peace in my routine, in the padded arms of knowledge, in the questions of the soul, in ancient rites and prayers and stories. It is the one thing I do enjoy, despite the dewy eyed uncaring youths.

I did not expect the administration to upend my peaceful routine. Beginning next week, when classes start for the year once more, I will no longer be teaching my classes alone. I am to have a young woman as an assistant, and a barely post pubescent one at that! An "expert in occultism", I am told. Mrs. Tanner, the Chancellor, put it this way: "Your students are not engaged in your teaching, Sebastian, and attendance and enrollment are suffering. This is an attempt to garner more interest in the subject, and for your class." I fought the urge to curse the brown wiry hair off of her head right then; to grab the silly rainbow glasses she wore on the thin perch of her nose and toss them across the room, for no other reason than to see the shock on her face, and to release the anger that had kindled itself in my chest, the same anger that, like a phantom, had been clinging to me tenaciously throughout the day. Instead, I composed myself and folded my hands in my lap.

"I assure you, I am more than capable of introducing occultism into the curriculum," I told her, in a way I hoped was both calm and convincing. "There is no need to force upon me another person who will most likely end up in my way. It would be unfair to this new teacher, to put him in such a position."

There was a brief twinkle in Mrs. Tanner's eyes, then, "You mean to put her in such a position." She paused to let this sink in before she continued. "I am afraid it has already been done, Sebastian. She starts next week. Her name is Annaleah Grace, and she will be here tomorrow to meet you and take a tour of her new campus. I expect you to be gracious."

I closed my mouth at this. Gracious indeed! "Of course, Mrs. Tanner," I said. What else could I have said? The outrage was there, like a hot coal, but I refused to lose my dignity. It seemed I had little choice in the matter, so what would be the point of showing her the enormity of my displeasure? I am not in the habit of making myself into an ass.

I'm glad I that I took up my pen. Writing seems to have calmed my nerves considerably, though I'm no happier with the situation. Perhaps, going forward, it would suit me to keep this journal of sorts, lest I uncharacteristically, in my infernal fury, hex the tongue out of someone's mouth.

I wonder about this Annaleah Grace. I was told she is young, a mere baby of twenty-three. What could she know? How could she possibly add anything of use or interest to my classes that I myself could not, were I given a chance? Ah, such speculation is futile. There is nothing to be done about it now. Tomorrow I meet her.

I am not entirely sure that I will not give her a hard time.

~SJB

Chapter Two

The Untethering

Annaleah drifted comfortably in the space between consciousness and sleep, her mind gently shifting from the significance of tomorrow's meeting to more fanciful, whimsical things. Muted lights flickered beneath her lids, forming images that flowed from one pattern into another, a kaleidoscope of movement and color.

As her breathing slowed and deepened, she felt her focus become more internalized. Leaving the sensations of her body behind, ethereal pictures danced before her, pulling her further into unconsciousness. As the world of dreams began to take shape, she felt a peculiar awareness that she was weightless, as if she were floating through the ether towards whatever land her dreams would deliver her to. It was a calm, peaceful experience, one she let herself be transported into without effort or concern. She was no stranger to meditation, and that was what this felt the most like to her; a wonderful, serene meditation where a profound order was reached. Chaos seemed like a distant notion, discord like a rumor yet to be proven. Here, in this perfect microcosm of serenity, her impression of weightlessness increased. It deepened into a feeling of floating, an untethering from all that was not incorporeal. It felt like being released, a freedom which brought a budding elation.

The jubilation was something she fully embraced, wanting more. Seldom had she felt so liberated, so in the moment, so close to something unfathomable and paradisiacal.

Then, something cool, hard and flat pressed against her cheek. It was sudden and unexpected, and it startled her into opening her eyes. Confusion gave way to fear, as she tried to understand what was going on. Was she was pressed against...the ceiling? How could that be? She wanted to turn over to see if it was true, and as the thought was formed, she found herself turning over, without conscious effort.

She looked down and there she lay on the bed below, her long blonde hair pooled out over her azure pillow. Her creamy skin looked supple and spectral as the moonlight filtered in from the open curtains. Her lips were parted slightly as she slept, her expression placid. Emanating from her midriff was a shining silver cord, which snaked its way upwards to her astral form, connecting them both together.

As she gazed down at her sleeping form, something to her left caught her eye. A furtive movement from the shadows revealed a large hulking figure that was quick and somehow sinister, peeling itself from the darkness and carrying within it the promise of unfathomable wickedness.

Annaleah watched in terror as the monstrous form moved to hunch beside her. Curiously unable to look away, she took in the abhorrent shape that was darker than the blackest shadow she had ever seen. A strange mix of horror, wonder and confusion raged within her; never had she seen anything like this in all her years of exploring occultism. She had read of shadow people and evil creatures, but this was her first time seeing what she had for so long researched. It looked as if it were made from congealed oil, undulating within itself. Its head and shoulders were humanoid, but its arms were too long for its body, thin, spindly and insectile, terminating in barbs. These it waved over her, performing strange movements over her sleeping form. A chittering sound came from it, as if it were speaking a bizarre incantation in the language of some terrible, insect God.

Annaleah tried to scream, but no sound came. Now instead of a wonderful, weightless feeling, she was paralyzed with fear, unable to move or cry out. As if hearing her unuttered wail, the creature turned its awful head and fixed its gaze on her where she floated against the ceiling. It scrutinized her with glowing scarlet eyes, which emitted a foul light enough for her to see the horror that was its mouth. Jutting out from each side of its open jaws were what appeared to be mandibles, each one spread out wide and wavering, the sickening sound of chittering coming out of it louder and stronger, building upon itself like some repugnant prayer to a God she couldn't even begin to contemplate. Terror pierced her, pinning her motionless to the spot in which she hovered.

"Oh Goddess, please let me wake up!" Annaleah pleaded in her mind, unable to say the words aloud. Still the creature chittered, now ceasing its strange movements over her body. As the sound intensified it stood up, reaching a long arm upward. Its blood red eyes shone with ferocity, malice thickening the air between them.

Annaleah was certain she was about to be skewered, panic now a super nova inside her. "WAKE UP!!" She pleaded with herself, "Oh please wake up!"

Suddenly, she was falling. The sensation of weightlessness was over all at once as she plummeted back towards herself. To feel her soul re-enter her body was immediate and jarring. It stole the breath from her and made her heart gallop. Instantly she sat bolt upright in bed, winded, gasping for the breath her soul's entry had stolen from her.

She instantly looked to the spot where the creature had stood, and was only faintly relieved to see nothing there. She scanned the room for the presence, and even though she saw nothing, she could still feel it in the room with her. She was bathed in a sheen of sticky sweat, still too stunned to scream. Exhausted, she crumpled onto the bed, too spent to cry.

She had an idea as to what the creature must be, something that clawed its way from the depths of Hell, be it a demon, a shadow person, or a malevolent thought form someone had conjured to terrify her. Why was it here, she wondered, and why now?

Annaleah was a white witch, one who did no harm to others, believing in the law of three; what you send out into the world, weather it is good or bad, will return to you threefold. She had always done her best to be polite and to offend no one. What had she done to attract such a malicious creature to her? Whatever the reason it had visited her, she knew one thing. It had meant to harm her.

Gathering whatever modicum of strength she had left, she lifted the pentacle which hung on a silver necklace against her chest. Squeezing it in her hand, she said, "Mother, Maiden and Crone, come to my side and bathe me in your light, protect me from that which seeks my harm and from all forms of darkness and negativity. Give me strength to repel that which is formed in shadows, and never leave my side. As I will it, so mote it be."

***

From the darkness of the shadows, where the moonlight failed to fall, it hid, listening. It saw the astral light of protection fall upon Annaleah, and enraged, turned to go back to where it had come from.

Through gnarled teeth and dripping mandibles it wailed, though Annaleah, now returned to her body and no longer in astral form, could no longer see nor hear it. So close, it had been, to ripping out the silver cord and being rid of her forever.

Now the Light had come, and was ever growing around his prey. Should he dare to stay longer, it would grow bright enough to sear his etheric form, perhaps even wounding him permanently. This little human was powerfully protected.

In one last act of hatred and defiance, it stretched over her praying form. Careful not to touch the light of protection surrounding her, it screamed and shook with the force and effort of its cry.

Let her have tonight. They would come for her soon enough.

Chapter Three

The Meeting

At nine-thirty the next morning, still bleary eyed and weary from her nightmare, Annaleah found herself outside the office of Chancellor Gladys Tanner. Her hand paused at the door, about to knock, when she heard voices coming from inside. Her heart began beating quickly in her chest, was she late? She turned, glanced at the clock behind her, and noted she was exactly on time. She was about to knock again, when she heard her name mentioned from behind the door. Curious, she let her hand drop and leaned closer to hear what was being said about her.

"I understand your initial skepticism, Sebastian," she heard a woman say, "but Ms. Grace has an exceptional resume. She graduated at the top of her class in High School at only sixteen and sailed through her college courses. She has an uncanny grasp of world religions, which I think you might actually find refreshing. I know you're used to teaching classes by yourself, but this is a move made by the faculty in an effort to revive a course we feel is gaining fewer and fewer students."

Next she heard a man's voice, low and calm, but so deep, dark and smooth that she was instantly reminded of black velvet. "In that case, Chancellor Tanner," Annaleah heard him say, "it would be an honor to have her as an assistant. I am concerned, however, that being so young, the students will not take her seriously and while she may know some of the more recent developments in the subject, I find it difficult to believe she will be well versed in the more arcane areas."

Something about his voice made Annaleah nervous, and strangely, a little excited. Perhaps it was the masked calm she perceived hidden in it or maybe it was the slight accent, which she couldn't place. In any case, hearing him speak caused a physical reaction, not entirely unpleasant, within her. She felt the blood coursing harder in her veins, heard it rushing in her ears as her heart beat faster. This time when she raised her fist to knock, her hand met with the door, and the three solid knocks were a bit harder and louder than she had intended.

As she heard someone approaching to answer, Annaleah found herself hoping that it would be the Chancellor that opened the door. She was anxious to see her friendly eyes peering out from behind those colorful glasses. She had already been nervous, but hearing that voice had done something to pique her nerves. She needed a kind pair of eyes to reassure her. While it would only take a moment to gather herself together, it was a moment she was in great need of.

"Ah, Ms. Grace, welcome, right on time I see," Chancellor Tanner said, smiling at her after opening the door. She stood a good head and shoulders taller than Annaleah, who was used to everyone being somewhat taller than her petite five-foot form.

Relieved, Annaleah took a deep, fortifying breath and steadied herself. "Please, call me Annaleah. It is nice to see you again Chancellor Tanner." The taller, older woman held the door open, her face wearing a genuine expression of warmth.

"Likewise, Annaleah. Please do come in. Professor Bainbridge and I were just enjoying a bit of coffee, would you like some?" She gestured to a dark wooden coffee table set with silver dishes. Annaleah's eyes fell on the antique style coffee urn and she smiled. She loved coffee. Her nerves begin to settle and she did her best to summon a strong, confident attitude.

A previously seated man rose from a crimson colored wingback chair, with such an effortless and fluid movement that at first Annaleah was not certain what she was seeing. He was dressed almost entirely in black, from the deep polish of his shoes, to his pitch black suit and shirt. He wore a red kerchief and tie, the same color as the chair he had risen from, but the splash of crimson only seemed to make his clothing even darker. He was tall and thin, but his clothes were well tailored and she could tell that he kept his physique in top form. His pale face was angular in a way that suggested aristocratic lineage, his cheekbones sharp and pronounced below smoldering brown eyes, so dark they were almost black. His nose was on the longish side, thin and slightly hooked at the end, but in such a way that it only added to his air of nobility. He wore his ebony hair long, straight and parted in the middle. It fell to just below his shoulders, where it seemed to lose itself in the fabric of his dark suit. When their eyes met, it affected Annaleah in such a way that she almost gasped audibly. He was incredibly handsome, to the point where it almost hurt to look at him. Not heeding her intuition to look away, Annaleah allowed herself a long moment to drink him in, ignoring the threat that sang to her, warning her that he might be dangerous.

"Annaleah Grace, meet your fellow teacher of World Religions, the mystical arts and philosophy, Professor Sebastian Bainbridge." Chancellor Tanner's voice had an amused, light lilt to it as she stood back and looked from one to the other.

Professor Bainbridge was on his feet and extending his hand to her, before Annaleah was aware that he had moved. She took his hand in hers, and as her flesh met his, she felt as though, for a moment, time had slowed down. He had, without a doubt, the softest hand she had ever felt. His eyes seemed to stare straight into her, and where she wanted to find respect and acceptance as a fellow teacher, she found instead a spark of smoldering intensity, followed by a cold and deep calculation as if he were trying to taste her essence and know every secret of her soul. It felt as if things stood out of time as his deep black eyes met and searched hers. He stood wordlessly grasping her hand in his own for what could not have been more than a couple of seconds, but it felt as if when his hand met hers, something extraordinary had happened. It made the air charged with electricity almost too thick to draw into her lungs, and when he finally spoke, Annaleah let the air rush out of her in a heavy sigh.

"It is my pleasure to meet you, Ms. Grace," Professor Bainbridge said in his exotic voice, his eyes still not leaving Annaleah's. Finally, he released her hand, and smiled what seemed a dangerous smile. She fought for composure, still not sure what had just happened, or what was still happening now.

There had been many times in Annaleah's life that she had been cornered and bullied into feeling inferior to others. Her school years had not been kind to her. She was so academically advanced, many of her peers saw her as a quirky, strange anomaly. She was used to the jeers, the cruel comments and to being bullied, even by some of the teachers. It also hadn't helped that she was an emotional person, prone to writing poetry and fantasizing. Her grade school years had been the most painful, she'd been innocent and wanted only to fit in and to play with the other children. She'd spent many days alone and many more in tears, either hiding in the girl's bathroom, in the library, or in the woods behind the school, certain she was different in only the worst of ways.

She had always been a small person, but she had been much smaller than her peers when she was in elementary school. An especially cruel child by the name of Shandy had been her main tormentor. Shandy had been a big girl, hefty and robust for her age. None of the other children had wanted much to do with her either, but Annaleah had always been her main target. On the days she hadn't been able to elude Shandy, she had often come home with small cuts and bruises from Shandy.

Being picked on for being little was only the beginning of her misery. For as long as she could remember, she had worn a small silver pentacle that had once belonged to her mother around her neck. The pendant provided her with a source of comfort and protection.

"What is this piece of junk?" Shandy had asked her one day, grabbing the sacred piece of jewelry tightly enough for Annaleah to fear she would break it.

"It's nothing, just a necklace," Annaleah had answered, hoping to escape without damage to her pentacle.

"Looks like one of those Hoodoo necklaces to me. Is that what you are, some kind of devil worshiping Hoodoo girl?"

A small group had gathered, knowing that if Shandy was involved, there was a good chance a fight would ensue.

"No, it's not like that. I know there is evil in the world, but in my religion I don't think of it as a devil like most people do."

Shandy had let her necklace go, and even though she had pushed Annaleah after releasing it, Annaleah let out a huge sigh of relief that her pentacle had made it out of the skirmish intact.

"So you don't believe in the devil, what, you think you're above believing in him? Do you think he can't hurt you if you wear that crap around your neck?" Shandy had puffed herself up, towering over her, flexing her arms as if she was about to throw a punch.

Annaleah had said nothing, breaking eye contact to lower her head, hoping nothing more would come of the confrontation.

"Answer me devil girl!"

When Annaleah still remained silent, Shandy began the taunt that would follow her throughout grade school, middle school, High School and even into college.

"Devil girl. Devil girl!" Shandy called out, waving her arms, playing to the crowd. The response was immediate, and the children who stood around began to close in, chanting in a sing-song manner.

"Devil girl, devil girl, devil girl!!"

"Stop it! Please, stop it!" Annaleah cried.

"What are you going to do about it devil girl?" Shandy asked, a wild look in her eyes.

"It's not like you're going to throw a punch at me. You aren't going to do anything, because all you are is a scaredy cat devil girl."

The chants got louder, the sneers on the faces of the other children now seemed to press in harder against Annaleah, making them appear as if they were swaying before her.

Unable to stand any more, Annaleah had turned and run, dropping her books in her haste to be away from the jeers of the other children.

"Run devil girl, run!" Shandy had yelled after her.

"Go home and have Mommy kiss you and make you feel better. Little cry baby devil girl!"

High School had been no better, the jeers and taunts had graduated into deeper cruelties, and harsher words. One time someone had put a dead crow hanging by a noose in her locker, with a note tied to the rope saying, "Cursed and killed by the devil girl."

It wasn't the act of someone trying to torment her that had disturbed her the most. It was the fact that someone had murdered an innocent animal just to make some kind of hideous point. She had untied the bird from the noose, trying her best not to cry lest the one who had committed the heinous act see her and know that what they had done had crushed her.

She had wrapped the bird up in a scarf and placed it in her backpack, intending to give it a proper burial when she got home. Someone had seen her though, and rumors had spread that she had taken the bird home to try to bring it back to life. Annaleah was accustomed to these things by now, and though they still hurt her, she did her best to keep to herself and not show others what effect it had on her.

She had found her strength though, with the help of her best friend, Seth, whom she had met in the fifth grade after one particularly bad run in with Shandy. This time it had come to physical blows, and Annaleah had sat on the front steps of the school hugging herself and crying, letting the blood from her cut eye flow freely down her face, to mingle with her tears.

Handing her a tissue to stop the blood flow, Seth had sat next to her and said the first of his many kind words to her.

"You know she's picking on you because she's jealous of you. You're smart and kind and she wishes she could be too, but she doesn't know how."

Not used to such kindness, Annaleah's tears had flowed even stronger. Moved that someone had finally showed her a modicum of compassion, she had thrown her arms around him and wept against him as he held her, as if he had always been her best friend.

As the years passed, he had taught her about self-respect, the gift of being unique, and the importance of being true to one's self no matter what others might think. She summoned Seth's gentle, blue eyed face in her mind for some much needed support, drawing strength in knowing he was sending positive energies her way for this meeting. Chancellor Tanner had thoughtfully told her prior to this meeting that Professor Bainbridge was not the most amiable of people, and would not take kindly to her being his assistant.

"He won't bite you by any stretch," she had said, "but he might do his best to make you feel uncomfortable. He has been set in his routine for quite a few years, and though we, the staff of this University, feel it is in everyone's best interest to have you on board with us, I doubt Professor Bainbridge will see it that way."

She had been warned. Going to her center for a brief second, Annaleah straightened up and tilted her chin upwards, purposely looking Sebastian in the eye. She smiled, doing her best to mirror the intense look he had bestowed upon her just moments ago. She might have been intimidated, but to Hell with letting him know that.

"The pleasure of our meeting is mine, Professor Bainbridge, and please, call me Annaleah," she said, her normally light voice a bit sturdier for emphasis. She saw the corner of his mouth lift ever so slightly, and his eyes twinkled for just a moment, as if he was amused.

"I'm aware my age is an issue for you," Annaleah continued, " but I promise you, it won't be an issue in regards to my intellectual abilities or in my ability to teach this class. I'm not here to take over, and I won't attempt to teach your subjects, I know you're much more skilled there than I am. I'm just here to introduce occultism, mysticism and superstitions found throughout the world. I hope that we can work together to teach the class to benefit the students." She held her gaze meeting Sebastian's, strength exuding from her heart, even if she was trembling on the inside.

"By all means, Ms.... excuse me, Annaleah," Sebastian said, all but purring at her in what seemed to be a mocking way. "I am sure we will be able to come to an agreement as to our teaching styles and how to best proceed with this arrangement. I have already finalized my curriculum for the first semester, but I will find a way to include your areas of expertise."

Chancellor Tanner cleared her throat. "Well then," she spoke, her voice light, "Annaleah and Sebastian, I will see you both on Monday on the first day of school. I hope both of you enjoy your weekend."

Chapter Four

Ruminations

Saturday, August 6th

Annaleah's hiding something. It's driving me mad that I can't immediately see into her deception; knowing things of this manner is something which I pride myself in, even if I don't make it widely known. It's in their micro expressions, in the temperature of their skin, in the way they hold themselves. Her secret however, eludes me. It was more like something I could sense in her aura, some great wall built up to protect something important. But what? It's put me on guard against her, despite her overall essence of innocence. I'm not used to putting my guard up against anyone; I am rather used to it being the other way around.

I don't trust her, but she intrigues me. How is it that she can maintain a sense of wide-eyed wonder and innocence, and yet exude something powerfully secret, the likes of which even I cannot penetrate? She is a nervous little creature, too. She walked into Gladys's office as if she had all the confidence in the world. Does she think I failed to see how she trembled when she looked at me, just like all the others of her sort, no doubt judging me on first sight with no cause yet for doing so? Did she think I missed the catch of breath in her throat, or how her body shook when she attempted to speak to me as an equal? Would she think someone such as myself unable to find out her secret?

It also disturbs me enormously that I was caught off guard by her beauty. What do I care of the ephemeral allure of any human, no matter how great that beauty might be? I'm not of their kind, and it's never been a problem for me to be distracted by something so petty and unimportant. Still, her emerald green eyes flash across my mind, and I am left wondering if there is something wrong with me. How can I let myself be beguiled so easily? It makes me trust her even less.

I'm still shocked at Chancellor Tanner's decision to add her to my class, especially without asking me or even warning me that it was a possibility. Perhaps this is an indirect means to usurp me?

They respect me, they fear me, and yes, they judge me. They assume they know me, who and what I am. That they come to false conclusions and judgment towards me, infuriates me! I suffer their glances, I feel the weight of their disdain, and then they wonder why I won't suffer their company. Fools. It sometimes angers me to the point of contempt, then I find relief in imagining terrible fates upon them.

Alas, I am more civilized than they give me credit for. I have already suffered for my indignities back when I was…younger. I won't make the same mistakes again. But this anger, it flares in my soul and will not let my mind know peace, nor quiet. Do they not know the authority of this subject that I possess? Can they not fathom in their tiny minds just how extensive my knowledge might be? Don't they realize that, if the self-entitled, little bratty students could sit still for a moment and listen to what I teach, that they might learn enough to pass the course?

I cannot imagine such a life as theirs; to have all the things they need handed to them without striving for it. If they would pay attention for just a moment, they might actually find this learning pleasurable. Otherwise, what is the point of learning, truly, if it does not illuminate your spirit?

To think that my teaching is causing a decrease in students passing my class, that it's somehow my doing, is unforgivable. If these flesh beasts had just a tiny inkling of what they are truly dealing with! I'm smarter than to entertain the idea of enlightening them, but that I should suffer for a mistake I have not made, is an affront to all that I am. They ought to thank me for my distinguished civility! Instead, they insult me with a child, to teach that which I know better than they could ever hope to understand.

If this is a test of some sort, then I will pass. I resent it with every fiber of my existence, but I shall suffer it. I have suffered far worse, for far longer. It is true that suffering can add sheen to your soul, even if the only one to see it is yourself. Ha! If the other faculty and students saw the sheen I possess, they would die of shock. No one knows of it but me, and it will remain that way, as it always has.

As for Annaleah, I will not tear into her as I had initially wanted. Her innocence and her secret interest me. At least she is a respite from the intolerable monotony my life has become.

~SB~

Chapter Five

Courage

"So," asked Seth from across the diner's shabby little table, "was he as terrible as the Chancellor said he'd be?"

Annaleah shifted in her seat and took a menu from beside the napkin holder. "I don't know about terrible, but he certainly is intimidating. There's something...." Annaleah paused, searching for the right word, and shook her head as it eluded her. An image of his handsome face flickered across mind, and she felt herself blush. Even as cold as he had seemed to be, aloof and intimidating, every so often her mind would drift to him, thinking of the plush velvet of his lips, or the deep inky depths of his dark eyes.

Seth smiled and cocked his head slightly, looking at her as though he sensed the inner workings of her mind, but he said nothing.

"There's something different about him." Annaleah continued. I can't put my finger on it. I did hear them talking outside the door before I got there, and I know he's far from pleased with having me teach with him." She sighed, regarding the menu without interest. Laying it aside, she rubbed at her eyes wearily.

"You look more tired than usual," Seth told her. "You okay?"

Annaleah nodded slowly, "Yes, I'm alright. I wanted to tell you though, I had a nightmare last night. I just hope it isn't the start of another pattern."

Annaleah thought she saw a strange light pass through Seth's eyes, a flicker of intense blue that was over as quickly as it had come. She blinked in confusion, not sure if what she had seen was real, or if it was a product of her sleepy, over worked mind.

"What kind of nightmare?" he asked her, his voice heavy with concern.

"Well, not a very pleasant one, that's for sure." She said, trying to think of how to describe the creature from last night, then deciding against it. "Let's not worry over it for now, though. I'm sure it was an isolated incident. I'm more worried now about how I am going to handle my new job." Annaleah grabbed the salt shaker and began to turn it this way and that, fiddling absent mindedly.

"I need this, Seth," she said, looking at the salt shaker. "With Uncle John's hours being cut and his ill health, I need to help out at home as much as I can. I owe him so much."

Seth took her hand gently. "You aren't going to let your uncle down, no matter what you do," he said with compassion. "Don't let this Bainbridge dude get you down. You have excellent credentials and he should be honored to have you teach beside him." Seth leaned over and placed his hand over hers. Annaleah set the salt shaker in its place on the table and grabbed both of his hands with hers.

"You're smart, educated and beautiful," Seth continued, "What man wouldn't want that?"

Annaleah smiled at her friend, and squeezed his hand. "You always know what to say, don't you, Seth? The truth is, I think he feels like I am trying to pirate his class from him. That's a bad place for us to start." Annaleah looked towards the window and sighed, her eyes sheening over.

"I don't want the students to see contention between us," she said quietly. "It might disrupt their learning."

Seth lifted a blonde eyebrow at her. "Disrupt their learning? You're such a saint, never thinking of yourself and always putting other's needs before your own." Annaleah turned to him, smiling. His teasing was all in good fun, and it cheered her up instantly. She saw the glint in his eye and wry smile, and couldn't help but smile with him.

He withdrew his hands from hers and placed both of his hands together, pointing his blue eyes up at the ceiling, as if in prayer. "Saint Annaleah of Doltree Georgia, we are blessed this day by your presence." He laughed his melodic laugh, and taking his straw off the table, he opened the end of it, placed it to his mouth and blew the wrapper across the table at her. With a mock look of hurt surprise, she feigned a wound where it had hit her on the shoulder.

"Medic! Medic! I am wounded and in need of medical care!" They were still giggling when the waitress arrived to take their order.

"So, why don't you look this guy up? He stays at an apartment on the university campus, right?" Seth's eyes suddenly went more serious, his expression showing concern for her situation.

"I bet Chancellor Tanner would tell you how to find him," he continued, "Set up a meeting and try to get on the same page before you have your first class together, which is what, tomorrow? Make peace with him. Heck, I'll even go with you if you want."

Annaleah tilted her head slightly, thinking about Seth's suggestion.

"That's not a bad idea, Seth. I sure could use your support. The Professor is quite an intimidating man."

"Well, that settles it then," Seth said, perking up at the idea, "I'm coming with you."

Still in deep thought, Annaleah paused, trying to decide what to do. Should she even do this at all?

After a few more seconds of deep thought, Annaleah looked Seth in the eye, trying to convince herself this was a good idea, one that empowered her and would show the Professor she was stronger than he thought. Perhaps he would even come to see her as his equal, though she knew that was a long shot.

Images of the professor returned to her mind, the sheen of his black hair, the well-defined lines of his cheekbones. She forcefully pushed these thoughts away, though she couldn't deny that seeing his handsome face would be nice, no matter how bitter and reserved he was.

With a deep sigh she said, "I'm still not sure though." She looked sheepishly at Seth, feeling bad about changing her mind on him. "If you came he might see me as intimidated by him enough to bring someone for support."

Annaleah took the straw wrapper and began to fold it as she spoke. "I am intimidated, but I don't want him to know that I am. I want to try to find a place of respect from him, and I'm not sure he would respect me as much if I took you with me."

She gave him a look of regret. "As much as I would love for you to come with me, I think I need to go by myself."

Seth tilted his head and smiled at her, and she knew he understood. She let out a deep sigh of relief, and a feeling of warmth towards him washed over her. For a moment she let gratitude warm her heart, thankful that she had such a good person for a best friend.

"No worries though. I'll let you know how it goes."

"Please do. If he is mean to you, I might just have to rough him up,"

He said, his eyes sparkling merrily.

"My hero," Annaleah said, batting her eyelashes at him playfully. "Actually, I think I'll go see him right now."

Seth looked genuinely surprised. "Wow. Right this very minute? Shouldn't you at least eat your lunch first?"

"I'm sorry Seth. I know it's rude of me to leave you to eat alone, do you mind?

"Nah, you know me," he said, "I'm good. Sometimes it's peaceful to eat alone, to be left to delve into one's own thoughts." He reached over and patted her hand reassuringly. "Besides, I know how important this is to you. I'm serious about roughing him up though."

Annaleah rose to her feet and kissed Seth on the cheek.

"Thank you, Seth, I'll make this up to you."

She took the bill to the counter, and after paying she returned to their booth and placed a few dollars on the table.

"I paid the bill, and that's the tip." She flashed him a big smile, still feeling guilty about ditching him. "I feel really bad for leaving you. I hate to ask this of you, but can you bring my food to my house for me later? I think I'd look weird bringing a doggy bag to the meeting. I'm also afraid that if I don't do this now, I won't ever do it."

"Not a problem." He replied, flashing her a winning smile. "Thanks for paying the bill sweetie." He said, beaming at her as if he was proud of her strength.

"You're very welcome. See you later, Seth."

"See you later, Saint Annaleah," Seth said teasingly.

Annaleah's heartbeat quickened as she left the diner. Was she really going to do this? What if he was busy and she interrupted him? Would he dislike her even more? How was she even going to find him?

As Annaleah continued on toward the university, she took a deep breath to steady her nerves. She reminded herself of her credentials how hard she had worked to get where she was now. Uncle John's kind face came to her mind's eye, calming her instantly. He had been her father figure for as long as she could remember. Her real father had left her mother before she was even born, so she had no memory of him at all. Her mother had been killed in a head on collision when she was four. Uncle John had been babysitting her that terrible night, and in a sense, he had never stopped. Though she didn't remember much of her mother, other than a sense of loving her and being deeply loved, she had many of her mother's personal items, which Uncle John had saved for her.

He often told her tales about her mother, which always lifted her heart and made her feel closer to her through Uncles John's shared memories. He would never talk about her father, though. No matter how hard she pressed, her Uncle's resolve was always the same; refusal. His green eyes would harden behind his wire rim glasses, and his body would stiffen. "I am sorry child, but I will not speak of your father." So she had invented stories for herself; that he was a mobster running from the law, and had to abandon his family in order to assure their safety. Sometimes, he was a traveling poet who had wanderlust in his blood and could not help but answer the call of the road that beat in his heart. Other times, when the sadness sunk in, he was a just a no-good, cruel, hateful man who ran away from his family for no good reason at all. None of these situations, or any of the others she had invented, filled the hole in her heart that her father had left. Sometimes, she would see an older man on the street and wonder, "Is that you? Are you my father?" She had grown used to the fact that she would likely never see the man who'd fathered her. However, there were still times when, seeing an older man with especially green eyes, whose hair was spiral curled and blonde like hers, it would make her wonder if it could be him. She never dared to ask though, too afraid of what the outcome might be. It was easier to do what her father had done so very long ago. To just walk away.

Annaleah was soon walking through the wrought iron gates of the University of Doltree, barely remembering her journey at all, being so consumed as she was by her thoughts. The beauty of the late summer sun illuminated the mid gothic architecture of the University's main admissions building, where Chancellor Tanner had her office. The entire University was beautiful, with its large stained glass windows, turrets, domed doors and marbled pillars. It looked as if it had been built centuries ago in some mythical kingdom, when in reality it had only stood for less than a hundred years. The landscape was gorgeous too, with cherry pine and oak trees, and all manner of rainbow hued flowers planted in between them. It was a peaceful, charming place. She remembered that while growing up in Doltree, when walking or driving by the University with Uncle John, she would imagine what it would be like to be a child living in the college, only in her mind she changed it to a huge medieval castle.

"Annaleah, is that you?" called a voice ahead of her, jolting her out of her thoughts. It was Chancellor Tanner, her brown hair pinned up smartly on her head and her rainbow glasses framing her kind, smiling eyes. "I wasn't expecting to see you here until classes start. Is there anything I can help you with?" Annaleah smiled and quickened her pace to catch up with the Chancellor.

"Actually, yes. I'm lucky I ran in to you. I'm looking for Professor Bainbridge. I could tell he wasn't too happy about having me in his classroom, and I thought it might be a good idea to sit with him before classes start and try to break the ice. Maybe ask him what I can do in his class to help him before I am thrust into it, because the truth is, I am not really sure what to expect."

Chancellor Tanner turned to look at Annaleah, one eyebrow cocked. "Well, you're quite the brave one. I must warn you though; I don't think he'll be much more receptive at this point, but I do agree it's a good idea to try to touch base with him as far as teaching goes. You can most likely find him in the teacher's quarters across from the library. I think he might be there now, but if not, check the library. He can be found there a lot of the time as well, in the rare books section. Good luck to you."

"Thank you, Chancellor Tanner. See you Monday," said Annaleah, as she turned towards the teacher's quarters.

"You're most welcome, but do me a favor, Annaleah. Call me Gladys. Chancellor sounds so...stuffy."

"Thank you, Gladys." Annaleah said smiling, glad to be on the chancellor's good side.

"My pleasure. Have fun with Sebastian," she teased, winking at Annaleah before slipping inside the admissions building.

Chapter Six

Sebastian and Annaleah

The teacher's quarters were separated into two main wings, one for the male faculty, and the other for the female. The apartments in each were set in accordance of tenure, with the faculty having been there the longest and held in the greatest esteem receiving the more spacious apartments on the top floor. The building was used mostly for those teachers who wanted to be close to their classrooms and worked overtime during the school year, but was occasionally used as full time residences. Annaleah wondered where Professor Bainbridge's apartment would be. Guessing that he held a higher tenure, she headed for the top floor of the male teacher's wing, holding her breath most of the way. She didn't even know what she was going to say. Would he still be angry? Would he resent her even trying to talk to him?

She paused in the hallway and closed her eyes, trying to stop the furious beating of her heart. Why was she so frightened by him? What did she think he was going to do, throw her out of a window? Really, if he did get angry with her, was that truly so terrible? It would reflect badly on him, not her. True, classes would be difficult to teach in such a situation, but there was nothing he could do that warranted such dread in her.

Taking a deep breath, Annaleah opened her eyes, and almost fell against the wall in shock. Standing before her, dressed impeccably in a black suit with dark blue piping stood Professor Bainbridge. He was looking at her with one of his eyebrows cocked and his lips drawn together. His gaze seemed to wash over her as he peered at her, a slow steady energy that radiated curiosity. He obviously hadn't expected to see her here.

Fighting for composure, Annaleah stood as tall as she could, upset at herself for having been caught off guard. "I'm sorry Professor Bainbridge; I didn't see or hear you arrive. I was just looking for you. I was wondering if we could have a word."

"Forgive me for spoiling your reverie," the Professor said in his low, smooth voice. "I didn't mean to startle you." His face remained stoic and his voice calm. Neither of them moved for a moment, each regarding the other. "I was just going to my quarters, Miss Grace. We can have a word in there."

Once again, he seemed to glide as he moved, his steps graceful and fluid. The breath Annaleah was unaware she had been holding left her body in a whoosh as he stopped beside her to unlock a door. He led her inside his apartment, and Annaleah took a moment to look around. The energy within his apartment was powerful and masculine, without a hint of a womanly touch. It was all beautiful and meticulously maintained.

The wallpaper was gorgeous, boasting a shiny black background with silver embossed fluer-de-lis patterns. Several classical paintings were hung on his wall, and she recognized The Nightmare by Henry Fuseli. It was her all-time favorite painting, in fact, she had done her High School final on it for her Humanities class. She was a bit surprised to see her favorite painting in his apartment, and found herself gasping at the coincidence.

Annaleah wondered briefly if she should comment on the painting, and decided against it when she saw Sebastian looking at her with a sour expression. Time to get on with it.

"Before we begin, please, have a seat." He said politely, gesturing at a beautiful cobalt blue wing back chair.

After Annaleah seated herself, he too sat, steepling his fingers and looking at her.

After settling into the chair, she tried not to fiddle nervously. She told herself to breathe normally, and to look him in the eye so he would not see she felt like a ten-year-old girl being sent to the principal's office.

She met his gaze. His eyes studied her as if he was and insect he was trying to pin down on a display board. It was as if he were trying to make her submit to him.

She had to admit that although beautiful, his eyes were also radiating a quiet sense of power, a pulsing energy that permeated everything in the room. Growing and building on itself, it made her feel slightly drunk, even hypnotized, as if she were disassociating from herself. She began to feel even more strange, as an odd pressure began to build up in the center of her forehead, where her third eye was supposed to be located. It wasn't a normal tension headache, the pressure felt more like someone was trying to probe into her thoughts, as if he was trying to control her. The thought that he may not even be human entered her mind. How else could he be doing this?

Subtly, Annaleah began to shield herself with a protective bubble of white light, but she found that maintaining the bubble while meeting the professor's gaze was more than she could do. Instead, she gently sent out her own energy, probing him to sense his intentions. She was met with his own protective shield, though her intuition told her he meant her no true harm. Perhaps he was just as intimidated as she was? Maybe he was showing off for her.

She looked away, breaking eye contact. She knew she was showing him that she was intimidated by him, which she hated, but she was unable to help herself. Even looking away from him she still felt slightly hypnotized. The feeling grew until she felt slightly woozy, as if the room had begun to spin.

Was he bewitching her? If so, he was more versed in occultism than she had thought. Should she reach inside the collar of her shirt and grab her pentacle? Maybe whisper a counter enchantment under her breath? No, she decided, she could counter his actions later, but here she couldn't let on she knew what he was doing. It would let him know she was on to him, and then he would likely try to intensify his effect.

Steeling herself to look at him once more, she noticed he had lowered the intensity of his eyes somewhat, though the mesmerizing, powerful energy was still there. His eyes were the darkest eyes she had ever seen. Looking into them, she almost forgot why she was there. It was as if something had taken over, and all that existed were his deep brown, almost black eyes.

"I hope you don't take offense Miss Grace, but I find it rather bold of you to come seeking me, and in my personal quarters at that. Please, tell me why you have come."

So, Annaleah thought, he wasn't going to call her by her first name. Was this a sign of respect, or just a way to distance himself from her so he could intimidate her? Quickly, she took a brief moment to call to her Mother Goddess for protection, and for guidance to help her say the right things. She also called out to her higher self to guide her through this meeting.

After a deep sigh, Annaleah said, "I have come to ask you to give me a chance to show you that I am worthy of teaching beside you, and also worthy of your respect. I may only be a few years older than most of your students, but I assure you I have unique credentials on the subjects that we'll be teaching together. I don't want either of us to start the year off on a bad note, or with animosity between us. I feel it would be harmful to our student's ability to learn." Annaleah found these words coming from her lips, but it was almost as if she were listening to herself from somewhere far off. She felt mildly sleepy and a somewhat disassociated, but at the same time, she was feeling more confident about herself and what she had to say to the man before her. Curious indeed.

"I promise you I'm not here to take over your class," she continued. "I understand you have been teaching here for quite some time and are a respected member of the faculty. It is my hope that I can gain your trust, and that we can find a manner of teaching together which suits us both and which the students find conducive to their learning. I will not presume that we will become friends, but I would like for us to try to make each other feel as comfortable as possible in the classroom, so that the students have the best learning atmosphere."

The silence that followed Annaleah's words seemed to go on forever and the air around her seemed to grow thicker and charged with an energy she couldn't quite put her finger on. It was almost as if it was touching her, undulating and pulsing, trying to throw her off balance. It felt like it were trying to pull her energy up and out of her, and in order to gain it back, she had to follow it. She felt a strong sensation that she wasn't wanted here, that she was invading his space and privacy. The feeling was urgent and insistent, and it made her heart beat too quickly in her chest. What in the world, she wondered? Was he trying to hypnotize her with his eyes and make her feel as if she needed to run?

She continued to look into the professor's eyes, even though she was fairly certain that they were the source of the strange energy. He sat motionless, staring at her. His expression was hard to read, his eyes fathomless and deep. Were she not so uncomfortable in this moment, she might have lost herself in their depths. She realized that even though she felt strange and off kilter gazing into his eyes, she didn't want to stop. His eyes were gorgeous and captivating. She felt drawn by them, wanting to swim in them as if they were twin oceans she wanted to drown in.

After what seemed to be quite a long time, the professor said, "Miss Grace, what do you know about coming of age rituals in other religious cultures?"

The question caught her off guard, and she was slightly flustered. Though she knew a little about the subject, it wasn't something she was well versed on, and she couldn't find anything to say, which embarrassed her.

Before she could answer, the professor reached for a book and handed it to her.

"I suggest you do some light reading before classes begin. Out of respect for your coming to me, despite your obvious discomfort, I will tell you that this is where I plan on starting my class." He paused for a moment, and cleared his throat. "Our class. Now, if you will excuse me Miss Grace, I have some things which I must attend to."

Annaleah took the book and rose to her feet, grateful this meeting was at an end. As she walked to the door, she heard him speak behind her. "As for respect, I feel it is a thing which is best earned, on both of our parts."

Annaleah felt him close behind her as he walked her to the door, his presence so palpable it overwhelmed her senses. Though he stood behind her now, the feeling of conflicting energies still washed over her. It was almost as though he were trying to seduce her, but behind that it was something deeply secret, as if he was trying to hide something about himself from her. Though he didn't make any overtures at her, the energy was slightly sexual, as if he exuded sexual power. Maybe that was her own imagination though. Mixed in with all of that was the dizzying sense of being bewitched, toyed with and then discarded.

If a person could feel another's energy tangibly through the flesh, she felt sure that this man's energy would be the sort that could seep deeply into her skin, burrowing all the way to her soul. It was slightly sexual, though he didn't make any overtures at her, it felt as if he exuded sexual power. Maybe that was her own imagining though, as even though he remained rather professional and aloof, she felt strongly drawn to him. She could almost feel him on her skin, hot and dangerous.

As soon as she reached the door and crossed the threshold, she was relieved to find the air felt easier to breathe.

"I bid you good day Miss Grace," he said from behind her as he began to close the door. When she was alone in the hallway, she had to fight all her senses not to run for her life. Thunder echoed in her heart as it galloped in her chest. Her breath came too quickly, and she hoped she wasn't on the verge of a panic attack.

What had really happened in there?

Holding the book in her hands, Annaleah walked down the hallway, feeling as if she were a little girl coming out the dragon's cave, having barely survived. Was she going crazy? He had done nothing to threaten her, yet the energy of his eyes still followed her. She still felt lightly intoxicated, the intimidation he focused on her now began to make her skin crawl.

Trembling slightly, she exited the building, and found herself fighting tears. She was angry that she had been so afraid. Angry that she had let him make her feel so small and insubstantial. Angry that she had let him dominate her. Yet beneath the anger, a subtle thread of pride wove itself around the rage, a small voice within her told her that she should feel proud; at least she had been brave enough to take the initiative to go see him. She was sure not many people would have done that. The emotions fought with each other within her, further confusing her and making her want to cry all the more.

She knew she was going to have to work hard to gain his respect, but for now she had to focus on regaining herself. Still fighting off frustrated tears, she fished a pair of oversized, dark lensed sunglasses out of purse and put them on and began to make her way home.

Chapter Seven

After the Meeting

Outside the campus, Annaleah felt herself coming back to herself. The trees reached out toward the sky, lush and beautiful. She breathed in their scent, letting the power of nature restore her.

After a few more calming, fortifying breaths, Annaleah took her cellphone from an outer pocket of her purse, and speed dialed Seth. A few rings later, she heard the call connect and instantly felt better.

"Saint Annaleah!" He said cheerfully, "How did it go?"

"I'm not really sure," She told him. "I mean, he wasn't outright rude or mean to me or anything like that. In fact, he gave me a book to read to give me a heads up on our first class on Monday." Annaleah felt a knot begin to wind through her stomach, as she recalled the uncomfortable situation with the professor only moments ago. What would the first class be like, she wondered? Though she was excited to be in her dream job at the university, she also dreaded being under the control of his powerful energies.

"Well, that's wonderful, sounds like you got through to him. So why is it you sound upset, and why are you unsure as to whether or not it went well?" he asked.

Being a student of occultism I almost want to say he has some sort of bewitchment going on." She told him.

"Even though it made me uncomfortable to look him in the eyes I found myself wanting to do just that, even if it was just to assert that I was his equal. Yet, when I did, I found myself saying what I needed to say, but…" Annaleah was beginning to get flustered again, not knowing what to say. Had the professor done that to her too?

Annaleah took the phone from her ear and held it out from her, as she tried to find the right words.

Taking another breath, Annaleah brought the phone back to her ear.

"Sorry about that Seth, but this situation has really discombobulated me. It was as if politeness was at extreme odds to the energy he was giving off, it totally confused me."

"It's alright Annaleah. I brought your lunch home for you. Meet me at your house and you can talk to both me and Uncle John."

"Okay, I'm on my way home right now. See you in a few minutes."

Annaleah ended the call and returned her cellphone to her purse as she tried to better understand what had happened between her and the professor. He was a teacher of World Religions, which meant that he would have had to study a bit of mysticism and the occult here and there. He had already shown he had more knowledge than she had thought, given the way that he had impregnated the energy of the room. Maybe he had done some sort of spell, or at least had warded his home against people he didn't want there. That had to be it, wards were known to work that way. His home was his sacred space, and if she had made him feel that she had violated his space, then the ward would have acted to make her feel as uncomfortable as possible so that she would leave. What of his eyes then? She had never heard of anyone warding their eyes before. The warding of his home made sense, but it was something more than that. It was something that she had never come across before, and she planned to find out what it was.

After her talk with Seth and Uncle John, she planned on doing some reading. Maybe it was time to do a spell of her own. Though she was not altogether lacking in confidence now, she still felt like a small girl when she was around Professor Bainbridge, so she decided to look for another sort of spell. Perhaps she needed to do a deep cleansing from his energy, and then surround herself in a protective bubble of white light.

Reaching inside her shirt, she lifted the small silver pentacle that hung on a silver chain and brought it to her lips. "Mother, Maiden and Crone, be with me. Help me find the answers which I seek." She whispered these words very softly, more said inside her own head than out loud. She had met enigmatic people before, but this professor was something entirely different.

A small voice inside her whispered to her quietly, but firmly, "Be careful, Annaleah, you could be playing with fire. Watch yourself."

Chapter Eight

Home Again

Annaleah shook her head, surprised and off put with the firmness of the voice. Fire, she mused? Her heart sank in her chest as she lowered her head, feeling deflated. This was not the sort of news she wanted to hear from her spiritual guides. Was it fire from the professor himself, from the situation of teaching with him, or something completely different she hadn't considered yet? Her intuition said it was the professor, and it was yet another disconcerting blow added to the events of the day. "Oh Goddess, please, don't let me have made things worse." She prayed in earnest, her head still lowered. Tears threatened to flow, but she blinked them back, taking a deep breath and using all the willpower she could muster.

As confused and upset as she was, she knew one thing for sure. She never wanted to feel the way she had felt in his apartment ever again. If she could dig up enough on him to understand why he was the way he was, then she would be the one in the position of power. Not that she would make him squirm the way he had made her squirm, but at least she wouldn't feel as if she were some tacky little girl he had been forced to endure.

Rounding the last corner to her home, she held her head up, the tears now replaced by her own inner strength.

After reaching her home and hugging Uncle John and greeting Seth, Annaleah took a seat at the kitchen table with the two people she cared for the most in the world.

"Seth here tells me you had quite a time with your co-teacher, Annaleah," Uncle John said. "I can't imagine why he would be cruel to someone as beautiful and sweet as you." His green eyes smiled as much as his lips, radiating with the love he felt for her.

"He wasn't really cruel per se, Uncle John," Annaleah told him, opening the Styrofoam container that held the lunch she had ordered earlier. "He was…" She paused to think about how to describe the strange situation with the professor. "He was more intense and calculating. I know he didn't want me there, but he never came out and said that either. He was more the energy he radiated and the ambiance of his apartment. It's like he wanted me to be afraid of him or to quake before him so he could feel some sense of power." She picked up a fork and stabbed at her chef's salad, her mind still processing the events of the day, trying to see if she had missed anything.

"Why would someone want to do that?" Seth asked, his blue eyes flashing with irritation. "It sounds like he is just some sad old man with no self-confidence that wants to make you feel inferior to the point that you concede and leave his class to him. Don't let him do that to you, Annaleah. You're strong, bright and gifted, and you deserve this."

Annaleah quickly swallowed a mouthful of salad and said, "Oh no, he is far from lacking in self-confidence. It exudes from him like some sort of hypnotic, frightening, glamour enchantment. In fact, on my way home, I was wondering if he had done some sort of spell work toward his home. The level of power behind this guy is unreal. I've never felt anything like it. It's very strange, to say the least."

"Can I see the book he gave you, dear?" Uncle John asked. "Just out of curiosity."

Annaleah took the book from under her purse and handed it to her uncle. Taking it in his strong, calloused hands, he read the title out loud, "Sacred and Secret Rituals of the World. Well, that sounds rather mysterious. Quite the thing to start the school year with, isn't it? Have you looked at any of it yet?"

"No, not yet," she answered, "but I plan to soon. I only have a few hours before I should go to bed. The first day is tomorrow."

"Why on earth didn't the Chancellor give you more time to prepare?" Seth asked. "Or hire you earlier?"

Annaleah took another bite of salad before answering. "Well, she did tell me over the phone that initially she was going to hire someone else. There were three other applicants for the job, but she didn't like any of them, so she had postponed her decision until the last moment, hoping some alternative would arrive. It seems my papers got misplaced, and she only found them recently. She said that she called me as soon as she read my credentials, certain I was the right one for the job. She apologized for the short notice, but said that if I wanted the job, it was mine. I don't have any time to prepare, but this job is something I need." She paused for a moment and looked at her uncle, smiling. "It's something we need."

Uncle John blushed and looked away from her. "Oh now, you know I can take care of myself. I still work most days, even if my hours are shorter. If this job turns out to be more of a curse than a blessing, you know I will get along just fine, and so will you." He returned his attention to the book and flipped through the pages.

"You are so humble," Annaleah said gently. "You have taken such good care of me for so long. Let me take care of you just a bit. Even if you don't feel you need it, indulge me."

He looked up from the book, and a piece of paper slipped out and fluttered softly to the floor, landing next to Seth's foot. Seth looked down curiously, then bent over to retrieve it.

"What does it say, Seth?" Annaleah asked, getting up from her seat to come over and look for herself. Seth's entire body went rigid, and when she looked at her friend, his eyes flashed from blue to a deep indigo, and there was something familiar and a bit frightening about it. Before she could be certain of what she saw, the flash and the color were gone, and it was only her oldest friend, Seth, looking at her with a confounded expression and the deep blue eyes he'd always had.

"I dunno, looks like some kind of occult diagrams to me. Hey, you okay?" he asked, looking at her as if she had gone a bit feeble minded. Still looking at him, Annaleah was mystified at what she had just seen, or what she thought she had seen. What in the world was going on lately? Was she going crazy?

"No, nothing," she answered. "I'm fine. Here, hand it over and let me get a better look at it." She steadied herself with a deep breath, shrugging off what she thought she had seen in Seth's eyes, and took the paper. It was a series of several odd diagrams, drawn in a particular and precise way.

"They look like sigils," she said, turning the paper over to see if there were more on the other side. There weren't. Uncle John got up from his seat and stood with Annaleah to look at the paper. He adjusted his glasses on his nose and peered at the paper. "What's a sigil?" he asked.

"It's a magical symbol, kind of like a signature. It is used to call forth or to represent the powers of a spirit, angel or demon," Annaleah answered. Uncle John and Seth glanced at each other nervously.

"You be careful of this professor, Annaleah. I don't know that I would trust him if he has things of this sort secretly tucked away in his books," Uncle John said, a look of fear in his eyes. Seth too, looked concerned.

"Oh come on guys, you know I can take care of myself perfectly well. I have studied this subject extensively for years. He might have thrown me for a loop and caught me off guard, but trust me; I am going to do my best to make sure it doesn't happen again. So what if he has a piece of parchment with sigils on it? He teaches World Religions, remember? It's probably something from a class and nothing 'woo woo' or crazy, okay?"

Annaleah was a bit surprised at both Seth and Uncle John. Didn't they trust her? What was up with Seth's eyes changing colors? She thought she'd seen the same thing happen in the diner when she mentioned her nightmare. And why were they looking at her as if they were scared for her? What on earth had been going on the last couple of days? It was almost as if by just meeting this oddly intense professor, he had tilted her world off its axis.

"I think we're both just concerned for you," Seth said, his voice lower than normal, "I know he is a World Religions teacher, but having a sigil to call forth an angel seems kind of odd to me."

Annaleah was surprised to hear him say this, she had said nothing of it being an angel's sigil.

"How do you know that it's an angel's sigil?" she asked curiously.

Seth looked surprised, his eyes going wide before he regained his composure.

"I mean, umm…. It looks like an angel's sigil. It doesn't look like something evil to me, or at least the energy it puts out isn't evil."

Annaleah and Uncle John looked at Seth. She was still confused at his comment. What had made him say that?

"In any case, while being cautious is a good thing," Seth continued nervously, "maybe you should give this guy a chance. It could be that he is really nervous and just put out such a demanding energy because he didn't know what else to do. I say give him a chance."

Annaleah placed the slip of paper back in the book. "I'll keep that in mind, Seth; really I will. Thank you, both of you, for listening to me. I've got to go study now. I only have a little while to try to get things figured out for class." Kissing them both on the cheek, she took the book and went upstairs to her room to study.

Chapter Nine

Curiouser and Curiouser

Sunday, August 7th

I must say, this Annaleah Grace creature has garnered even more of my curiosity. As I'm certain she felt a high level of intimidation during our meeting with the Chancellor, I was surprised to find her lurking about the hallway outside of my apartment, in hopes of "having a word with me," as she put it. She has more courage than I gave her credit for. I know, once inside my home, it must have been even more difficult for her. Surrounded by the energies of so many different things which all hold my energy signature, which would have reflected back to her. Why, it must have been overwhelming. I almost felt pity, watching the pulse of blood surging in her neck, knowing that her heart must be beating as fast as a tiny, cornered bird's would have.

It seems this girl wants my respect, and my cooperation in teaching alongside her. Not such an unusual request, but it interests me that she could even speak to me with the level of fear held in her eyes.

Her pupils were dilated and her hands shook, which amused me. Yet she still found the words she sought and spoke them well. Most people would have excused themselves and gotten out of the situation that caused such a heightened state of fear, yet she looked me in the eye, and I am well aware of the effects of that.

I have worked hard over many years to obtain the effects of a certain great charm, so others could not see the true form of my eyes. It has the rather interesting side effect of slightly hypnotizing others if they gaze at me too long. For a moment there, I was certain she would figure it out! Still, there is something about this girl that perplexes me and lures me into deeper pensive contemplations. She hides something vast and important, but she hides it so well that it appears she has erased her own knowledge of it. I have never quite seen the likes of it, in all my many years. She is the first person to have me confounded in so many years that it is useless to try to count them.

Who is this beautiful woman child, is there a reason she has been thrust into my path? Why do I find myself thinking of her when no other human in all my time here has ever caused me to reflect on them, let alone be interested in them in any way whatsoever? She has the energy of one much more powerful than her age or mannerisms suggest. Who or what is she really?

Where on earth did the Chancellor find her? She is not a normal girl by any degree. I will not, however, let her or this situation get the better of me. I am here to teach and to do a job. I'm a firm believer in the idea that everything does happen for a reason. Thus, I believe she has a reason to be here. What that reason is evades my understanding at this point, but I have been privy to many, many things in my long life which, when reflected upon, have happened as they needed, and with great reason.

Tomorrow begins the first day of a new year at the University. I am beginning to think it might not be as dull and monotonous as I had dreaded it would be. While I do not relish the thought of having another person in my class teaching alongside me, potentially derailing my entire course, I find the change in circumstances more...palatable. The fact that Annaleah came and faced me while terrified when doing so, well, that gives me a certain satisfaction. Satisfaction that she fears me, certainly, but also that I shall not have some simple minded, silly girl teaching my class.

I digress. I must begin the final preparations for tomorrow's class. I am quite interested to see how it will go.

~SB~

Chapter Ten

The Nightmare

Annaleah found herself in a familiar, terrifying place. Her bare feet were coated in layers of red Georgia clay. Her white night gown, damp with perspiration, clung to her, also soiled with the thick red mud. The night's air was alive and electric, carrying in it the fear, anguish and pain of the events unfolding around her. Screams punctuated the energies around her, war cries and weeping intermingling with the loud screaming. Tears came to her eyes, welling up as the battle raged around her and she smelled the coppery scent of spilled blood.

All around Annaleah a battle that had occurred eons ago unfolded. Tall beings fell from the sky, feathers scorched, scarring the land on which they fell. Here, before her, brother fought brother, some with swords and other weaponry, some with bare hands, teeth and claws. These winged men towered over her, and she watched, unseen, as the fangs of one creature tore into the flesh of another, crushing bones and severing limbs. She didn't want to see, and yet she couldn't look away, forced for reasons unknown to witness the savagery. Shrill cries shook the trees and vibrated the earth, making her cover her ears for fear that they would bleed. The smell of burned flesh and feathers mingled with the blood and stung her eyes, bringing more tears to blur the horrific vision around her.

There were thousands upon thousands of these beings. Some were scattered in dead or dying heaps upon the ground, while others who still fought were so engaged in battle that they either did not see or did not care that they stepped on the dying ones, that they smashed with their large feet the remains of the dead as they waged more savagery.

Annaleah was splashed with blood as she walked on, not knowing where she meant to go. She never knew where to go when she found herself here. The blood staining her nightgown had a terrible, sickly feel to it, dirty with sin, guilt and all manner of contagion. Wiping at the blood in a state of near panic, she felt it sting her skin as if it were poison.

She wanted to run, but didn't know where to flee. The winged men and women were everywhere, some with deep indigo blue eyes, others with silver. Some wore armor that glistened and seemed to protect them from the worst blows, while others were naked or nearly so. Sounds of metal piercing flesh, bones being crushed, the screams of the dying and battle cries of victory all assaulted her, overloading her senses as much as the sights which were bizarre and inconceivable. She watched as a tall, muscular being bathed in a golden glow grabbed one of his brethren, and with his bare hands, began to tear the wings off of the struggling creature. The golden light of the attacker seemed to grow as he strained to break the bones and sever flesh from flesh. Already weak, the darker, dirtier creature struggled with as much might as he could, his silver eyes contorted into a mask of perfect misery and excruciating pain. Blood flowed freely from his shoulders, and his cry tore at her heart. It was not the cry of savagery, nor was it the cry of death upon his blood stained lips, rather, it was the cry of utter dejection, pain and suffering. More than that, it was the cry of something that not only had lost, but was lost, utterly, hopelessly and irrevocably. Once the wings had been completely severed, the towering creature above him shouted something in a language both beautiful and terrifying before flinging each wing away in random directions. The wounded creature convulsed, blood and spittle foaming in his mouth, before bursting into flames, screaming his song of pain and dejection.

Annaleah sank to her knees, covering her eyes and weeping. "No more!" she screamed, not knowing what else to do. Suddenly, the creatures fighting nearest to her paused, and seemed to notice her for the first time. For a moment, all fighting stopped while they looked intensely at her, as if to pierce her soul with their gaze. The ones with the golden glow stood their ground, while those with the silvery eyes seemed to gain new strength. Instead of fighting each other as they had before, those with silver eyes joined as one to advance upon her, eyes and teeth flashing, sinew and muscles flexing in preparation for the wrath they would to inflict upon her.

In her desperation to escape, Annaleah fell, twisting her ankle and falling into a muddy puddle of wet clay. As she fought for courage, adrenaline surged through her, and she barely felt the deep gash open in the flesh of her leg as she fell against a sharp rock within the mud. Her blood began to flow into the water, a striking, crimson contrast to the texture and color of the soaked earth.

Cowering and wounded, Annaleah prepared herself for the descent of teeth, claws and nails into her flesh. She screamed until her throat felt as if it were on fire. Instead of her skin being ravaged and torn from her however, she was being shaken. Hard. Her eyes snapped open, her arms and legs flailing in some meager attempt at self-defense. She was slightly shocked at what she saw, further adding to her confusion. Uncle John was holding her, trying the best he could to both shake her awake and bear the blows she was throwing. His glasses had been knocked off his face, and she saw that he was afraid, but not for himself.

"Annaleah, wake up! It's just a dream, wake up! You're safe!" Uncle John said over and over, until finally, she registered the truth of it. She stopped her frantic attempts at defense, and drew her hand to her mouth, horrified that she had been battering her beloved uncle.

"Oh, Uncle John," she said, her voice quivering. She could no longer hold her tears back, and she began to sob. She bent her head and placed her face in her palms, trying not to show Uncle John just how upset she was. She didn't want to upset him any further. It could hardly be helped though, as her chest heaved as the sobs overtook her. She wept for knowing she had lashed out against him, and for the horrors she had just undergone in her terrible dream.

Uncle John, seeing her return from her nightmare back to her waking self, released her and spoke soothingly. "Oh my sweet girl, don't you cry. You've done nothing wrong. If I could take these terrible dreams from you I would, it isn't fair that you suffer them."

Annaleah threw her arms around her uncle, and he held her, rocking her and smoothing her hair. After a short while, she looked up at him and said, "They saw me this time, Uncle John. They never heard my screams before, nor have they ever seemed to know I was there at all, but they knew I was there this time. The dirty, battle scarred ones with silver eyes all stopped fighting their enemies and converged together and came at me. I know it was just a dream, a horrible and terrifying dream, but after all these years it has never changed. Why now? Why did they see me now?"

Looking at his niece sympathetically, Uncle John said, "It's probably the stress you're under, Annaleah. You have a very important day tomorrow, and the stress of meeting the Professor and confronting him likely had something to do with it. Please, try not to worry. Let me get you some warm milk to calm your nerves; it always worked for you when you were a child." He held her face gently in his hands, and raised himself up ever so slightly to place a kiss on her forehead. "I will be right back, sweetheart. Just remember, you're okay."

"Thank you, Uncle John. The warm milk sounds wonderful." Annaleah wiped her tears from her face and smiled back at her uncle. He bent to the floor to retrieve his fallen glasses, then stood and walked towards the door. "I love you, Uncle John, thank you so much, for everything," she said, her heart brimming with gratitude for all he had done and all that continued to do for her. He turned in the doorway, the lines of worry in his face going soft as love flowed into his expression.

"Love you too, Annaleah. Be right back."

As he left, she threw the covers off, intending to get up and wash her face in the bathroom. Dark red Georgia clay caked her bare feet, and a foul crimson liquid splattered her legs. The sheets she had been lying in were also saturated with dirt and blood. Little bits of grass and sticks had dried in clumps within the red clay, sticking to her flesh as a macabre collage. Scratches, ranging from light marks to deep, bleeding gouges marked her flesh, mixing with the red dirt. Her ankles and feet were so thoroughly caked that she saw it had completely covered her toes to her calves, as if she had been bathed in clay and gore. Where she had fallen against the sharp stone in her dream, she bled freely, the blood washing some of the leaves of grass further down as it quickly made its way down her leg.

The pain hit her shortly after seeing the severity of her situation. She bit into her clenched fist, more tears squeezing from her closed eyes. It was raw and pure, the hot blood felt as if it were searing her as it continued to bleed out, the wound itself reminding her of a gaping maw created from hell itself.

This had never happened to her before. Her heart raced as she searched for an explanation, trying to block the pain from her mind. She knew in her heart what is must mean, and it terrified her. She had really, truly been somewhere terrible, she had somehow been transported to another reality, another dimension, and had returned with the proof of her travels smeared on her, bleeding from her, and radiating harrowing pain from her body. How could this be? It didn't even seem like a possibility, but here she was, shaken to her core and staring at the evidence. If this had happened meant it could happen again. This realization pierced fresh fear into her heart. If she brought back sticks, clay and fresh wounds, could she bring back the beings from that world into this one? She trembled, terror permeating her ever breath, every heartbeat heavy with its essence. Would she bring danger to those she loved?

Annaleah had to calm down before Uncle John returned. Taking a deep breath, she ran her fingers through her hair and wiped the tears from her face, feeling utterly exhausted.

"Mother, Maiden and Crone, please help me to calm down," she prayed silently, "I don't want to scare Uncle John."

Deep waves of calmness washed over her, the terror leaving slowly as she exhaled, a subtle peace flowing inwards to her soul as she breathed in. After several meditating breaths, her self-control slowly came back to her, and she relaxed.

As she continued to take deep, calming breaths, she took the sheets from her bed, wadded them up and threw them in the closet. She didn't want Uncle John to see this; he had enough to worry about. Padding lightly on dirty feet, she called down the stairs to her uncle. "Uncle John, I am going to take a shower, can you leave the milk on my night stand?"

She heard him rustling about downstairs, then his voice called up, "Sure thing sweetie." She got out a fresh set of sheets, a towel and a new nightgown and headed to the shower.

She had been dream walking again.

Chapter Eleven

Shaken

Monday morning, August 8th 3:15 AM

It is not often that I'm in such a state as I now find myself in, and, having imbibed my last few fingers of whisky, I find I'm no calmer than before I had partaken of the spirits. For whatever reason I've taken up these pages. I am grateful for them now. The relief and catharsis provided in this journal are more than I would have given them credit for before I began. I'm hoping by the time I am finished with this entry, some level of calmness will have returned to me, that my mind will clear of the horrific images burned into it years ago, and now, just recently, revisited upon it.

I do not dream often, nor do I imagine those like me dream often either; it was not built into our nature to do so. Tonight however, I dreamed. Oh such terrible visions! Memories that scar the very fiber of the soul, searing the depths of it to the core, wounding, breaking, burdening, twisting. There is no forgetting such things, no healing over the scars with layers of soft, pink flesh. Some wounds never heal; some pains will never cease, but can only be forced back into the darkest shadows of one's being, given a long chain and a playground in the blackest parts of the soul. It is best not to visit this place often. Indeed, it is prudent to guard one's self from this hateful place, and ensure no one ever gets close enough to see it within.

The burning, oh, the hateful smell of burning feathers, of flesh ignited and blood spilled freely over the torn earth! I saw again how the sky itself was dark and bruised by all those who fell, screaming, burning, bleeding and fighting as they fell, leaving trails of feathers and blood in the air behind them. So many sounds at once, screams and war cries, pleading prayers that fell deaf to the one to whom they prayed. Metal on metal, bones crushing and blood flowing so freely that I could hear it being absorbed into the earth. Brother against brother, the innumerable deaths of those who once could not die. So much suffering, so much pain, the sense of betrayal hot and thick in the air. Madness, decay, fear, pain, the first ever palpitations of hatred.

Tonight, I dreamed of it all again. It was as if I were living it once more, being punished over and over again for sins never meant to be committed. I saw those I loved torn apart, I felt their blood wash over me like a cursed rain. I heard their cries and could do nothing to help. The war raged on around me, but I was unable to do anything to affect my surroundings, as if I were a ghost in my own dream. I was trapped and helpless in this forsaken, Goddess cursed place, surrounded by death, war and madness. I was back in a place that no being should ever have to revisit, and for the first time in so very, very long, I was afraid.

I awoke with a scream in my throat, choking with the effort not to let it loose. The visions of my dreams still burned behind my eyes, and I shook as I rose from my bed. Why on earth, after all this time, would I be dreaming of this? I am seldom one to lose my composure, but to be forced to relive even a single second of that! Why these dreams would revisit me is beyond my understanding. I know they cannot be healed, but they can be sealed off, shuttered and forgotten, condemned to be sequestered and quarantined for the remainder of my days. Why have they broken free? What has happened to call them forth?

I cannot help but wonder, does this have anything to do with the woman child who has come into my life, the beautiful and strange girl called Annaleah? I can sense she has some sort of power, but it is so controlled. Is she even aware she possesses such ability, does she know how the air itself seems to hum around her, or am I simply seeing something that isn't there? I wish I knew, but I am much too exhausted to contemplate it further.

I feel none the better for having written this, only more wearied. Perhaps I deserve this, for what I have done, or maybe for that which I did not do. If this is my punishment, then I shall bear it with dignity. It is the least I can do. For now, however, I must put this away and hope that the remainder of my night is without further event. My first day of classes will occur with or without me having had sound sleep, so for now I must finish this and hope that no more dreams come. Tomorrow will be difficult enough, training a new teacher, without me being sleep deprived and in a foul mood.

~SB~

Chapter Twelve

Breakfast with Uncle John

Annaleah woke the next morning exhausted and feeling slightly hung over, even though she had not partaken of any alcohol the night before. The light streaming from a crack in her curtain made her wince and want to bury herself under her sheets, ignoring the day's importance. Never one to concede to her pain or discomfort, she threw the covers back from the bed, hoping not to see any more mud or debris from her dreams. There was nothing on the sheets she had changed before collapsing back into bed, thankfully into dreams she didn't recall.

She had dressed her wound before she went to sleep the night before, and only a little blood stained the bandage. Wincing as she sat up, she took a deep breath to steady herself before she got up and put weight on her wounded leg. The throbbing ache was something fierce, but she knew the importance that the day held for her, so she willed herself to bear it as best she could. Praying once more to her Goddess for strength and forbearance, she reached over to her bedside table and took the aspirin she had laid out last night, knowing she would need it this morning.

Annaleah could hear Uncle John downstairs, fixing her breakfast. The smell of fresh ground coffee and bacon made their way up to her, and she smiled, despite her lack of sleep. He always got the finest coffees, dark, rich and smooth with no bitter after taste.

Heading down the stairs slowly, Annaleah took the book the Professor had given her the day before, which she had read only a very little of before falling asleep. She planned on seeing if he would let her sit on the sidelines for the first few days to observe his class and teaching style, before being immersed into teaching herself. If he did expect her to teach today, she wasn't sure how she would handle it. She simply did not have the energy mentally or physically to do so.

Uncle John was wearing his fuzzy green bathrobe over flannel pajamas, his light brown hair sticking up in various places, obviously uncombed. He hummed as he worked over the stove, swinging his hips a bit as he cooked. The table was set simply but tastefully, a vase full of summer flowers in the center. He had picked climbing hydrangeas and mixed smaller bunches of it in with black eyed Susan and the sleepy bells of columbines in hues of blue, pink and red.

"Where did you find the columbines, Uncle John?' Annaleah asked, leaning over the table to admire the blooms. They were her favorite flower, and that he had found some and put them on the table meant a lot to her. Suddenly she wasn't so tired and wasn't in as much pain any more.

Uncle John spun around on his heel, wooden spoon in his hand, a big smile on his kind face. "Miss Delland grows them in her garden," he answered her, "along with the other flowers. I fixed a leaky pipe for her in return for those. I think I made a fair trade." Uncle John set the spoon down, poured them each a cup of fresh coffee, and began to place their breakfast onto plates. Annaleah watched her uncle for a moment, smiling, then walked over to him and placed a kiss on his cheek. For a moment, he looked a bit startled, but then his face relaxed and he beamed back at her. She might be in her early twenties and considered a woman now, but he would always see her as his little girl. He looked at the young woman standing before him, who, having survived the abandonment of her father, the death of her mother, being bullied most of her school years, and so many other things, had borne her fair share of burdens without resentment at her fate. Being different than others had only made her work harder in her studies, and made her love those that loved her as she was all the more. She had become quite the young woman.

"I'm proud of you, kiddo," Uncle John said, handing her a plate of food and then seating himself at the table. "I want you to have a good day. Don't let anyone or anything get you down, okay? Not even that Bainbridge guy."

Annaleah took her seat and looked at her plate. It was piled with eggs, bacon, toast and strawberries. Uncle John must really be proud of her, he rarely cooked, and it all looked so good. "I won't let anyone get to me, Uncle John," she promised, spooning scrambled eggs onto her toast. "Thank you so much for the breakfast, and for the flowers too."

"Columbines were your mother's favorite flower too, you know," Uncle John told her, his eyes looking just a tiny bit sad. "She used to plant them in our garden with your grandmother when we were little. She said the fairies liked them, and that if you left small gifts under them for the fairy folk, you could make a wish and it come true. I believed her, too. I saw her put a bit of chocolate under them every so often, but I never asked her what she wished for." He sighed, a faraway look in his green eyes. "She would be proud of you. Of all you have gone through and remaining unbroken, of all the hard work and long nights you spent studying. It would have meant so much to her."

Annaleah reached over her plate, plucked a pink columbine from the vase and placed it behind her left ear. "Then I'll wear this for Mom," she said softly, "so that where ever it is that her spirit may be, she can see her daughter honoring her memory."

Uncle John smiled at her, and seemed to be perfectly content in the moment. "Well, now that's just beautiful, my dear. You're going to melt that Professor's heart. Teaching class will be easy because everyone will be looking at you and telling you what a lovely creature you are."

Annaleah laughed at this, and winked at her sweet, silly uncle. "Let's hope so," she said, thinking how wonderful it would be if things would go that way. Bless Jonathan Alan Grace, for all the right things he said. He knew just how to make things seem like they would be okay. If it were true that the day went according to how to morning did, then today would be a fine one indeed.

Chapter Thirteen

Just Before Class Begins

The Georgian sun was already warm in the cloudless azure sky, its heat blissful on Annaleah's skin as she walked to her first day of classes at the University. She only had a few periods to teach a day, the earliest of which was at ten AM. It was about half past eight now, but she had wanted to arrive early to see what the Professor expected of her today. Though her wonderful morning with Uncle John had eased a lot of the tension from last night's terror, she was still more tired than she would have liked, and she hoped it wouldn't affect her sensibilities too much.

As her trendy black kitten heels fell upon the pavement in a rhythmic cadence, her thoughts turned to the man with whom she would be teaching. She wondered how old he was and where he was from. He couldn't be past his early forties, she guessed, for there were no discernible lines in his face. Though far from stuffy and boring, he dressed too maturely to be much younger than that, and, although he was quite stylish, he didn't follow the trends of those in her age bracket. As to where he was from, he was most certainly not from the South, that much she was sure of. His voice was low and rich in timber, his words perfectly enunciated, but not strained with effort to be so. There wasn't a trace of a drawl, though he did have an accent, like a cross between a noble English Lord and a Russian aristocrat.

Turning the last corner onto the campus, Annaleah saw several students. She smiled at some and said hello to a few others, her heart beating with excitement with the possibilities of the day. Balloons and a banner welcoming the pupils had been hung at the entrance to the main hall, where the classroom she would share with Professor Bainbridge was located. The sound of laughter, music and the buzz of conversations filled the air around her, as well as a few university cheers from some of the returning students, mostly the football jocks she mused, from the look of their letter jackets. The University had a very good football team, with many prestigious trophies and awards to show for it.

The door to Annaleah's classroom was slightly open, but she knocked anyway, waiting for the Professor's voice to invite her inside. Instead, after a brief moment, the door opened and she stood looking into the dark eyes of the Professor.

"Miss Grace, you don't have to knock at the door of your own classroom. Please come in," Professor Bainbridge said, opening the door and walking back towards his dark wooden desk. "You are rather early. Is there something you wished to speak to me about?"

"Yes sir, actually there is," Annaleah answered. "I did do a bit of reading from the book you gave me, but I was wondering exactly what you were expecting of me for today. You and I weren't given a lot of time to get to know each other, or to come up with a way to teach together that suited us both. I really just want to be on the same page as you, Professor." Though she still felt a bit intimidated by him, she spoke with confidence, proud of herself for not shaking as she had in his apartment.

The Professor regarded her stonily, his dark eyes narrowing slightly, as if he were deep in thought. After a moment he said, "Actually Miss Grace, there won't be much to do today beyond introductions and a basic speech as to what the class is about. The curriculum will be handed out, books given, etcetera." The Professor took a seat behind his desk, opened a drawer, took out a book and handed it to Annaleah. "This is the main book we will be using in class and a copy of the curriculum. I should have given these to you yesterday, but you seemed quite happy to be gone from my apartment. I believe you have plenty of time if you'd like to read over it before class starts."

As Annaleah took the book from the Professor, she noticed his hands. They were pale with long fingers, more like those of a pianist or an artist than a teacher, she thought absently. "Thank you, sir. I will look at it now," she said as she turned to leave, heading towards a bench outside to settle in and read over the book as she waited for class to begin.

Professor Bainbridge remained at his desk, focused on some faraway place that only existed in his mind. He was still perturbed by last night's dream, having not had one like it in quite a long time. Dreams of that manner did not occur without reason. They were usually the precursor to something important, serving either as a warning or an omen of some kind. Having been so close to her only moments ago, he was now certain Annaleah was part of it, though he was no closer to figuring out how. He tried to concentrate on how she fit into last night's dream, but all he could think about was how she affected him. When she was beside him, something about the flower in her hair had awoken in him something he wasn't sure he had ever felt before. It was an uncomfortable fluttering in his stomach which rose like a flame into his chest, making his heart beat faster. It was as if the smell of the flower had floated through the air to intoxicate him. Combined with her presence, it enchanted him, making him feel weak. The bloom nestled divinely in her hair, its scent not too strong, but very sweet. He saw the way her hair flowed around it, like a blonde cascade of curls that ended just above her bottom. She looked innocent, sweet, fresh. Her deep green eyes appeared wide with wonder and youth, full of life and all the enchantment that came with it.

He didn't like the way his heart beat faster when she was near, or the way he had to clench his jaw to steady his composure. It was unlike him to react to anyone in such a way. In all his years, never had any woman had such a powerful effect on him. He clenched his jaw at all these new feelings, trying to guard himself against them. How dare she seem so innocent, when he was sure she was not as innocent as she presented herself to be. He began to resent her, and the feelings she elicited from him.

Taking a deep breath, Sebastian pondered the fact that she had entered his life just before a string of strange events began happening. Had she sent these dreams he wondered? And if so, why? Who or what, was she that gave her the power to send dreams, and why did he have such a visceral reaction to her, when no one before her had ever set his mind spinning or made the air about him suddenly seem more alive?

Perhaps she was some sort of spell binder, maybe even a succubus, using glamour to enchant him, so she could fulfill some secret, mysterious plan. She seemed innocent, but he was not going to let himself be fooled. He tried to imagine her as a succubus, one of those wicked demons that seduced men and then stole their souls.

Images of a dark room lit by a single candle flashed through his mind, her flesh hot against his skin, her kisses burning his lips. The vision stole his breath, surprising him greatly. What was really going on? It was best to distance himself from her, whatever she was confused

his senses, and he couldn't afford more thought now with the class to
start so soon.

She certainly seemed more in her element today, and though it was
a good thing, he wondered what had changed. No matter. He knew he
wouldn't have to wait too long before the meaning of the dream became
evident.

Focusing on the day before him, he opened his books and looked at
the list of students who would be in his classroom shortly. It was time
to put away his personal musings and become the Professor again.

Chapter Fourteen

The Owl

By the time Annaleah returned to the classroom, a small desk had been set at the front of the room, several feet away from Professor Bainbridge's. A nameplate bearing her name had been placed on it, front and center, along with a plain black mug full of pens, a few university books and a notepad. She walked over to her new desk, smiling broadly.

"The Chancellor wishes you to know this desk is only temporary. When your time permits, she would like to see you so that you may procure another more suited to your tastes," the Professor said, watching as Annaleah opened and closed the drawers. She was about to tell him that this desk would suit her just fine, when the bell rang and the last of the students filed in. Not really knowing what to do, she took her place behind her desk and waited for Professor Bainbridge to introduce her.

The Professor walked to the front of the classroom, and all eyes fell upon him. "Good morning students, welcome to World Religions. In this class you will learn many things, one of which is respect. You will give whomever is speaking your full attention and you will raise your hand before you speak. I'm a great admirer of rules and order, and I expect you to act accordingly while you are learning in my class. There are to be no cell phones on during my class. If one rings it becomes mine." Several students, groaning at this disclosure, pulled out their cell phones and turned them off.

"I must also make it clear," the Professor continued, "that if you are taking this class as a means to fill your credits and not as something to take seriously, you will not be handled with children's gloves and given a mark that you have not worked fastidiously to earn. This is not going to be an easy class, but I hope it will be one that you find both enlightening and rewarding.

"There has also been a change from last year's methodology, which I am sure will be quite refreshing for those of you who have taken my classes before. I will be joined in teaching you by Miss Annaleah Grace. You will treat her with the same respect and attention that you would give to me. For the first few weeks of class, I shall be training her for the most part, so I also expect that she will have some questions for us as well. Please join me in welcoming Miss Grace." He stretched his arm towards Annaleah and turned slightly to look her in the eye. She rose from behind the desk and walked to the front of the class, and he moved aside a bit to give her room to speak.

"Thank you, Professor Bainbridge. Good morning everyone, it is a pleasure to be here with you all," Annaleah began, looking at the faces of the students before her. Some looked at her with respect, while others did not look at her at all, regarding their nails or the clock over her head with more interest. "I am honored to be teaching World Religions with the Professor. While I do not hold such a prestigious title myself, I am both a student and a teacher of the occult and of things arcane. I will do my best to teach you these things during my time here."

A woman dressed all in black raised her hand. Annaleah nodded at her. "You mean things like witchcraft and Satanism?" asked the girl. There was a small bit of laughter and someone hummed the Twilight Zone theme.

"Quiet!" the Professor said. "Please continue, Miss Grace."

"Yes," Annaleah answered. "They will both be included, among other things. There are many types of witchcraft as well, and not many of them include pointy hats and warted noses. We will discuss things such as how the media and Hollywood influence the subject of the occult, how other religions treat witchcraft, voodoo, and other practices, as well as many other subjects. I have been a student of such things since I was a child."

The girl who had asked the question about witchcraft raised her hand again. "So what was it exactly, that really got you interested in witchcraft and the occult, and do you see yourself as a witch?" she asked, seeming genuinely interested.

Annaleah glanced at the Professor, unsure whether or not he was willing to let her have so much of the floor on the first day of class. He was leaning slightly on his desk, and seemed interested in what she had to say. His expression suggested he didn't know why she had looked to him at all, and that she should answer the question given her.

Annaleah felt her cheeks go hot, as she tried to find the right words to say. She hoped no one noticed the color rising in her face. "Honestly," she answered, "it's not really something I have been asked before. I guess I would have to say truthfully, as odd as it might sound, I got interested because of dreams. I began to have some rather odd ones when I was a child. Dream dictionaries and other books just didn't seem to have the answers I needed."

A young man dressed head to foot in various shades of brown raised his hand. "Yes?" Annaleah asked, pointing to him.

"So what made you turn to the occult for answers?" He asked, with a slight accent that Annaleah couldn't place. She noted that most of the students who had previously been fiddling or otherwise not listening now seemed to be giving her all of their attention. She felt both relieved and on the spot. As she thought of a good, honest answer to give, she also wondered how the Professor thought she was handling things on her first day. Was she doing well? Did he resent her speaking too much? As she tried her best not to look at him again, she answered the question.

"It was the lack of other options," Annaleah answered. "I knew that my mother, when she was still alive, was a white witch, and it seemed only natural for me to pursue this course. Oh, by the way, yes, I am a witch. Or, as I might be more properly classified, I am an eclectic pagan who follows mostly the Wiccan rede and deities. To give you an idea of what I was trying to find information on, let me ask you a question. Has anyone here ever heard of dream walking?'

The girl who had asked the first question raised her hand. "Isn't that a Native American thing; something about visiting another person's dreams?"

"That's right, very nice," Annaleah said, relaxing a little. "In fact, not much else can be found on the subject of dream walking, other than it is something which takes a lot of skill and practice to do and requires a certain ethic when practicing. I have, as of today, only found two books ever focused on this subject, and only one of them was an occult book."

Annaleah was starting to feel a bit more in her element, interested in what the students had to say. However, she could feel the professor's gaze upon her, and was doing her best not to look at him, keenly aware of the effect his deep eyes had on her. She was enjoying the interaction with the class, and was afraid that if she looked once more at him, she would lose her composure, and therefore her respect, from the students.

Suddenly, there was a thunderous crashing noise at the window, as something large and brown flew into it hard, cracking but not shattering the glass. Everyone jumped in unison, startled. Cries of "What on earth?" and "What was that!?" filled the room, as they all tried at once to go to the window to see what had smashed into it.

"Everyone back to your desks at once," said the Professor in a loud, firm voice. "There is no need to panic. I assure you we are not being attacked. Miss Grace will go outside and see what hit the window, but until she comes back in to tell us what happened, I expect you to remain seated and calm in your desks." The students looked from him to the window, clearly wanting to stay and see was going on. It was not just Annaleah however, that was intimidated by the Professor. Most of the students looked at him with wide eyes and went back to their seats, despite intense interest in what was going on at the window.

Professor Bainbridge turned to look at Annaleah, his eyebrow raised slightly and his lips tight, as if to ask her why she hadn't gone outside to investigate yet.

Swallowing at the chastising expression, she made her way outside to see what had caused such a commotion.

As she approached the window outside, she saw large, dark brown feathers lying strewn about in the grass, as well as a few still floating in the air. A brown, feathered form, still moving in the grass, sent out soft distress calls. Curious, and a still a bit startled, Annaleah removed her light summer jacket and moved slowly toward the injured creature.

It was quite a large bird, with big, bright yellow eyes that blinked rapidly, and a hooked beak that was slightly open, panting. Large dark tufts of feathers topped its head like great, fluffy ears.

When it turned its big yellow eyes in her direction, she recognized it as a great horned owl, stunned and frightened, trying frantically to get up, but too dazed and injured to do much more than move its head and one wing slightly. Annaleah continued to approach it slowly, so as not to frighten it more than it already was.

"You poor dear," Annaleah said sadly, kneeling beside the owl. She expected it to do its best to fly away, or at least get as far from her as it could. Instead, it turned its head toward the sound of her voice, its large yellow eyes seeming to look straight into her very core. It ceased its distress cries and began to make an odd cooing sound.

"That's right sweetie, I am not going to hurt you, it's okay. I'm going to try to help you." Annaleah wasn't sure why she was talking to the owl, knowing it could not possibly understand her, but still hoping that it would register the calm in her voice. She moved slowly and placed her summer jacket over the owl, amazed that it didn't seem scared or disturbed at her proximity or at her placing her jacket over it.

"You sure are a beautiful bird," Annaleah crooned, gently tucking her garment around it. "I'm going to pick you up now, ever so gently, okay beautiful? I'm going to bring you inside and try to get you some help. Don't be afraid." Saying a quick prayer, and trying to imagine her hands filled with light, Annaleah picked up the bird, which squawked just a bit, but then settled down as she wrapped the rest of the jacket around its body. She held it softly, and looked down at the big, bright yellow eyes that looked back up into hers. She stood slowly, making her way to the classroom inside, the owl held gently before her, one arm under it and the other one on top of it, making sure it was secure but not held tightly enough to cause it more pain. As she walked into the classroom, several students gasped and she saw the Professor's expression darken considerably.

"It's a great horned owl," Annaleah said. "I have no idea what it's doing out during daylight hours, or what caused it to fly into the window, but it is hurt and it needs help." Almost at once, the students got up from their desks for a closer look at the injured animal. The sudden movement and the appearance of so many other people startled the bird, which began to struggle in Annaleah's arms.

"Back to your seats immediately," the Professor said, looking angrily at Annaleah. This time, curiosity won out over intimidation, and with his students still trying to push closer for a look at the animal, he quickly ushered Annaleah out of the class, closing the door behind them once they stood in the hall. His dark eyes burned her.

"What is the meaning of you bringing this animal into the classroom?" he demanded, "I sent you outside to see what was going on, not to make a mockery out of my class." The bird was starting to struggle in Annaleah's arms again, frightened by the professor's tone of voice. Seeing an injured animal struggling hurt her heart, and awakened something protective inside her. How could he get angry that she was trying to help a bird that so clearly had injured itself? How could he think his class and respect was more important than the welfare of another living creature?

"With all due respect, sir, this bird needs help. I'm not trying to make a mockery of your class at all, but I can't, with a clear conscience, just leave this owl to suffer." Annaleah felt herself shaking again, weakened by something the Professor held behind his black eyes. Dark, smoldering eyes which seemed to wash over the deepest parts of her soul and see into her darkest secrets. It was absolutely unnatural the effect his eyes had. His eyes were purely hypnotic, and some of the most handsome she had ever seen. Even while still under his scrutiny, and still being shaken up at the turn of events, Annaleah found herself thinking of just how good looking he was. She was ashamed at the effect he had over her. Yet, strangely, it seemed more than just that, as if the tie to him was profoundly intrinsic and she was helpless to the pull of his masculine beauty. It was more than just his intensely fine looks, however. It was something mysterious and heady, something whimsical and confusing, but it was something she could no longer deny.

The injured animal in her arms made a curious sound, its beak only slightly opened, as if it were sensing the intensity of the moment. This certainly was not the way Annaleah had wanted or intended to start off her first day of classes.

The door opened behind the Professor and the girl dressed in black that had asked about witchcraft poked her head out the door. "Excuse me, I don't mean to interrupt," she said, "but my friend's mother, Mrs. Adams, teaches the Animal Husbandry class here at the University. I'm sure she would be willing to take care of the owl."

Not waiting for the Professor to speak, Annaleah sent silent prayers of thanks to the Goddess, and walked quickly to the girl at the door. "Yes, thank you. That would be wonderful!"

"Would that be alright, Professor Bainbridge?" the girl asked, exiting the class fully. The Professor closed his eyes, the corners of his mouth turning down and his lips tightening. Without speaking, he nodded slightly and gestured for them to go before stepping back into the classroom.

"Don't mind Professor Bainbridge," the girl said, moving closer to Annaleah to look down at the owl. "He is the resident eccentric, dark, moody professor. You'll get used to him eventually. I have taken his class before and failed. He's a real hard ass. I need passing grades in his class though, so here I am again. My name is Rachael; it's nice to meet you. I would shake your hand Miss Grace, but I see your hands are busy holding the owl."

"Oh, please call me Annaleah. Miss Grace sounds too formal," Annaleah said as they began to make their way to the Animal Husbandry class. "At least, outside of the classroom. I have a feeling the Professor might have a problem with you calling me that in his class. What is his deal, anyway?"

"Good question," answered Rachael." He is a very private person; no one really knows anything about him, so all we have is speculation and rumors. I do know it is not wise to get on his bad side though, or the entire year will be hell for you. Don't kiss his ass either though. He hates that too. He is an odd little bug, but he is kind of hot." Rachael winked at Annaleah and snickered.

"Yeah," Annaleah said, starting to feel better, "if you like the menacing temperamental type." They walked for a few moments in silence, crossing the campus to a smaller building.

"So what do you think an owl is doing out during the day time?" Rachael asked, holding the door open for Annaleah. "And what made it fly into the window?"

"I have no idea," Annaleah answered. "I was wondering that myself. I do know that owls are considered a bad omen in some cultures though." The bird made a noise of protest at this, almost as if it understood what Annaleah had just said. "In others, they are seen as birds of great wisdom and are not an omen of death, but a warning to hear the words in between the words being spoken and to discern the truth around you that's trying to remain hidden."

"Aren't they also considered messengers of departed loved ones as well? Rachael asked. Annaleah smiled, thrilled that Rachael knew so much about the spiritual meaning of owls.

"Yes indeed, I'm impressed you know so much about owl lore."

Rachael smiled, "I'm into the Native American totem animals, animal medicine and such. I like a little light reading in my spare time."

"That's wonderful, so what else do you know about owls?"

Rachael furrowed her brow, and after a moment answered, "They're great spirit communicators, and also seen as a traveler between this world and the spirit world. They were sacred to Athena, the Greek Goddess of wisdom, art and war tactics. They are quite a powerful bird, and gorgeous too."

"I remember seeing a movie when I was younger, one of my older sister's favorites, about the Greek gods and such,' Rachael commented.

"Athena had an owl named Bubo. It was a pretty good movie."

"Bubo. I like that." Annaleah looked down at the owl in her arms, wrapped in her jacket. Its deep yellow eyes were half closed, whatever distress it had been in earlier apparently forgotten. "Shall we call you Bubo then?"

Having reached the classroom, with a neatly polished "Mrs. Adams, Animal Husbandry" plaque screwed into the door, Rachael knocked three times. She looked down at the bird, her dark red lips smiling wide, "Well Bubo, here you are then. Your healing is at hand. Come meet Mrs. Adams."

Chapter Fifteen

Bubo

Mrs. Adams was a tall, thin woman with large, pale blue eyes set in a kind, slightly wrinkled face. She wore her graying hair pinned into an old fashioned bun on the top of her head, and wore a long navy dress with many buttons. The effect was rather matronly, but also somewhat comforting. She smiled at them as they entered.

"Hello Mrs. Adams. I am sorry to intrude on your first day of classes," Rachael said as the class turned their attention towards her. "But we are in need of your expertise. This is Miss Annaleah Grace. She's the new teacher working with Professor Bainbridge in World Religions," Rachael continued, addressing the class of about a dozen students as well. "She was just introducing herself when this great horned owl flew right into the window, and injured itself," she explained.

Mrs. Adams walked over to Annaleah and gently shifted the jacket wrapped around the owl. Very gently, and with some trepidation, she looked closely at the owl and ran her fingers over its wings, trying to see if the owl flinched in either fear or pain. When it didn't, she slowly lifted one of its wings, again looking for a reaction from the bird. As the bird didn't seem to be bothered, Mrs. Adam's released its wing and continued to study the bird in Annaleah's arms, which looked rather content, given the circumstances. "Oh my, well that certainly is unusual, isn't it? Out in the daytime, are we pretty one?" Looking back up at Annaleah and Rachael, Mrs. Adams put her hand softly on Annaleah's shoulder. "It is wonderful to meet you Miss Grace. I wish you all the luck teaching with the Professor. Maybe having a young beautiful woman at his side will soften him around the edges somewhat. I think that would be wonderful for just about everyone."

There were some snickers and laughter from the students behind her at this remark, and Annaleah felt her face grow hot. Her feelings for the Professor welled up inside her, quickening her heart and embarrassing her all at once. Really, how could she have such intense feelings for a man whom she had just met, and who had treated her so stonily? She was confused, and this further added to her feelings of unease. She looked away and smiled nervously, hoping her discomfort wasn't obvious to everyone in the room.

Mrs. Adams winked at Annaleah playfully and addressed her class. "So, can anyone tell me why a nocturnal bird such as this beautiful owl would be out during daylight hours? I'll let you think on this for a moment while I take a look at the bird. Ruben, will you please get me a blanket from the closet?" There was a gentle wash of talking between the students as a young man dressed in jeans and a red polo shirt walked over to the closet, and, after a moment's rummaging, walked to Mrs. Adams with a soft blue blanket.

"Thank you, Ruben." Slinging the blanket over her arm, Mrs. Adams walked to her desk and began to move things off of it and onto bookshelves, empty desks and her chair. Once this was done, she spread out the blanket and motioned for Annaleah to bring the owl to her. "I don't think our friend here is too bad off," she said, "Most birds of prey that get seriously injured actually die of shock long before their injuries prove fatal. This one seems rather calm for what it has just been through, and having so many humans around doesn't seem to bother it a bit. This entire situation is most unusual."

"I'm really not sure what it could mean either," Annaleah said, furrowing her brow in thought. "I've never seen or heard of an owl acting like this before, it just doesn't make sense." Looking at the bird, Annaleah felt strongly attached to it. What in the world was going on, she wondered? So many strange things had begun to occur since meeting the professor, was it possible he had summoned the bird? If he had, then why had he acted so angrily at her for having gone out to rescue it? None of it made sense to her, no matter how she tried to figure it out.

"Annaleah, since you are the one holding the bird, I am going to ask you to very slowly and very gently, open the jacket around the bird. Then, I want you to try to set it upright on the desk, on the blanket, so we can see the extent of its injuries."

Looking into the owl's eyes, Annaleah felt a strong sense of familiarity, as if she could sense the bird's energy. She felt a sense of peace coming from it, as if somehow it was sending her a message that it knew her. The strange energy moved her, warming her heart even as it confused her with the lack of a logical explanation as to how this could be happening. Was this a spirit of a lost loved one? A spirit guide come to her in the form of an owl, so that she would know, through the animal's spiritual medicine that something extraordinary, meant just for her was happening? Her heart opened at the thought, and even though she was aware of the stares focused on her, the feeling continued to grow as she looked at the great bird.

Annaleah looked from the owl in her arms to the class, who were all still looking at her with rapt attention. She walked over to the desk, and, looking down once more at the owl, told it softly, "Ok Bubo, I am going to unwrap the jacket, ok? See that blanket there? That's for you. I am going to put you on it, okay?" The owl looked up at her calmly, and blinked its deep yellow eyes. Annaleah felt somewhat silly, and blushing slightly, looked back to the teacher. She was making a fool of herself on her very first day of teaching. What could the class and Mrs. Adams be thinking of her? Had they seen her face flush earlier at the mention of the professor? "Oh please don't let them think I'm crazy," she silently prayed, hoping to regain her strength and composure.

"I know she can't understand me, but I feel I should try to explain what is going on to her anyway."

Mrs. Adams looked at her with a warm smile. "No need to explain. I think it is wonderful that you are talking to her. She might indeed get a sense of calmness from the tone of your voice."

Annaleah nodded, and looked down again at the bird. "Ok, here I go then." She shifted the bird around in her arms, so that she was holding it with one arm, and began to unwrap her jacket from it with her free hand. After being placed on the desk, the owl swiveled its head to face Annaleah, its amber eyes focusing upon her with a look of intensity. As it gazed at her, the bird spread its wings out to their full extent to test them, which elicited a unanimous sound of awe from everyone in the classroom. Its wingspan had to be at least four feet.

As their eyes met once more, Annaleah felt a sense of awe wash over her, as she was hit with wave after wave of what felt like adoration that emanated from the bird. It had to be something more than what it seemed to be. Though she knew that there would likely be a rational explanation made by Mrs. Adams and the class, and echoed by her as well, she knew this was something spiritual, with a deeper meaning than she dared to ponder at this moment.

After what seemed to be many moments, Mrs. Adams regained herself and addressed Annaleah and Rachael. "I am at a loss for a reasonable explanation for all of this. Great horned owls are notorious for being aggressive birds that don't like humans very well. This one must have been raised by humans from a very early age. There is no other reason for it being so calm. It seems particularly fond of you, Miss Grace. It also looks unharmed. I think it is a very lucky bird indeed to have survived crashing into a window at all, let alone doing so without any noticeable injuries."

"This is totally amazing," Rachael said, looking at the bird as it began to preen itself. "I think it has to be some sort of omen. Annaleah and I were just talking about it on our way here."

Annaleah's sense of a calm awe was suddenly gone. It was one thing to teach about omens in her own class, but talking of such things in this class was quite another.

Visions of Shandy filled her mind, and memories of the endless torment at her hands made Annaleah clench her fists as she tried to push the ugly memories out of her mind.

"Seeing an owl at daylight is seen as a very bad omen," one of the students, a young woman with brown plaited hair, at the back of the class said. "Even as a sign of death. I don't believe that though. Maybe it was being hunted by another animal, or its natural prey was scarce, which forced it to hunt during the daylight hours."

Annaleah was relieved to hear this, and let out a breath she had not known she was holding. "Thank you, Goddess," she whispered quietly.

"Excellent Candace, very good thinking," Mrs. Adams said. "Many times when you see an animal out of its natural habitat or operating outside its normal hours, it is because of disruptions in hunting. It also could have been chased out of its habitat by something, be it man or something else in nature, like a fire."

"No, I think it is something more esoteric than that," Rachael said, her large brown eyes full of wonder as she watched the bird. "Here we have a new teacher of the Occult and the arcane, and on her first day an owl flies into the window, cracking it, yet here it is unharmed. It is not afraid of humans, and when Annaleah told it she was going to put it on the desk, it just went there on its own, as if it understood her. That my friends, is not just odd, it's freaking otherworldly. On our way here, Annaleah told me some cultures see owls as messengers from spirits. Maybe this owl has a message?"

Annaleah thought what Rachael had said was very likely, though she found that such explanations were frowned upon and widely laughed at by most others she came across. She expected laughter from the students, or for someone to outright disagree or even be openly rude. No one did; they all stared at the bird, which was clearly in no state of shock.

"It's true," Annaleah said, "Some people think that owls can carry the soul of a loved one, and come to the aid of a living relative or friend. I am of the opinion that owls have gotten an undeserved bad reputation as far as omens and superstitions go. They have very powerful spirit medicine. Some Native American people think that seeing an owl is a sign that the trials and burdens that you or one very close to you carries have been lifted. Even though they could be associated with death, one doesn't always have to think of death in the most literal of terms. For instance, in tarot cards, most people freak out when they have the death card pulled, thinking it means either they or someone that they love will surely die. Death can mean the ending to a certain period in your life so that you can move on to something better, or it can mean the death of troubles, and the death of worry."

Mrs. Adams walked up to Annaleah, and putting her hand on her shoulder once more said, "While I find this all most fascinating, I have to tell you I am a bit nervous about having a wild bird of prey in my classroom. Though it seems calm now, it could, at any moment, decide to try to attack one of us. While I would love to continue this, I simply cannot risk my safety, or the safety of anyone in this room, and that includes the owl. There are certain laws about birds of prey, and great horned owls in particular. I'm afraid I'm going to have to phone the department of natural resources. With their blessing, I know of an animal rehabilitator who will help the owl."

The class erupted behind her, most of them in protest. Annaleah didn't want to leave the owl, even though she knew it was the most logical and ethical thing to do. She thought about it being the soul of one departed come to watch over her and her heart filled with hope.

Annaleah knew that handing the bird over to someone with knowledge of how to help it was the best thing to do, yet her heart wasn't ready to give the owl to someone else. What else was there to be done that would make sense? She couldn't keep the bird.

Her mind worked furiously to think of something as Mrs. Adams pulled a cell phone out of her pocket. If she had to let the bird go, then perhaps she could let it go outside herself. They had all agreed that the owl didn't appear to be injured. It was worth a shot.

"Please, let me try something first?" Annaleah asked Mrs. Adams. "If it doesn't work, I will make the phone call myself. Is that okay with you?" The other teacher nodded her consent, and moved back.

Annaleah turned to Rachael, hoping her request would be granted. "I have a huge favor to ask you, Rachael, feel free to say no. I have no idea if it will work, but this is the only thing I can think of."

"Of course, what do you need?"

"Your leather jacket," Annaleah answered. A look of realization at what Annaleah was about to ask of her lit in Rachael's eyes, and for a moment, Annaleah was afraid she was going to say no. After a brief moment though, Rachael shrugged out of her leather jacket and handed it to Annaleah without a word.

"Thank you," Annaleah whispered in Rachael's ear, "I owe you one." Taking a deep breath and steadying herself for what was about to come, Annaleah began to wrap the jacket over her forearm, securing it with the leather belt attached to the jacket. All eyes were on her.

"Bubo," Annaleah said simply. The bird ceased its preening and looked at her. Taking another breath, Annaleah held out her arm to the bird, and called it again. "Bubo, come." The owl opened its huge wings and, to the astonishment of everyone in the room, flew to Annaleah, and landed gracefully on her jacketed arm. Cries rose up from the previously silent students, surprise and awe in their words and expressions.

Annaleah exhaled her held breath, her heart hammering in her chest. She looked at the beautiful bird on her arm. Someone asked how she did that, another exclaimed it had to be a trick of some kind, that she was the animal's handler, and then everyone started talking all at once, the excitement electric in the air.

"Quiet, everyone, quiet!" Mrs. Adams said in a forceful but not unkind voice, waving her hands for emphasis. Once the students had settled down, Mrs. Adams turned back to face Annaleah. "I'm not sure how on earth you have done such a thing; I have never in my life seen anything like it. What you have just done stretches my levels of comprehension to an almost uncomfortable point. I do commend you though. Am I correct to assume that you will be releasing the owl back outside?" Her voice was soft but bright with astonishment.

"Yes, I will be," Answered Annaleah.

"Well then," said the matronly teacher, her eyes now full of childlike wonder, "Can we come with you?"

Not waiting for an answer, the students rose from behind their desks, obviously not willing to let such an opportunity pass them by.

Still in a state of awe, Annaleah looked into the bird's eyes. Trying to connect with it in her mind, she said, "Please trust me. I know you must be scared, I'm a little nervous too." The owl bobbed its head slightly, its eyes still looking at her, as if it could indeed hear her speak to it with her mind.

Leading the line of students outside, Annaleah walked slowly, getting used to the weight of the owl perched on her outstretched arm. It was heavier than she had expected it to be.

What if someone raced out of the classroom, and frightened Bubo she wondered? Would the owl take flight and be loose in the school? Would she be fired for bringing inside, or even worse, arrested? What if, Goddess forbid, the owl tried to attack one of the students or teachers?

Even as she worried, she felt a beautiful sense of calmness rush over her, a warm wave of trust that she was sure was sent from the bird.

"I will do my best," it seemed to say.

As she continued down the hall, Bubo's grip tightened on her arm. Annaleah could sense uneasiness from the owl as the noises from the school echoed in the hallway. Doors opened and closed, and the background sounds of classes in session must have been quite foreign to the owl. Bubo was trying her best, Annaleah knew, to keep calm and not break the bond of trust that she had forged with her.

Trying not to further spook the bird, she did her best not to cry out as she felt the sharp talons slice through the leather, and into her flesh.

"Oh no," she thought as she tried to ignore the pain in her arm, "I hope Rachael isn't mad her jacket just got torn."

The owl looked up at her, its body hunched as close to her arm as it could get. She swore the look in its eyes was apologetic.

Once outside, the students and their teacher formed a loose semi-circle around Annaleah and the owl, their eyes full of expectation. Annaleah found herself not truly wanting to let the owl go, feeling already somehow strangely attached to the bird she had only just seen for the first time not more than half an hour ago. Her heart tugged in her chest with a twinge of sadness, part of her hoping the bird didn't fly off to its freedom. Risking her fingers getting nipped, she slowly reached out a hand to the bird to pet it, and was pleasantly surprised when the bird nuzzled her hand affectionately.

"You have to go now, Bubo," Annaleah said softly to the bird. "It's been a pleasure to meet you, but you don't belong here. I hope to see you again someday." The owl blinked at her and made a soft sound, and then with a fluid, graceful movement, opened its wings and prepared for flight. Annaleah held her arm up high, thrusting it forwards to give the bird momentum. The great owl released her arm, its large brown wings fanning the air as it took flight.

"Goodbye, Bubo," Annaleah said as the bird made its way higher into the sky, and further away from her and the group of astonished students.

"Hey, it's okay," Rachael said, gently taking Annaleah's arm. "Maybe you'll see it again. In fact, I would be surprised if you didn't." Wondering how Rachel knew she was so upset, Annaleah instinctively rubbed at her eyes and was startled to find that there were tears there.

What a strange day it was turning out to be.

Chapter Sixteen

The Dream Keeper

The Dream Keeper outstretched his massive wings against the indigo of the twilight sky. Though normally loath to interfere, he knew things had to be sped up. The last dream he sent had opened their minds and their psyches, but they needed another push. Though they had felt the pangs of attraction for each other, they needed to be opened to it more, so much depended on it. If they did not become a team devoted to each other soon, it might be too late. Their stubbornness and fear were understandable, but time was running out. The situation was becoming worse, more lives of those like him were lost every day, lives that should never have been taken. His kind were meant to be immortal, created in the Heavens to glorify their Creator, to protect the Heavens and to watch over humanity. There had been so many wars, and so many of his kind had fallen that now when one of his brothers or sisters died in battle, there was no soul to cross over into Heaven, or to the Underworld. They simply ceased to exist, their energy quickly winked out and extinguished forever. It was unnatural. Energy of any kind couldn't just disappear, not without transforming into something else. This is why their deaths were often followed by natural disasters; earthquakes, a tsunamis or fires. There were, however, a small number of angels who dedicated themselves to collecting the quickly dissipating energy of the ones who died in battle, trying to preserve their energy in a way, by encapsulating them into objects and placing them in sacred sites throughout the earth. These angels were rare, but when there was a major battle being fought, they always seemed to be there, lying in wait to try and save the essence of those mighty ones of the Light who had died in war.

The Dream Keeper knelt at his altar, facing the West, his silvery blue wings opened wide. He plucked a feather from each wing and then let them fold neatly against his back. Holding a feather in each hand, he lifted them up so that the full moon fell upon them, letting them become "moonstruck" and thus enchanted. Praising the Creator, and with the deepest essence of love and light, the Dream Keeper began his chant in an ancient, beautiful language, his voice melodic and resonant, resonating deeply throughout his sacred space. He programmed a dream into each feather, one for each of the ones on the earth who played a pivotal part, though neither of them knew it. One was innocent, not knowing who or what she truly was, but powerful beyond her understanding. The other was full of bitter hurt and a deep sense of betrayal. Each was one of a kind, and they needed each other. His brothers and sisters of the Light needed them both, and so here he knelt, breathing words of enchanted dreams into each of his feathers, to bring the two of them closer together.

***

In her dream, Annaleah stood with bare feet on the moonlit path, deep in the woods she knew so well, behind the house she shared with Uncle John. The kudzu covered pines and Spanish moss draped oaks gave her a sense of familiar comfort as she gazed upon them. Here she had played since she was a child, learning the mysteries and wonders of nature. She had many fond memories here; One of which was as her only memory of her mother, Elise. Like Annaleah, Elise had loved nature, and Annaleah remembered walking in the woods with her and seeing her long blonde curls blowing in the wind around her slim face. In her memory, she was holding her mother's hand, and they were laughing and singing while trying to find interesting things to point out to each other. She couldn't have been much older than three, as her mother had died when she was four. This memory was sacred to Annaleah, and was one she saved to think of only sometimes, afraid if she thought of it too much, she would distort the sound of her Mother's voice, and of her laughter, one of the only things she had left of her. She wanted to remember it pure and real, so she kept the memory safely locked away in her heart, for the times when she needed it most.

Annaleah walked further along the path which opened into a small clearing far within the woods. A figure stood there, dressed in black and partially hidden in the shadows of the night. A sense of familiarity washed over her, as well as a sense of longing, though she was still unsure of who it was in the clearing. She stood at the edge of the woods, watching him, her eyes drinking in his form, or what she could make of it, and tried to understand what was happening. Her sense of urgency to go to whomever it was standing before her was mixed with a sense of foggy confusion.

The shadowed form moved slightly, the moonlight falling more fully on him, and Annaleah gasped in surprise as she looked upon Sebastian Bainbridge, but he was not as she knew him in her waking life. What little bit of skin she saw was pale and luminescent, as if arcs of light were within him, reminding her of white opals in their brilliance. He was much taller, at least eight feet, but it was neither of these two things that registered the most shock to her. It was his enormous wings. If he were eight feet now, then his wings were a full fifteen, reaching several feet over his head. They were full and glorious to behold, shimmering with a silvery white light that looked as if it were somehow alive. The feathers shone like the quality of his skin, but paler, a silver white so pure it almost hurt her eyes to gaze upon them. His hair was still long and black, but it too shone with its own light, a deep blue aura about it, as if the moonlight had come to life within it. He was beautiful.

Sebastian must have felt the intensity of Annaleah's gaze upon him, for he turned and looked right at her, where she stood trying to hide behind the branches of a small pine at the edge of the clearing. The moment his eyes met hers, she felt her legs lose a bit of their strength, for they were not the eyes she knew in the "real" world, but eyes she felt, without knowing how or why, that she knew intimately. His eyes had no pupils; the whites only held a large, colored iris that was silver and reflective like a mirror. She was frightened for a moment, though she sensed he meant her no harm. What was happening?

"Annaleah," Sebastian said, his pale, full lips smiling at her. He opened both his arms and the full span of his large, beautiful wings to her, radiating a sense of love, one which washed over her so completely that she felt hypnotized by him. The swelling of her heart became a flood of emotions, as if she had known and loved this creature for longer than she had even known herself, had known life or breath. Nothing made sense, and so she let go of sense all together and went with her emotions, which were so powerful they drove her out of her place behind the small pine, and towards Sebastian in the clearing of the woods.

As Annaleah moved, she noticed her feet were not her own feet, but those like the creature which called to her. They too, were pale, but instead of lit from within with a silver light, they radiated with a warm, pale golden fire, little arcs flashing here and there. As she walked, she noticed her body felt different in stature, not the tiny five-foot frame she was used to. She too, was much taller, though not quite as tall as the creature Sebastian Bainbridge had become. Moving seemed more effortless, as if her intention to move fueled her forward more than the movements of her feet. She was confused, but too blissful in her state of emotions to let the confusion settle in and ruin it.

Finally, Annaleah stood face to face with the strange and beautiful being that Sebastian had become. He looked down at her with a serene and loving smile on his lips, his silver eyes soft and gentle despite their otherworldly qualities. The moment seemed to last forever, emotions and meaning conveyed wordlessly, carried into her heart and mind, filling her with a deep, living sense of passion and longing. It washed over her and through her until it became all she could think, all she could feel, reverberating in each heartbeat, exhaled with every breath. Finally, she fell towards him, into his arms, consumed, on fire with longing for nothing more in the world but to be held by him.

Sebastian caught Annaleah neatly in his arms, and encircled her in his wings, holding her so close she felt she could melt right into him and together they would burn as one being. Tears came to her then, spilling down her cheeks and falling onto her breasts, a silver light coming from them as they fell. Sebastian opened his wings then and placed a finger under her chin, tilting her head up to look into his mirror eyes. As she saw herself in them, glowing and alive and beautiful, it felt so very right. Sebastian wiped the tears from her eyes, slowly, gently and with great care. His eyes never left hers as he bent his head down, until right before the moment when he caught her lips with his, and everything in the world ceased to exist but their kiss. In that sacred, glorious moment, as their lips pressed together, she was pierced to her heart with all-consuming adoration, and from behind her she felt a great motion, as if she had moved something with a great weight on her back. Confused, and a bit shocked, she broke the kiss, turning to see what was happening behind her.

Sebastian laughed despite her apparent confusion and said, "Oh Annaleah my darling, did you forget?"

Feeling a bit betrayed by his laughter when he could plainly see her distress, Annaleah asked, "Did I forget what?"

At this Sebastian outstretched his magnificent wings to their full height and length, blocking out the sky and the moon hanging therein.

"Your wings Annaleah; you forgot you had wings."

Chapter Seventeen

Mesmerized

With a sharp intake of breath, Sebastian awoke in the perfect darkness of his room. As he listened to the thunderous galloping of his heart, his mind spun as he tried to understand what had happened in his dream.

He trembled as he regained more consciousness, and though he willed himself to stop, the tremors continued to pass through him, wave after wave. It was no use to fight them, and he finally resigned himself to their grasp, gritting his teeth in frustration that he had lost control of himself.

Fragments of the dream washed through his mind. He had found himself in the middle of a clearing in a moonlit forest, in a form he had not taken in countless years. Feeling his wings on his back, the familiarity of their weight and the wind rushing over them in the coolness of the night had brought back memories both comforting and terrible. He had stood there, looking around him, wondering why he was there, and why he was no longer in human form. Before he had the chance to form any answers, he saw her. He thought of the luminescence of her skin as she walked from the shadow of the trees, the faraway look in her eyes before it came to her who he was, and the gaze of adoration in them after she did.

He recalled the warm flood of an emotion he had not felt in so long. It overcame him, radiating from his very soul as she glided to him, her golden wings gently folded behind her back. He hadn't fought the feeling, but had welcomed it, even enjoyed it as it filled him.

It wasn't likely for him to let his guard down in waking life, but those who worked in the Unseen knew dreams were another matter.

His dreams were an opening, a means to get his attention when there were few other ways of doing so. They certainly held his attention now.

Closing his eyes tighter as he remembered his dream, he fought with himself. He wasn't ready to let emotions weaken him, as beautiful and tempting as they might be. Yet part of him wanted nothing more than that, to let the tenderness he felt from her wash away the bitter hurt in him, to be freed of his burden by the touch of her lips on his. It required trust, and that was something he wasn't sure he had to offer.

Something was going on in the Unseen, something with remarkable importance. There was no other explanation for it. There was too much going on in too little time for it to be anything but guided by the hands of those who had once been his brothers and sisters. He knew Annaleah was a central part of it, but why her? Why was this beautiful woman-child so important?

And beautiful she was. Though his heart was scarred and he had all but forgotten the tenderness of raw, unadulterated emotion, the powerful elation he felt when he saw her in the dream was undeniable. He remembered how he had wanted to rush to her, to sweep her up in his arms, to kiss her until there was no more doubt in his heart. He would have done so, if he could have taken his eyes off of her. There had been a power and intensity when their eyes met, a linking of the spirit in a way that was more intimate than the touching of flesh.

As Sebastian remembered their kiss, he parted his lips, trying to relive the moment when her mouth had first pressed over his. His heartbeat quickened once more, and momentarily forgot his vow to himself to never love, to never trust again. For just this brief moment of time, he told himself, he would allow for this simple pleasure, this gift from the Unseen.

Something changed in him as he did so, and in his mind's eye he envisioned a silver blue feather gently falling through the air, illuminated by the moonlight.

Then Sebastian knew, it had been a dream sent by the arch angel Gabriel, the Dream Keeper.

If Gabriel had taken the time to send this message to him, whatever else it might mean, Sebastian knew one thing for certain.

War was coming.

Chapter Eighteen

Nephila the Jorogumo

Annaleah roused briefly from her dream, and finding herself in her bed, felt a pang of disappointment at leaving Dream Time. She could still feel the tingle of the creature's lips on hers. The creature...Professor Bainbridge? Since she had met him, she had tried hard not to look at him as anything but the moody, intense man she had just begun to teach with. She had to admit however, that try as she might, she had begun to see him as more than that. Closing her eyes, she permitted herself to think of him as something more, as a man, and as an attractive one at that. He did have a nice, full mouth, and his eyes, though dark as night and holding a strange power that puzzled her, were also in their way, quite handsome. His voice was low and his accent was rich and mysterious, and his particular way of enunciation was eloquent.

Annaleah smiled, the afterglow of her dream still full in her mind and spirit. She willed herself back to sleep to see if she could again meet the creature that the professor had become in her dream.

***

Once again, Annaleah found herself in the woods, still on the path, a little way from the clearing. The energy of the atmosphere around her, however, was not the same as it had been before. The moonlight did not lend its beauty here, nor its essence of serenity. Shadows, thick as syrup, clung to the trees, undulating in a way that made her feel dizzy. There was a sense of danger hanging heavy and thick in the air, a feeling that she was being watched by someone with evil intentions.

In bare feet, Annaleah spun around in a circle, willing her eyes to see into the inky darkness of the thick shadows, to find what or who it was that watched her. She didn't notice the silence around her was absolute, until she stepped on a twig and heard it crack under her foot, sending her heart hammering thunderously inside her chest. Looking down at the path she stood on, she saw what appeared to be several black specks move from the grass of the woods onto the path itself. Some were large; some no bigger than her fingernail. Only a few came at first, and then more followed, until there were many, all moving toward her.

"What in the world?" Annaleah thought to herself, as she watched the dark objects, trying to make out what they were. When realization hit her, fear struck her like a slap across the face and adrenaline surged into her blood. They were spiders. Hundreds of them, all crawling as one toward her, their insectile legs moving them closer to where she stood. Though she loved all of nature, she strongly disliked spiders. They never seemed natural to her, as if they were alien creatures dropped off by some evil otherworldly people to terrorize humanity. They had always frightened her, and now they were here in a horrifying hoard, moments away from converging upon her.

Annaleah ran. With every muscle in her body and every thought in her mind, she ran with as much energy and purpose as she could. She hoped to find the Professor in the clearing, waiting for her, to save her. Her bare feet hit the earth with almost no sound; the only thing she could hear were the movements of thousands of legs, the scuttle of carapaces on earth, and the threat of mandibles clicking behind her. The shadows in the trees coalesced into forms she could now make out, and these were even more terrifying. More spiders, some as large as her head, dropped from the branches and joined their brethren on the path moving towards her.

With a burst of speed, Annaleah made it to the clearing, where she saw a form hunched in the middle of it, motionless. She ran to the form, not noticing that the spiders had stopped at the edge of the woods, not coming into the clearing itself. As she approached the figure, it threw off its silky black cape, and stood up, startling her. A beautiful Asian woman stood before her, smiling wickedly. Her long black hair shone in what little moonlight the crescent moon and stars offered. Her skin was smooth and seemed to radiate a golden hue, though her skin itself was pale as alabaster. Her lips were stained scarlet as if with blood, a stark contrast to the fairness of her skin. Her deep brown eyes were lined in kohl, her lashes long and full. She wore a black and yellow silken kimono with intricate golden embroidery, and a silver pendant at her throat in the shape of a spider.

"Expecting to see someone else?" the woman asked Annaleah, smiling even more broadly before throwing back her head in maniacal laughter. Annaleah was frozen, too terrified to speak. The woman stopped laughing, lowered her head again and, smiling once more, looked Annaleah in the eye as she moved closer. "What's the matter girl, cat got your tongue?" The woman walked around her, slightly hunched forward as if she would lunge at any moment. "I see you have met my children, yes? They come out when it will rain, and also, in times of war. They were only trying to say hello, and you ran from them, you rude girl! You have offended my babies, and so you have offended me. Are you prepared to make it up to me?"

"Leave her alone, Jorogumo!" said a strong, feminine voice to their left. At hearing this, the woman before Annaleah spun towards the voice, her expression one of pure wrath.

"Do not call me Jorogumo! Who dares to call me by this name? I am Nephila. Who goes before me and orders me as such? I demand you show yourself!" There was a rustling, and the wind picked up a notch, blowing both Annaleah's hair and that of the terrifying woman before her. The air to their right began to shimmer. A form began to appear before them as if being formed from the rippling, spinning air solidifying before them. The air began to trace the form of a woman, who spoke as she gained more physicality.

"I am Marchosias, and it is time for you to go, Nephila. You have done enough. You do not have permission to be here." The woman who spoke had now become fully solid and every bit as beautiful as the one called Nephila. She was taller than Annaleah, with long, blonde hair, her face slim and fairy like. A pair of ebony wings were folded against her back, large like the creature the Professor had become, at least ten feet over her head, even as they were folded. She wore a white Grecian style goddess dress.

A look of fury and fear crossed Nephila's face, and it was clear she was livid as she focused on the newcomer. The woman who seconds ago was so beautiful suddenly opened her mouth and, with eyes impossibly large, made a terrible sound, like a scream and wail both at once, painfully high, loud and shrill. From her stretched lips came a tearing sound that, even over her wailing, Annaleah could hear clearly; the separation of flesh from flesh. Blood began to flow down the woman's face as her mouth tore open, and large shiny black mandibles emerged from the broken hole her mouth had become. Her widened eyes began to cloud over, becoming large black eyes that continued to split and divide until there were eight of them. Still, she screamed. Her body began to jerk as if she were wracked with strange spasms, the sound of broken bones accompanying each spasmodic movement.

The woman who called herself Marchosias seemed unfazed, though Annaleah was frozen in terror, unable to move or speak. Turning towards Annaleah and whispering in her ear, the woman said, "It's time to wake up, Annaleah." Still the sound of screaming, flesh tearing and bones breaking continued. Yellow and black arachnid legs began to protrude out of the body of Nephila. The woman with black wings placed her hand over Annaleah's eyes so she would see no more, and said again in a soft, comforting voice, "Wake up, Annaleah. Wake up."

Then, thankfully, the sounds of terror began to fade, and Annaleah felt herself falling backward, into total darkness.... Falling awake.... Falling blessedly awake....

Chapter Nineteen

Dream Walker

It only took Seth about fifteen minutes to get to Annaleah's house. She'd been sobbing as she'd asked him to come over. Though he could barely make out what she was saying, he was out the door in a flash. Always the night owl, he had been up anyway, doing a bit of reading on his day off from his artwork, which he sold to collectors around Atlanta for a decent price. His work was good, mostly paintings in an abstract style, of things of an occult nature. He enjoyed painting pagan deities or dragons, some fairy folks or mythical creatures. He did a bit of sculpture too. and those got the highest prices, as they took the most time and were a bit more difficult to do.

Seth let himself in with the key Annaleah had given him years ago when they had been friends for about a year. It had been a sign of her trust and faith in his loyalty. They had been so young back then, he recalled, smiling fondly. He hoped she had calmed down a bit so they could talk about what had upset her so much. He knew it had something to do with a dream she'd had, and that she was frightened. She hadn't wanted to wake Uncle John and worry him, and Seth understood that. She said Uncle John had to come home from work early that night, something he rarely did. His hours had been cut and he worked every chance he got, even though he was a sick man. He must have felt for him to come home from his job as an ER triage nurse at the Doltree hospital.

Uncle John took pride in his work and in his ability to take care of himself, as well as Annaleah. He had worked through being sick before, and, Seth guessed that knowing this too was partly why Annaleah was so upset. Uncle John was the last family she had left, and watching him get sicker and having to suffer with his chemo treatments broke her heart. She hid this from Uncle John though and was always cheerful and hopeful, full of nothing but helpful words and love, never letting him see how much it hurt her when he had one of his bouts. He had been doing well for a while now, both of them had been hopeful when none of his hair had yet fallen out from chemo. He had seemed to be getting better.

Knowing he had to come home from work must really have upset her. He knew she helped her uncle, as much as he had helped her since she was little. The oncologists had been quite surprised when they told him it was Hodgkin's disease. "This is a cancer we rarely see in adults. It tends to be a childhood disease," his doctor had told Uncle John. Seth knew Annaleah had wanted to burst into tears, but she had told Seth that she had grabbed Uncle John's hand instead, and told his doctor, "Well, if Uncle John has to get cancer, it would have to be the one children get. He is, after all, only a child at heart." That had been two years ago, when Uncle John was a stage two. He was a stage three now.

As Seth walked through the door, he looked at Annaleah, his heart sinking with concern as she slowly sat up on the couch. She was wearing her lilac colored silk robe over her nightclothes and had been curled up into a ball, her arms wrapped around her knees. Tears still stained her cheeks, and her eyes looked red and puffy from crying. Normally she would have jumped off the couch and ran to him, throwing her arms around him, but tonight he knew she just didn't have it in her.

"Hey Seth," she said simply. "Thank you for coming over."

"You look terrible. What happened?" Seth sat beside her on the couch, his concern blossoming in his heart and quickening its pace. She looked slightly dazed, and this worried him. He took her hand in his and held it gently, waiting for her to gather her thoughts.

"Can you make us some tea first, please?" Annaleah asked. "I would have made us some but.... I just feel so out of it right now, so drained. I have some chamomile and hibiscus in the cupboard over the stove. You know where everything else is." Her voice sounded so tiny as she spoke, as if she truly had been drained of all her energies.

"Of course," Seth answered. "I'm on it." He rose from the couch, kissing her on top of the head before making his way to the kitchen to brew their tea. He didn't say anything as he brought the teapot to a boil and prepared their mugs with four sugars each. Though it might have seemed a lot of sugar to most, he and Annaleah had bonded over the knowledge that they both shared an insatiable sweet tooth.

He let her gather her strength and her thoughts, not wanting to push her. It had been a long time since he had seen her this upset. It hurt him to see her in this state, but knowing he was there with her also made him feel better.

After a bit, Seth returned to the living room with two steaming cups of chamomile and hibiscus tea. He handed one mug to Annaleah and set the other on the coffee table in front of him before sitting down again beside her. She cupped the warm mug in her hands, seeming to gain strength from it. She looked even more pale than usual and a bit dazed. Her eyes were glazed and unfocused, and her face was almost expressionless. Her dazed demeanor worried him.

"I think I am dream walking again, Seth."

Seth leaned closer and put his hand on top of hers, his heart sinking in his chest, knowing whatever it was that she had gone through had shaken her terribly. She didn't look like herself, and for her to act like this frightened him.

"Tell me." Seth said, leaning closer to her. Seth remembered the time she had dream walked when she was younger, just entering puberty, and it had proved to be quite an issue for her, and for Uncle John, too. They had thought it was simple sleepwalking at first, when the police dropped her off back at home early in the morning. They had seen her walking barefoot in Hideman park, almost six miles from their home.

After it happened for the third time, the police told Uncle John if they saw her out past midnight again, he would have to go to court for violating a number of child safety laws. She had been insistent that she had been dreaming, and since it had been impossible for her to walk that far in such little time, with no blisters on her feet, he and uncle john had believed her.

In some dreams Annaleah had said she had fought these angel beings before, and indeed, the marks of her dreams did show up on her skin, which prompted Seth into doing research on dreams and dream walking. He had found out how rare it was to be a natural dream walker, and that most spiritualists had to train diligently for years to be able to dream walk. Usually it meant walking into another person's dreams and interacting with them there, but Annaleah seemed to be able to take it even further. The idea that she could slip from dreams into reality was a disturbing one. What if she found herself on top of a building and in her sleep, walked off of the roof, thinking she was somewhere else in her dream? Or what if she was dreaming of breathing underwater and transported herself to the bottom of one of the real world's oceans?

That idea that she could travel in the real world using dreams as a means of transportation was just thoroughly frightening. At least, it was if she had no control over it. What if she got stuck in a dream, and never woke up again?

Seth closed his eyes and sought his strength. "Well," he told himself, "That means potentially good things could come through too."

It was hard for Seth not to express his concern for her, but he knew she would shake him off if he did so. Instead, he squeezed her hand. He sensed there was more she needed to say, and her dazed demeanor told him it was going to be disturbing.

"The night before I went to my first class," Annaleah continued, "I dreamed an awful dream. Uncle John had to wake me up. He said I was screaming." Annaleah paused, her face crumpling with the force of her emotions. Seth could tell she was trying to control herself, but she was having a hard time. She needed him to be strong for her, so he reigned in his concern. He swallowed hard and waited for her to tell him the rest of what she had gone through.

"I dreamed of a war, but not between men. I was standing on the bloodied ground where angels fought with one another. Those with indigo eyes fought with the ones whose eyes were silver. The sky was dark, swollen and bruised, as if it suffered from battle wounds too, yet it continued to bleed forth more and more angels. Some were screaming and some were speaking in a language I have heard before in other dreams but could not understand. None of them seemed to know I was there. After Uncle John left, when I got up to go to the bathroom, I had mud on my feet. How on earth did I get mud on my feet when I was in my bed dreaming?"

Annaleah looked at Seth, her eyes now greener than usual, the tears bringing out their color all the more. Panic gripped deeply inside his chest, its icy fingers making his heart beat even faster. Why was this happening again, he wondered? What did it mean?

She took a sip of her tea and continued. "Tonight, my dream started out rather nice. I was in the woods, where my mother used to take me. I was on a path that led to a clearing in the woods, and there stood, of all people, Professor Bainbridge, only he wasn't really Professor Bainbridge."

The professor...? Seth was now certain he had something to do with all the strange things that had been going on ever since he had entered Annaleah's life. Even though he felt certain Professor Bainbridge was some sort of catalyst, Seth felt an odd certainty he wasn't quite as bad as he seemed to be. Perhaps he was here to protect her in some way. She had said the dream had started out nicely, so it made sense.

"I mean it was the professor, but he was.... different. He had wings, huge wings, and they were so beautiful. He was beautiful. His eyes were silver, not just the iris part, but his entire eye; he had no pupils at all, like his eyes were mirrors. He called to me and I felt like I had known him forever, so I went to him." She took a deep breath and looked off for a moment, as if her eyes were focusing on something Seth couldn't see. "It was so real."

For the first time that night, Annaleah smiled, the dazed look gone from her eyes and replaced by a gleam of wonderment.

"I could smell the crisp night air. I could feel the grass under my feet. I could hear the crickets in the woods and Gods, when he kissed me..." Annaleah trailed off, smiling just a bit.

Seth looked at her, amused. Kissing the Professor? That seemed a bit odd. It wasn t something he had been expecting to hear, but he was glad to see her smiling. He thought briefly of teasing her to break the lingering tension, but knew right now wasn't a good time.

If she was attracted to him, he was happy for her, she deserved a good man in her life. Assuming the professor was good, that is.

"Wow. I didn't see that one coming." Annaleah's eyes gained focus again almost at once, and she looked defensive.

"No, it isn't like that," Annaleah said. " It was like I said, as if I knew him forever, not as the Professor, but as the creature he was. He looked like one of the angels that were fighting in my other dream. Only his eyes didn't have pupils like theirs did. And Seth," Annaleah paused and looked him in the eye, "I had wings too! Though I didn't know it until just before I woke up."

"It doesn't sound that awful. I mean, the dream before that with the battle scene sounds terrifying, but the dream in the woods, it sounds like you kind of enjoyed it. What makes you think that one was dream walking?"

Annaleah considered this for a moment. "The dream was just, so intense, as if I really, truly were there. I woke up after this dream, but only for a second."

Annaleah smiled at Seth and gently moved his hand off hers. She picked her mug up and took a sip. Seth was glad she had calmed down a bit.

After she had set the mug back in its place, she took a deep breath and went on. "It was the dream I had after that which really upset me, and is the one that frightens me. I think there is something in my dreams that is trying to escape into this reality to harm me. I know that sounds crazy, but it's the truth. If what I dreamed of is going to try to come out of my dreams, then I'm afraid of what will come of it."

Annaleah hung her head, as if it were too full of emotion to hold upright anymore. A tear fell from her eye, and Seth gave in and wrapped his arms around her. He held her close to him, his mind racing. He would die in a heartbeat to protect her.

He hadn't heard of anything coming out of a dream into reality before, but that didn't mean it was impossible. The ramifications of this could be devastating. He could feel her shaking in his arms, and was surprised to feel himself shaking too.

"I need your help Seth. You know so much about dreams," Annaleah whispered against his shoulder. "I don't mind the dreams of walking in the woods and seeing a beautiful creature, but I have to tell you about the next dream."

He released her from his protective embrace, and she pulled away from him slowly, still shaking. As she lifted her head to look at him once more, the tears had come back, leaving trails on her cheeks.

Seth brought his hand to her face, and carefully wiped a tear away with the pad of his thumb.

"Don't cry," he whispered, though another tear fell. He gently wiped it away, too.

"I may not be the biggest or the roughest guy around, but I promise you I won't let anything happen to you. I promise to protect you in any way I can."

Annaleah took his hand and placed a kiss on it, splashing it with another tear.

"Thank you," she said as she tried to smile for him.

Seth slowly moved away from her to grab a tissue from the coffee table. She took it from him and began to dab at her face.

"I was in the woods on the path to the clearing again," Annaleah swallowed, "only this time I felt as if something terrible was there with me. The darkness in the woods seemed to be alive, and it was! I was being spied on by hundreds and hundreds of spiders. They dropped from the trees and came from the woods onto the path I was on. At first I didn't know what they were, but when I realized they were spiders, some of them as big as a basketball, I ran to the clearing to a hunched over figure. I thought it was the Professor, having just seen him moments ago in my other dream."

She looked down at her hands that held the tear stained tissue, wringing it as though it might give her some answers. "

"It wasn't. It was a beautiful Asian woman who called herself Nephila."

Seth gasped audibly.

"What is it?" her green eyes looked at him expectantly.

"Nothing, I'm sorry," Seth apologized. "It's just that name sounds familiar." Seth searched his mind for a moment, knowing that name meant something, but he came up with nothing. "I'm sorry, please go on."

Annaleah drank the last of her tea and then put the empty mug back down on the coffee table. "The woman knew she terrified me," Annaleah said. "At first I wasn't sure why. She was a beautiful woman wearing an elaborate kimono of black and yellow, but I knew she wasn't what she seemed. She spoke threateningly to me, but in a roundabout way. Something about offending her spider babies by running from them when all they wanted was to say hello. Something else about them coming out when it was going to rain and when war was afoot. I was so scared I couldn't speak. She got mad when I didn't say anything."

Annaleah stared blankly at the mug on the coffee table for a moment before she went on. "Then, suddenly, another woman appeared, forming herself out of the air. She was only a bit taller than me, with straight blonde hair a bit darker than mine, and she had wings like the creature the Professor was; only hers were black. She called herself...Marchosias."

Marchosias.... That name seemed familiar too, though he couldn't remember where he had heard it before. Why was he unable to recall such important sounding names, he wondered? Annaleah lifted an eyebrow, looking closely at him.

"Anyway," Annaleah continued, "Marchosias called this other woman Jorogumo, which really pissed her off. That's when she said her name was Nephila, and asked who dared to call her Jorogumo. None of this makes any sense, Seth."

Annaleah put her head in her hands, and sighed loudly, wiping at her face before she went on. "Marchosias told Nephila to leave me alone, and then Nephila began to change into a hideous black and yellow spider. Her mouth split open and mandibles came out; her eyes went dark and morphed into eight eyes. The other creature put her hand over my eyes and told me to wake up. So I did."

"My God Annaleah, that sounds terrifying!" Seth said. "I'm so sorry you went through that. I wish I could have dream walked there to you. I promise I'm going to do my best to figure this out for you. I'm not going to let her hurt you."

Seth wanted desperately to calm her down and reassure her, but he had to ask her something.

"Did you wake up with muddy feet?" he asked, looking down to see her clean bare feet, wondering if she had washed them before he got there.

"No, not this time," Annaleah told him, rolling back the sleeves of her lilac robe. Tears came to her eyes once more, spilling down her cheeks. Seth looked at her arms and saw dozens of red, raised welts on each. Shocked, he took her left arm to examine it further.

"When I woke up this time," Annaleah continued, "there was no mud, though I wish that is what happened. Instead as I woke up I felt something crawling all over my arms. When I threw the covers back, I had spiders on me, all over my arms. They bit me, over and over. I am amazed I didn't scream, but I couldn't, I was too scared. I managed to brush them all off of me and step on them, but not before they did this."

As if for emphasis, a shiny black spider crawled up the table leg and onto the coffee table, chittering and opening and closing its mandibles as it went.

Annaleah jumped up on the couch, but before she could scream, Seth smashed it with his bare hand, sending its now gooey body parts to different corners of the table.

Amped up on adrenaline, they both stared wide eyed at the table, their breath ragged and deep.

Snapping out of it, Annaleah dropped to her knees on the couch, covering her head with her hands, sobbing.

Seth was just as terrified as she was, now knowing just how much danger she was in. He rushed to her side, wiping his hand on his pants before he touched her.

Seth tried not to show how scared her really was for her. If she had brought those spiders back with her, then that meant not only could she travel through dreams, but that other things could, too. That meant her safety was in jeopardy. Who knew what crazy things she could bring back with her, potentially worse than spiders?

"It's ok, it's gone, I killed it." Seth said, trying to refocus himself on being strong for Annaleah. He didn't want her to see him shaking. She didn't seem to hear him though, and she was trembling more than ever.

He sat beside her and wrapped her in his arms again, not knowing what to say, but wanting her to feel safe. He rocked her, feeling helpless as he wiped a tear from his own face.

"It's not okay." she spoke against him. "It might never be okay again."

"You need to wake Uncle John, Annaleah, and let him to look at your arms. He will know if you need to go to the hospital. I don't want to frighten you but those things could be poisonous."

Annaleah jerked her arm back and began to roll her sleeves back down her arms. "No! I am not waking Uncle John up. He's not well, you know that. I don't want him to see me upset. If I do tell him what happened, it will be when he feels stronger. Besides, there are no red bulls-eye looking marks or streaks on any of the bites. That means whatever those bastards were, they probably weren't poisonous. They were shiny black spiders, about the length of my thumbnail. I promise to keep an eye on them though. If they get worse I will take the day off and go to the hospital, okay?"

"Ok Annaleah," Seth conceded, knowing he couldn't talk her out into it. Could a hospital here in the waking world even help her with bites from an otherworldly spider? The best he could do for now was to support in in whatever decision she made. If it turned out to be not in her best interest, he would be the first one there to help her then, too.

"It does sound like dream walking. Tell me the name of the women again, if I can look her up we might find some sort of way to fight her." He pulled out his smart phone. She told him, and after a moment of searching he found what he was looking for. "Got it; a Japanese creature of folk lore, like a ghost or goblin, said to seduce men with their beauty, only to transform later into a spider and devour their victim."

Seth looked up from his phone to his friend, worried. "I know that you know a lot about the occult and different folk lore of the world, have you ever read or seen anything about the Jorogumo?" he asked.

Annaleah shook her head, her blonde curls falling over her eyes, only to be quickly brushed away. "No, never. That's what makes it seem so real, so horrible and so threatening. She's a real creature, and she had her babies follow me out of Dream Time. Why, Seth? Why me? I am no one special, why are there angels fighting in my dreams and terrible demon-like figures trying to follow me out of my dreams?" Seth saw she was trembling and wished he had answers to give her, something to say that would make her feel better.

"I don't know, hon. I do know that you are special, very special. These creatures might know something you don't. We'll look into dream wards and rituals, okay?"

"What about the other name?" Annaleah asked, ignoring Seth's last comment. "Marchosias? Does it say anything about her?" Seth looked back down at his smart phone and pressed some buttons.

"Yeah," Seth answered, "apparently she is a demoness too, but not totally evil. I remember reading about angels and demons before and finding out that not all those who fell are evil, in fact, they can be quite helpful to humans if approached with respect.

"The same goes for angels. Though they operate on the Goddess's word and will, not all of them are keen on humanity. Some still blame us for the loss of their brethren, for the Watchers who were seduced and thusly cursed, and for the original fall itself. Some angels who fell are neutral and serve neither the darkness nor the light."

Seth continued to read for a moment. "Anyway, depending on the website, it seems this Marchosias is seen as both male and female. Since she showed herself to you as a female we will go with she. She was an angel of the order of Dominions, and though she didn't fall as the others did, she was forced to take a side when the first war in Heaven began. She didn't want the war to occur at all and was hoping matters could be resolved, but when the Creator wouldn't negotiate, she stood in support of negotiations with those who were to fall, and so was locked out of Heaven.

"She is a powerful negotiator between the angels and the demons, and an even more powerful warrior. She usually shows herself in her demonic form, a cross between a wolf and a gryphon with a serpent's tail. In human form, she is described as you saw her, blonde haired with black wings, but not really a woman yet, more of a teenager." Seth looked up from the phone and focused on Annaleah.

"So the question remains," Annaleah said, looking at Seth, "why are they visiting me in my dreams?"

"I don't know yet, Annaleah," Seth answered, "But I promise, we're going to find out."

Chapter Twenty

Summer Rain

Seth stayed with Annaleah through the rest of the night, watching over her as she slept to make sure she didn't have any more disturbing dreams. He borrowed her laptop to do research, looking over at her occasionally as she slept. She didn't seem to have any more nightmares, and she didn't dreamwalk anywhere, though she did toss and turn most of the night.

Seth hated to wake her when morning finally came, as she really hadn't had a restful night. However, he had no choice, as she had classes again this morning. Having the presence of mind to greet her with a hot cup of coffee, he gently roused her from the couch that had served as her bed. He handed her the coffee as she arose, rubbing at her eyes.

"What time is it?" she asked him, her voice thick with sleep. She sat up slowly, pulling the blanket over her. Still looking half asleep, she accepted the coffee he handed her, and sat looking at it for a moment.

"It's about eight thirty in the morning," Seth said. "I let you sleep as late as I dared, but your first class starts at ten. I knew it would take you a while to wake up fully, so I got you up. I wish you could take the day off and go to the doctor about those bites." Annaleah made a soft grunting noise of protest at this.

Annaleah sat the coffee mug down on the side table and leaned further back on the couch. "I'm so tired," she said. "I wish I could go back to sleep." Seth sat beside her, feeling bad for her.

"I know you do," he said, patting her leg sympathetically. "That's not just any coffee, though. It's coffee with two shots of espresso in it. I put cinnamon and sugar in it as well. Try to drink it." Seth turned to retrieve the mug, and when he turned back to her, she had pulled the blanket over her head. He laughed and pulled it down over her face. Annaleah made a small whining noise as he did so. He held the cup to her, and she sat up and took it.

"Did you find out anything else interesting while I slept?" Annaleah asked, looking at the laptop.

Seth nodded, feeling like his heart was beating too fast. He hadn't learned as much as he had wanted, but what he had found was a bit on the frightening side. She seemed to be able to do more than what was written of in the books he had read that night. "Well, we know dream walking usually just involves a dreamer's ability to visit another person's dreams. It's also something that usually has to be practiced and takes great skill. Yet for some reason, not only can you do this, but you also seem to have the ability to travel to other places you dream of. Not only that, you also appear to have others beginning to dream walk into your dreams. This is some pretty intense stuff. I haven't been able to find out as much as I want to yet, but as soon as I find out more I'll let you know. I'll study more when you're at class. For now, go ahead and get ready, I'll drive to you the University."

After another cup of espresso laced coffee, Annaleah had mostly woken up and was ready for her day at the University. It was raining outside and the sky was the color of slate, promising storms to come. With a heavy sigh of resignation, she resolved to be as strong as she could, knowing that even though rain had a tendency to make her even more sleepy, with a bit of willpower she would be able to overcome it. She refused to let the rain set a somber tone to the day, nightmares or not. There was no more room for negativity today, no matter how it might gnaw at her in the inner recesses of her being.

Still, she hoped she would be able to stay awake. Annaleah sighed and pulled on her brown and pink paisley raincoat as she left the house. She hoped the long sleeve shirt she wore under her coat hid the spider bites well enough to avoid curious eyes.

Seth drove Annaleah wordlessly to the school, leaving her to be lost within her own thoughts. As she listened to the rain hit the roof of his VW rabbit, her eyelids became heavy, and she fought to keep them open. Deep in her chest, she felt the weight of her tiredness, like a fist that was pushing down on her. It even seemed as though it took extra effort to draw breath, and with the peaceful cadence of the rain, it was all she could do to stay awake. Consciousness itself seemed to be an illusion, dancing in and out of her awareness, blurring the lines of reality and what lay beyond it.

Once at the University, Seth pulled up to the gates to let her out.

"I'll meet you here after classes," Seth told her as she exited the car. "Try not to worry too much about things."

"I promise," Annaleah answered, smiling at him. "When we meet I have to tell you about the owl. I think I forgot to tell you what happened yesterday in all the commotion of last night."

Seth looked at her, puzzlement creasing his forehead. "Owl?" he asked.

"Yes. I will tell you after classes OK? Bye for now Seth, enjoy your day." She waved at him briefly before turning and heading into the building.

She was still a bit early, so Annaleah decided to walk to the teachers break room in this wing of the school, just to see who was around and to ease into the day. It looked and felt earlier than it was, due to the dark storm clouds and steady rain. She was also hoping for one last cup of coffee before classes began. She could use the caffeine to wake her up a bit more and to help settle her thoughts over everything that had been going on in the past few days. So much had happened in such a little amount of time that it left her head spinning when she tried to think about it.

A few teachers Annaleah hadn't met yet were in the break room, some reading or working on papers. Others were chatting quietly over coffee. Annaleah made her way to the coffee, delighted to see someone had just recently made a fresh pot. Choosing a mug at random, she lifted it and saw a shiny black spider hiding underneath. Startled, she almost dropped the cup, gasping loudly as she fought to keep the mug in her hand. A few questioning eyes turned her way. In lieu of an explanation, Annaleah pointed at the spider, which was scuttling away toward a crack between the counter and the wall. The gesture didn't do much to stop the questioning looks, and some of the older teachers even looked at her with open disapproval.

No longer in a mood for coffee, Annaleah decided she would just head for her classroom. She'd hoped the Professor wasn't there yet. She'd had so much happen to her so quickly and she didn't want to add having to deal with the quirky, snarky Professor, at least not just yet. As she walked down the hallway, the thrum of rain hitting the roof and the sound of her heels hitting the cold linoleum floor seemed oddly comforting. She told herself the spider meant nothing; that they liked to hide in dark places and that it was only a coincidence that one had appeared after her terrifying dream. Only, the spider had looked exactly like the ones she woke to find on her arms in a swarming, biting horde. She wrapped her arms around herself, trying not to think of it at all. She forced a picture of her classroom into her mind, in an effort to find something, anything else, to focus on. She began to have a strange, sleepy, floating feeling, as if nothing were real. Was all of this still a dream?

As Annaleah rounded a corner in the hallway, she saw the Professor walking several steps ahead of her. Her reaction to seeing him surprised her slightly. She expected a sense of being let down, having wanted the room to herself for a few moments before classes began. She would have expected dread at having to deal with him. Rather curiously, she felt her heart speed up and her face flush in a rather pleasant manner. Maybe it was because of the ebony leather trench coat he wore to stave off the rain, or the way it fit him. It had been tailored to accentuate his physique, and Annaleah imagined she could see each line of his muscles move as the leather whispered over them. The coat fit his body snugly before it flared out just above his hips. When he walked, it billowed out behind him. The effect was somewhat ethereal, making him look almost as if he were floating. She felt a fluttering sensation in her belly, and a sense of nervous anticipation.

As she followed behind him, willing her heels to be silent on the cold tile floor, Annaleah found herself wondering what the Professor was wearing today, or if he wore cologne. If he did, what sort of scent would he choose? She hadn't noticed any on him before, but he seemed like a man who would appreciate a classic, alluring fragrance. Something with sandalwood maybe, or amber she thought. She began to feel even more sleepy and light headed, her thoughts running in a pattern somewhat unlike her.

As she followed the Professor, she noticed the walls, ceiling and floor all seemed to swim faintly before her and her vision began to go a bit dim. Her heart started to beat faster in her chest, and her breath became a bit harder to draw in. The feeling of floating increased, and she suddenly found herself so dizzy that she had to stop following the Professor and lean on the wall for support. In reaching forward, she misjudged the distance and stumbled, falling loudly against the wall before collapsing onto the floor.

Ahead of her, Professor Bainbridge spun on his heel, and when he saw her, a startled look spread over his handsome face. Annaleah was dazed and slightly embarrassed as she watched him heading toward her, the surprise in his expression changing to one of open concern. Her thoughts faded to ones that amused her, though in a vague corner of her mind, they registered as silly and out of place.

He seemed to be moving in slow motion as he walked towards her. The billowing if his leather trench coat was strangely attractive to Annaleah, and reminded her of a priest's robes. It flowed out behind him and appeared to leave trails in its wake. "Oh I'd love to confess to you, Father," she said under her breath, giggling.

As he reached her, he put his arm under her in an effort to bring her to her feet. Smiling up at him, she looked deeply into his almost black eyes and sighed dreamily. She tried to stand up, but found she was too weak, and almost fell back to the floor. He opened his mouth and tried to say something to her, but she couldn't hear the words he spoke. She was too stuck on the shape of his plush lips to care about what he said.

Annaleah's vision was fading, her ability to make sense of things already almost gone. As the edges of darkness won out, she noted that she was in the Professor's arms, wrapped up in what seemed to be an embrace. This gave her a sense of silly, girlish joy. She smiled up at him, quite happy, even if unwell and confused. The last thought she had before the darkness claimed her was of the Professor's scent.

"Leather and summer rain," Annaleah said aloud, smiling up at the Professor before the darkness became absolute.

Chapter Twenty-One

The Thawing/ Gabriel Is Summoned

Wednesday, August 10th

The past few days have proven quite the reprieve from the monotony I penned previously. Indeed, the happenings within my life as of late have shown themselves to be anything but monotonous. I'm still trying to process everything, for knowing what it means changes a lot of things. Truth be told, I was actually quite comfortable in my routine. Safe in my world of self-imposed isolation, separated from others and convinced of my superiority over humanity, these "flesh beasts" as I have long called them. I have found something within myself changing, and though at first I was unsure of my liking of this change, it continues to work itself within me regardless of my opinions. It illuminates parts of me that I hid in the darkness so very long ago. I find my thoughts to be more introspective, something that I was not prone to doing, even as little as a week ago. Though some of the things which bring their faces up to the light of my self-pontifications aren't too easy to gaze upon, it's something I feel has needed to happen for such a very long time. Having been so long overdue, the process is somewhat uncomfortable, if not painful. Most of the things I'm beginning to illuminate with the light of understanding are things that I buried long ago, telling myself I should never revisit them. I'm actually quite surprised I'm not more resentful of the process, but instead I find it most welcome, despite the discomfort.

It's all because of her, Miss Annaleah Grace. Her entry into my life has shaken it so completely that I am most certain things will never be the same again. Only a few days ago I was unsure of her, resentful even.

She was going to change my teaching life, possibly take my job, and I couldn't bear her for it, though I don't think I treated her any differently than I treated any of the others.

She isn't like the others though, oh no, not by a very long shot. She is something altogether different; though I am not sure she knows it. In fact, I'm fairly certain this creature is unaware of who, or really, what, she is. This makes her one of the most innocent beings I have ever come across. This innocence is rare, and it is beautiful. I must protect it, for even though I have been damaged so deeply by the event I have come to refer to as "The Betrayal," I have found that I still have the ability to process and understand emotions. For too long I have kept all but the most mundane emotions locked tightly away. Those that made me feel too deeply or made me show others I had anything to do with any form of weakness were avoided at all costs. I saw strong feelings as a sign of a weak fortitude, and even a display of foolishness. But I was the fool, though I hate to admit it. Self-preservation was all that mattered, as well as being respected. I didn't mind that it segregated me. I even enjoyed the fear. It protected me.

I think dreaming of her as I did is what began the illumination. Knowing that Gabriel, the Dream Keeper, had sent the dreams heightened my realization. His involvement told me that there was much more going on than I allowed myself to see. Such a dream he sent as well! Never have I allowed myself to take part in what I perceived to be the ultimate in human idiocy; love. There was a time when I loved far greater than I deemed any mortal able to love. Loving so deeply and completely had borne me the greatest wound I have ever been inflicted with in all my many, many years. It pained me so deeply that it wounded the fiber of my soul, making me lock it away from sight, from others as well as myself. Most importantly, myself.

I awoke today with a sense of impending…something. I was unable to put my finger on it. I was still being haunted by the dream I had of Miss Grace earlier. As I mentioned, I have never allowed myself to dabble in the more elaborate of emotions, but something about the whole situation left me unsettled, in more ways than one. That I was unable to toss the dream, and what it aroused within me aside also pointed to its greater meaning, and so I allowed myself to linger in it a bit. I told myself it was only to understand its place in my life and to prepare me for what was coming.

Having placated my sensibility, for the first time in so very long, I was able to feel what it was that made one's life, separated from the Creator, bearable on this earth. Letting it settle in upon me was like opening Pandora's Box. Hope rushed forth, holding hands with Trust and Faith. These three faces I hadn't seen in many eons. These flesh beasts. I began to pity and envy them both at once. I thought they could never come close to the deep love known in the Heavens an eternity ago; the pure, deep love for the Creator. It is something none of them can ever know, until their time here on earth is done. This is why the Creator made life on earth a bit more enjoyable, for they had to trust in the existence of the Creator, without knowing it as a certainty, as we did. These humans, (I can no longer call them flesh beasts, out of my new found compassion toward them, as well as the fact that I have lived for so long among them as a human myself) were given love, a physical body to enjoy and express it with, and the ability to bear offspring. These things were not given to my kind, for what is better than seeing the face of the Creator every day and basking in the pure, radiant love therein?

I digress, yet again (sigh!) The day began with rain. After a cup of coffee and a shower, I decided it was time to contact Gabriel and ask him what was taking place. Angelic invocations are not the easiest rituals to perform, and must be done with the utmost care and attention to detail. What is called today "Enochian Magik," can be terribly dangerous if not done with supreme accuracy. Of course, I have a bit of an edge on my human counterparts, though having been separate from my angelic brothers and sisters for so long, I too, must submit myself to ritual to gain an audience with them. I have misplaced my original sigil of power, but it didn't take me long before I had another constructed and ready to use. I had to do another ritual prior to this however, for one such as me can't remain in full human form easily in the company of another angel. It disrupts our illusion. This pre-ritual was to ensure the glamour of my human form was not torn apart, leaving me in my true, shameful, "fallen" reality.

It is always an amazing thing, to have an undisguised angel appear before you. The energy of the room was at once purified, thrumming with the energy of purity and grace. It began with a tiny ball of light, one so bright that I could not look upon it with my pupil-devoid human eyes. Yes, this is why my eyes appear to be black. I can't disguise the fact I have no pupils from humans. It is much easier to just make the entirety of my iris black, knowing most people would see them as very dark brown. I know that looking too long into my eyes can produce quite interesting effects as well. From this lustrous, fiery spark, Gabriel grew in his beautiful glory, until his stunningly bright form illuminated the whole of the bedroom into which he had been summoned. Tears spilled down my cheeks, as I stood within my summoner's circle. It had been millennia since I had seen my brother, and he has not changed. I told myself it was because of the radiance and intensity of the light that I wept, but I knew the lie I was telling myself. I can't recall the last time I shed a tear, let alone many.

In a few moments, Gabriel adjusted the intensity of his glowing brilliance to a comfortable level I could more easily endure. His long blonde hair flowed loosely down his silver-blue winged back, his eyes a deep shade of indigo which flashed brighter every so often with the power of holy, divine love. Like most of our brothers and sisters, his face was angular and lean, his skin pale and lit from within with arcs of light. As he stood before me, his face bore the expression of deep love, as well as a sorrowful, paining sadness.

"Hello Seraphael. It has been too long, my brother." I hadn't heard Gabriel speak in so long that time had ceased to be meaningful. I wasn't sure what to say; the tears still flowed freely down my face.

Smiling, he opened his wings and arms to me, and I went to him as a human would, in a manner of supplication.

For a moment, brother held brother, thoughts and emotions conveyed wordlessly. After a short while, Gabriel whispered in my ear, "All is not lost to you, as you think Seraphael. It's good to see you, and to see that you are weeping warms my spirit. There is so much hope for you. Do not supplicate yourself, you are my brother and my equal."

"Your equal?" I asked, not unkindly, but rather incredulous. "Surely you have not forgotten!" I drew away from him then, confused, but unwilling to become angry. He simply continued smiling at me with serene compassion.

"Not everything is as it seems, Seraphael. However, it is not my place to show you this. I believe you have summoned me for another reason?"

"Yes, Gabriel I have many questions, but first, what is happening to me?" I touched my face to indicate what I meant, wetting my fingers with my tears. "I have been in human form for thousands of years now. I know how to move among them, as well as how to avoid any suspicion from them. I know how to live without any fear of getting caught up in human emotions or petty dramas. Yet within the space of a few days, so much has changed."

Gabriel regarded me for a moment, compassion in his indigo eyes. "You must have lived too long with the humans, dear brother. Time has no meaning; it is of no consequence in the greater scheme of things. It is an illusion created by man to put their understanding of reality in order. Having said this, Seraphael, many things are happening. You are evolving, changing as you must. Though you have seen tears as a weakness for most of your human existence, you are beginning to see that they are not a weakness at all. Tears are cleansing and purifying, brother. As you cry, you are allowed a moment to contemplate that which makes you weep, and perhaps to rectify things. Suffice to say Seraphael, it has been long coming."

I nodded, digesting with my heart the words that he spoke.

There is never a lot of time when spirits are summoned, but I felt my time with Gabriel was running short so I continued.

"What is the nature of this Annaleah Grace? Why is she so important that you sent me such a dream of her?" I inquired.

"Annaleah's father asked me a long time ago to watch over her, and so I have. She is a very important little one." I thought I noticed a look of deep affection cross Gabriel's face as he spoke of her. "Have you felt yourself finding it harder to remain in human form around her?" he asked.

I took a moment to ponder this, not really knowing if I had or not. "I'm not sure I have," I answered honestly, "though she does evoke in me a sense of strangeness, as well as a sense of familiarity. I feel as if she hides something."

Gabriel must have found this funny, for he began to laugh merrily. "She herself does not know, it is part of what makes her so special and so innocent. She is here for a reason. Those of the darkness seek her, and if they find her, they will devour her without mercy. Some already know she is here. If you have not seen them yet, rest assured, you soon will. War is coming, my brother, and this time, you are going to have to fight."

I felt anger at this last remark, an old terrible pain beginning to burn in my chest once again. I loved my brother still, and it was because of this that I fought to repress it.

"I don't wish to upset you," Gabriel continued. "There is so much you still don't know. Annaleah is part of that. I can't stay for much longer. I will be needed soon. You don't have to protect her if it is not your will to do so. I will tell you, however, that it is in your very best interest to make sure no harm comes to her." As he spoke the last sentence, his image began to lose the edge of its luminosity, a sign he was ready to leave. I didn't have enough time to remain upset in his presence, so I abandoned my anger at what he had said. Instead, I embraced him one last time before releasing him from the circle I had invoked him into.

When he was gone, it felt as if he had taken the air itself from the room as well. I hadn't felt so utterly dejected and alone since "The Betrayal" itself. Seeing Gabriel, I had also seen a reflection of the Creator, and felt comforted by it. Now he had left, taking that reflection with him, I felt the old, ancient sting of abandonment again. I fought the desire to weep, forgetting the tears that were already streaming down my face. I wiped at them, tempted to lose myself in them for a while, wondering at the last time I let myself openly cry. I realized then what great strength it took to allow oneself to weep, especially when every atom of your existence told you to bury everything deep inside.

I glanced at the clock instead, noting that I would be needed at the University soon. It was time to put all this away, and get back to mundane life. Or so I had thought. Everything seemed to go as if it were a normal day after I left my apartment, though only for a little while. The fearful glances of the humans as I walked across campus to my classroom were evident, as usual. Previously, it had never bothered me that others never looked at me with more than a passing glance. Today, it made me feel invisible and inconsequential.

And so I entered the building, shaking the rain off my black umbrella before placing it in the umbrella rack near the door. I could keep up the facade, I told myself, even knowing how things had changed. I had only been walking down the hall for a moment or two when I heard a commotion behind me. When I turned, I saw Miss Grace, looking confused and quite pale. Alarmed, I went to her side, and at first, was going to ask as to her condition. It became quickly apparent, however, that she was not herself and in fact rather ill.

A curious thing happened then. I noted that even though she was in a bad way presently, she was quite beautiful. Despite her whitened pallor and the sheen to her pale green eyes, she was a lovely creature. I began to feel her mind reaching towards mine as well. I could tell in her eyes that she was glad to see me, though I couldn't fathom why. Instead of fear, intimidation or loathing, for the first time I could remember, a human looked at me with open affection. I felt her fondness towards me fall upon my heart as if she had sent lightning to strike me.

I could see she was still at risk of falling, as it became apparent she was going to pass out at any moment. I gathered her in my arms, telling myself it was so she would not hit her head on the hard floor when she lost consciousness. When I had settled her in my arms, she turned her pixie like face towards me and smiled the sweetest smile anyone has ever smiled at me. Her eyes were blinking rapidly, and I knew she wasn't going to stay with me much longer. Curiously, before she blacked out, she looked me right in the eye, without any sense of discomfort on her part. This in itself is rather alarming! I have seldom, if ever, known of anyone to look deeply into my eyes without either looking quickly away or falling into a strange sense of a trance. With a sweet smile, almost like that of a child, "Leather and summer rain." I sensed the adoration she felt transfer from her soul into mine as she spoke this, though I haven't a clue as to what it means. I wanted to ask her, but after she spoke, her eyes closed, and consciousness left her.

Class has, of course, been canceled for the day. I stayed with her as the ambulance arrived, though they wouldn't let me inside with her. The Chancellor assured me that Annaleah's next of kin would be notified, and that she would be well taken care of. I didn't miss the Chancellor's look of curiosity at my concern for a woman whom I had openly despised only a few days ago, though she also seemed quite happy to see my concern.

I'm going to have my lunch and then head down to see Annaleah. I am not certain what has happened to her, but if my hunch is correct, those of the darkness are behind it. My spirit has just begun to rekindle itself, and I am fairly certain Miss Grace is the reason behind this. If Gabriel says war is coming and I must fight, then fight I will.

I will fight for her.

~SB~

Chapter Twenty-Two

Annaleah meets Satanael

Annaleah was floating, the darkness through which she drifted alternating between a deep grey mist and an absolute black. This darkness seemed to be a tangible thing, something that, if she reached out to touch it, would have the texture of velvet one moment, and a wispy cloud the next. Her thoughts were tangled and made no sense, lasting only a few moments before focusing on something else. She felt drunk, confused and more than a little frightened.

In this place of confusion and obscurity, sounds began to reach her. They were distorted, as if she were hearing them from underwater. A strange beeping sound reached her, and then people speaking.

"Unknown slow acting toxin," a woman said. "We need a vial of antivenin, STAT!" This was answered by a man asking, "Antivenin to what?"

A stinging sensation in Annaleah's arm brought a brief moment of lucidity, as she felt a needle pierce her skin. There was an abrupt flash of light as she opened her eyes. She saw the worried faces of both Seth and Uncle John, their concern etching deep lines beneath their eyes and tugging at the corners of their mouths.

The sight of Seth and Uncle John faded as Annaleah began to fall back into the arms of darkness. She descended faster now, moving more quickly through layers that felt more dense. Her senses began to reassert themselves as she began to feel fear and the hateful presence of dread heavy in her heart.

Through this Stygian she fell, her fear steadily growing. Out of the murk, forms began to emerge, but she could only make out a few features. She saw disembodied silver eyes that quickly turned from a shiny metallic shade to that of a milky, cataract white before bursting and running their fluid into the gloom around them. She saw sharp, hooked teeth spattered with fresh crimson liquid, gnashing and grinding before once again fading from sight. Here and there she saw a claw, a horn, or the flutter of a rotten wing before they dematerialized back into the darkness. Around her she heard terrible sounds, screams, moans and wails followed by hideous, maniacal laughter. From here, the sound of heavy chains rattling and dragging; from there the sound of flesh being torn. The scent of rotting, burning flesh entwined with an acrid mix of sulpher, blood and gunpowder.

Annaleah slowed her descent slightly as she continued to fall through this terrible place. She felt herself become marginally more solid, and told herself that this was really happening. Maybe not in the reality that she normally lived in, but that it was a reality of sorts. This frightened her even more, and she wished desperately to be in her own dimension.

She heard impish laughter and felt small tugs at her hair and clothes. She turned to see what it was attacking her, but only caught a brief glimpse of a leg or tail before it was claimed again by the darkness. From all around her, she heard her name spoken from many different voices. Some were whispers, others loud, but all sounded intent on doing her harm, or at the very least, contorting her sanity. Though some laughed and others sounded sing-song as they called to her, she could feel the underlying intent of evil in their voices, and it frightened her.

"ENOUGH!" she screamed, covering her ears, her eyes blurring with tears. As soon as she said this aloud, she felt herself hit the bottom of where ever it was that she had dream walked into. The landing was not as hard as she had expected, but it was still hard enough to knock the breath from her. She remained where she had fallen for a moment, crying with her eyes closed, afraid to look around and see where she was. She felt what she thought was grass beneath her, and wondered briefly if Hell had grass.

Then the rattling began. It sounded as if thin slices of bone were sliding against each other, a sound that turned Annaleah's blood cold. It was quite loud, as if whatever produced it must be at least ten feet tall. If this were a snake, she thought through her terror, it must be the most horrifying one ever known in any realm. All the more reason to keep her eyes shut. Along with the sound came a low, resonating growl that came from everywhere at once and filled the air with its vibration.

It began as a low, throaty timbre and rose just sharply enough to become a little louder than the sound of rattling bones, letting her know just how much danger she was in.

Annaleah didn't want to open her eyes, but curiosity won out over fear, and she found herself looking at something that stopped her heart for several beats. Before her was a chimerical creature, its head lowered to the ground, putrid breath streaming from its flared nostrils. The head was huge, shaped like that of a monstrous dog, though it was covered in large boney scales. As she looked closer, she could see these scales covered its entire body, each one vibrating against another, producing the wretched rattling noise. The creature's eyes were burning intensely, and though one glowed a faint red color and the other a sickly green, they looked human. The mouth was curled into a menacing snarl, the lips black and roped with drool, barely covering sharp daggers of yellow teeth as long and thick as her fingers. The neck was thick and stout, and though covered in scales, there was evidence of powerful musculature. The body was that of an enormous cat, from its paws to the curves of its legs. It held itself in a predatory stance, as if ready to pounce on her. From the shoulders of this beast grew giant white bat wings, bloodied and torn, spread wide in the air before her, as if to let her know of its dominance over her. Arched over its back was a long white scorpion tail, its deadly stinger dripping thick, colorless venom. Instead of being covered with a carapace of any sort, the tail too was embedded with scales of bone, all vibrating against each other. No other part of this creature moved, making the beast appear to shimmer.

Annaleah was too frightened to move, though the sounds this strange creature made rose in volume so much so that she desperately wanted to cover her ears. Tears streamed down her pale cheeks as she imagined what this thing might do to her, the pain it would inflict on not only her body, but upon her very soul. For this was the sort of place where souls went to be punished or destroyed.

Annaleah closed her eyes and sent up a silent, heartfelt appeal to her Goddess. It was a simple prayer, but because of its sincerity, laden with power. "Please," she intoned with all the strength her emotions could muster. "Help me."

From high above came the piercing screech of an owl, followed by the fluttering of wings. As if startled, the terrifying creature before Annaleah raised its head to look for the source of the sound, and folded its wings back slightly, ceasing its own growling and rattling. Annaleah, emboldened, also turned to look. It was Bubo, eyes intense, beak open and claws spread and ready for an attack.

"Bubo!" Annaleah cried, sending gratitude up to her Goddess for hearing her. The nightmarish creature turned away from the advancing owl at hearing her speak, and gazed at her hatefully, which proved to be a mistake. As its huge head turned to look at her, Bubo flew by Annaleah, the wind from the owl's mighty wings bringing a rush of fresh air. As the beast opened its mouth to growl again, Bubo caught the side of its head in her claws and tore at its flesh. The creature reared up on its hind legs, the mighty wings spreading as if it were about to take flight. It tried without success to swipe at Bubo with its sharp ivory claws. The roar of anger and pain the creature gave was equally as terrible as the growl, and much louder.

Looking around for something she could use as a weapon, Annaleah saw some large stones lying in the sparse grass. She grabbed one of the larger ones and took careful aim at the beast that fought Bubo. To her delight and amazement, the stone struck the creature and embedded itself in its sickly green human-esque eye. Howling in pain, the beast shook its head, trying to shake off Bubo and loosen the stone from its socket.

"That's quite enough!" said a loud male voice, and though it rang with authority, it was also seductively melodic. At once, the creature stopped its frantic efforts to disengage the owl and the stone, and dropped its head in a sign of submission and respect. Bubo also stopped fighting, and, releasing her claws of scaly flesh, flew to Annaleah's side.

Looking around for the source of the voice, Annaleah spotted what she thought was a very tall man, surrounded by a bright reddish-orange aura, walking towards her. He moved through the gloom with supreme grace, as if he were gliding over the ground. His clothes were black and fit loosely, flowing behind him like ink as he came closer. His hair was long and blood red, and moved around him slowly as if it were alive, though there was not a sigh of wind in this forsaken place. The long tresses flowed beside and behind him in a mesmerizing manner, as though he was under water and the currents were moving his hair languidly. Behind him were what appeared to be large wings, the same bloody red color as his hair. Though they were folded tightly to his back, Annaleah could see that they were much different than those she had seen on the

Professor, and inspired terror instead of awe. They appeared to be made of scales and leather. She couldn't tell if they were wet, or just shiny and slick. The man's face was very pale, his features sharp and angular. He looked almost fairy like, though far, far more dangerous.

A voice spoke inside Annaleah's mind, one she found at once to be familiar and strange. A woman's voice told her, "Don't look into his eyes, Annaleah, whatever you do." Before she looked quickly away from him, Annaleah saw the man smile wickedly as if he had heard the voice too.

"I hope Tantibus here hasn't scared you too much, Annaleah. That wasn't much of a welcome I'm afraid," said the man whose hair seemed to slowly dance of its own accord. Like a slow fire, if fires burned under water, she thought, still not daring to look at him after the warning. His voice was hypnotic, musical and serpentine. He turned to address the beast, whistling for it to come to him. The creature obeyed, its head lowered as it came to his side.

"Be still, Tantibus," the man told the beast. Reaching long, thin fingers towards the stone embedded in the beast's eye, he plucked it out, and then began speaking in a tongue Annaleah recognized at once from her dreams. Almost immediately, the creature's wounds were healed.

"Now then," said the man, straightening. "I see you have one of your guardians with you, Annaleah. Very well. I have no wish to fight with you. I have come to make you an offer. I am Satanael, and you, my dear, are in my domain. You have come to the very outermost part of it, as should you have come any further your survival would not be assured. I can make certain for you, however, that no matter where you go, you will be safe. You have power within you child, the likes of which no one has ever seen before, but you lack the ability and knowledge to control it. Let me show you what you are. Let me be your teacher. I will give you all that you desire, fulfill every dream. I will make you rich beyond imagining, more beautiful than Helen of Troy, wiser even than King Solomon. I can teach you to harness your power so that none oppose you. There must be so much confusion going on within you now, little one. So much is happening, and yet you have no idea why. Look at yourself in my presence child, you are glowing. Can you feel your blood coursing faster, hotter, stronger? Do you know what you are?" His words were like a musical chant, spoken with a serpentine accent, seductive, dangerous and otherworldly.

Annaleah did feel different, as if she were both bursting apart and coming together all at once. She noticed that the man before her did not appear to be as tall as she had thought, and then she realized he had not shrunk, but she had grown. She looked at herself, and saw arcs of light moving like fire beneath her skin, like those she had seen in her dream with the Professor.

"You see," continued the man before her, "you are not who or what you have thought yourself to be your whole life. You, my dear, are quite special."

He looked away, as if reflecting on the importance of the words he was about to tell her. "Why do you think you are having these dreams? Why do you think you are changing in my presence?"

He shook his head and made a tasking sound. "So misunderstood all of your life; ridiculed, mocked, even openly despised. The humans among you could tell you were different, and they hated you for it. That is what humans are so very good at, hating and fearing those who aren't like them. They could feel it every time you were near them, but none of them ever took the time to figure out why you were different or what made you that way."

Satanael paused, leaning closer before he continued. When he spoke again, his voice had deepened in its timber.

"How lonely you must have been, yet you never hated them for it, did you? It only drove you to stand out and to be who you are, even though you still aren't sure what that means. Your innocence is precious. It is a beacon to those of our kind." Satanael straightened up and took a breath, watching her keenly. "You see, you and I are not so very different. Though we may walk different paths, we are of the same lineage." His voice held a sense of pride, as though she should know what lineage he meant. "I say to Hell with those who didn't try to understand you, who opposed you for your remarkable, wonderful differences from them. They didn't deserve to breathe the same air as you!"

Satanael spoke so convincingly that Annaleah looked at him for a moment, but avoided his eyes. He looked passionate and angry, his mouth drawn in a tight line.

"I will never let you feel lesser than anyone else again, nor will I tolerate others disrespecting you. I will show you what it is that you are, Annaleah. Come to me, be my disciple. I will tell you everything."

Annaleah considered his offer. Her heart raced and her breath became ragged with anxiety. Her mind spun blindingly fast inside her skull, which made her close her eyes to steady herself. It was a tempting offer, but one laced with danger. She could feel trickery oozing off of him. Though he was skilled at hiding it, still it hung in the air between them, a silent but present energy in the air.

Yet, she wanted answers. He was powerful, that much was an utmost certainty. What was it that he knew, and could it be possible that he would indeed protect her?

He leaned back, his arms crossed, giving her room to contemplate his offer. He looked so self-assured, as if he knew she would say yes to him. Annaleah looked briefly to his face, still avoiding his eyes. Smugness clung to him.

His words had held power, seduction, and the promise of a certain knowledge withheld from her for far too long. He emanated an energy that was calming and intimidating in equal measure, something akin to an enchanted delirium. Still his hair moved about him, like serpents dancing a dance of disillusionment.

There was too much trickery about him, and Annaleah's instincts told her to run. This was not a man who could be trusted, powerful and full of promises or not. His offers were tailored to suit her temptations. Her wishes were played upon, his seductive voice plucking at the strings of her wants to elicit an unyielding desire to say yes.

"Resist him, Annaleah!" the voice cried again, snapping her out of her daze. It was spoken with desperation. Clarity came to her again, washing away what felt like a hypnotic enchantment. He was a trickster, and a liar, this she knew instinctively. She had to fight him, and she had to do it now before she lost her willpower and gave in.

"Don't say yes," Annaleah told herself in her mind, as she struggled to disentangle herself from his enchantment over her. "This is Hell and you are talking to the Devil Himself. He is the master and father of all lies, he is tricking you!"

Annaleah prepared to tell him that she had no intention of following him, when she opened her eyes and accidentally caught his gaze. His eyes were strange, deadly and beautiful, the same blood red as his hair and wings. As she looked into them, panic fluttered in her heart, as she remembered the warning not to look into them. It was too late, she was instantly hypnotized, drawn into his mind by his sheer force of will. She saw herself dressed in fine clothes and wearing beautiful jewelry, adored by both men and women. She saw herself writing strange symbols and felt the knowledge of countless generations fill her mind. Great power filled her veins and surged in her blood, making her more self-assured than she had ever felt before. She saw scenes where others bowed before her and accommodated her every wish, fervently hoping to gain her favor in return. She felt herself being seduced by the man who stood before her, his lips hot fire on her skin, his skillful ministrations bringing wave after wave of ecstatic pleasure. There were diamonds and gold draped on her, silk sheets, champagne, berries, chocolates and candles. Heady, intoxicating incense smoke filled the opulence of the room.

"All of this is yours, and more," his voice spoke within her mind. His words were low and soft, dripping with seduction, and they soothed her fears, as if each word uttered had reached inside her soul and stoked her into submission.

Somewhere off in the distance, Annaleah heard the familiar call of her owl guardian, this time echoing loudly and with determined ferocity. Hearing the screech, she was brought back to the desolate darkness, the spell broken as Bubo flew against this mysterious man. It was almost painful to be released from his enchantment. Feeling somewhat drunk after looking into his eyes, Annaleah tried to take in the scene before her. Bubo had flown at Satanael, her wings flapping angrily in his face in an effort to break the eye lock. Satanael reached out and grabbed Bubo effortlessly, throwing her down beside Annaleah. Bubo fell with a cry of distress, feathers floating out around her.

In horror, Annaleah rushed to Bubo's side and knelt beside her, reaching out to smooth her feathers as tears began to stream down her face.

"Bad choice, Annaleah. I want you to remember this when my legions are ripping you and your loved ones' limb from limb. I am not an unreasonable being, child. I offered you all that you could have ever wanted." His voice sounded thicker, laced with disappointment and a modicum of sadness.

"I would have made you my queen!" he said, awe coating his voice, "In return I get your guardian's wrath. I have been nothing but kind and respectful to you, Annaleah. This is how you answer my offer of such gifts?"

Again he made the tsking sound, and shook his head.

"Such a pity. Now go. Prepare yourself for war."

As soon as his last word was uttered, Satanael stood no more before her. The creature called Tantibus was gone too, as if they had never stood before her at all. Annaleah looked down once more to see if Bubo was alright, and saw that the owl was glowing with a soft golden light. Curious, she touched the bird gently, and gasped when the owl did not move or respond.

"Bubo!" She cried, more tears stinging her eyes.

"It's alright, Annaleah, " said the same female voice that had spoken in Annaleah's mind earlier. She turned toward the source of the voice and saw a woman bathed in golden light. She was dressed modestly in a simple white lacy dress that fell just above the knee. Her hair was long, blonde and curly, her eyes a piercing shade of pale, burning green. She wore a pentacle around her neck on a silver chain, and no shoes on her feet. She looked like Annaleah, if Annaleah were a bit older, and smiled at her with love in her eyes.

"Bubo will be just fine. She is a special bird, an avatar. She offered to carry my spirit to you. She is still while my spirit is free, but she will be okay, I promise. Do you know who I am, Annaleah?"

Annaleah walked closer and nodded her head. "Are you my...mother?" The woman smiled at Annaleah, her eyes sparkling with love and warmth.

"That's right. I am your mother. I am so very proud of you, Annaleah. Look at you, all grown up. You're so beautiful." Annaleah reached out to embrace her mother, but went right through her form.

"I am not a physical being anymore, even in this place," her mother explained. "Though someday you and I will be able to hold one another again. You haven't much time left here, honey. You dream walked here to this awful place, but there was no way I was going to let you come alone. You need to know so many things. You must talk to Seth. Tell him what you saw here. He knows a lot more than you think. It is time for your Uncle John to tell you what he knows of your father, too. He may say some things that might hurt you, but you'll know the truth from the lies."

There was so much Annaleah wanted to say, so much she wanted to ask. It wasn't fair her time was almost up. She had never wanted to come to a place like this, but now that things had turned for the better, now that she was with her mother, she didn't have much time. It wasn't fair.

"I am always with you, my darling. Don't ever forget that. You are so much more special than you now know, and I'm not saying that because I'm your mother. I'm saying it because it's true. I love you, Annaleah."

Through her tears, Annaleah said, "I love you too, Mom."

Then she felt a sensation of floating, only this time it wasn't exactly falling, it was more a feeling of being sucked upwards very quickly. Again came the confusing sounds of voices that Annaleah couldn't quite understand. She was falling upwards at such a quick speed that she didn't see anything this time, in fact the rush of wind was so great that she did not open her eyes, until all at once the feeling of being pulled upwards faded.

She heard the beeping of a machine, and voices again, and when she tried to open her eyes, found that the room was brightly lit, and full of doctors and nurses.

"She's back!" A young nurse with a loose blonde bun said, smiling. She was quickly pushed aside by Seth, who gathered Annaleah up, hugging her gently.

"Oh my Gods, Annaleah, we were so scared!" he said, his voice filled with relief. Uncle John joined Seth at Annaleah's side, tears glistening in his eyes. Both were moved aside by the nurse.

"I know you are glad she is okay, but you need to let her rest. Please, sir, let her back down, " the nurse said, with a chastising look on her face. Seth slowly lowered Annaleah onto the bed again, kissing her on the forehead.

"I'll have Uncle John tell the Professor you're okay. He was here for quite a while. He didn't seem all that bad to us. He was really worried about you." Seth said.

Annaleah's heart leapt in her chest. The Professor had been to see her? That was a rather curious thing. A vision of her in his arms filled her mind, followed by the scent of leather and warm summer rain.

Annaleah focused her thoughts on Seth and smiled up at him, patting him gently on the face. She held her hand out to Uncle John, who took it in both of his. She tried to speak, but found that she couldn't. The nurse, seeing this, began to usher Seth and Uncle John out of the room.

"She is going to be fine, I promise. She is not quite out of the woods, and she needs to rest. We will take care of her. Come back in the morning and she'll be in better shape to speak with you. Go home, take care of yourselves, and we'll take care of her."

Seth and Uncle John looked at Annaleah, clearly not wanting to leave.

She nodded at them and pointed at the door, her way of telling them it was okay to leave her. Sighing, Seth said reluctantly, "Ok, but we will be back first thing in the morning. We love you, Annaleah."

Annaleah kissed her hand and blew an imaginary kiss towards her family.

There was going to be a lot to talk about tomorrow.

Chapter Twenty-Three

The Plot Thickens

Annaleah found herself once more on the moonlit path in the woods that led to the clearing. The night air was soft and warm; the sensation of it blowing across her skin and through her hair was vivid and calming. She knew she was in Dreamtime again, even though the breeze and the dewy grass wet beneath her feet felt as real as her waking reality. As she walked along the path, a sense of profound peace fell upon her, settling in her heart and uplifting her spirit. The cicadas serenaded her as the clearing came into view. A single figure stood in the center waiting for her. She stood just out of the moon's light, letting the shadows fall upon her form. As she walked closer, Annaleah saw large black feathered wings folded loosely behind the figure's back. A sudden jolt of fear pulsed in her heart as she remembered the winged girl from her dreams with the Jorogumo.

"Don't be afraid, Annaleah," the winged girl said, "I am here to help you. Please come join me in the clearing. I promise, you're safe." Pushing the fear from her heart, Annaleah made her way to the clearing, again noticing how her body felt. Instead of her small five-foot body, she felt tall and lean, her movements effortless and graceful. She saw flashing arcs of golden light pulsing in her arms and hands, her skin itself was paler and more luminous. Though the sensation of this body was strange and new to her, it also felt genuine, as if it were her true form that she had been locked out of all of her life.

"It is your true form, Annaleah," the woman said as Annaleah joined her in the clearing. "You have been made to forget it in your human world." As Annaleah looked at Marchosias, she noticed the young woman's eyes appeared as if their iris' were swirling, colors undulating within them and blending into each other. The result was slightly mesmerizing. "I will explain," she continued, her expression one of seriousness. "I am here to defend you, to fight by your side when the time comes." She looked down at Annaleah's arms, her eyes holding an apology. "I'm very sorry about your spider bites. I was busy fighting the Jorogumo in this realm, and I wasn't able to stop the spiders from crossing into your world. Nephila has been dealt with for what she did to you. She may try to attack you again, but for now she is unable."

Annaleah closed her eyes, and brought her hand up to her head as she tried to understand what was going on around her. There was so much to process. Both Satanael and Marchosias had mentioned fighting, a coming war, and now Marchosias was mentioning fighting beside her? She was confused, and a little scared, too.

"Marchosias, please, tell me what is going on," Annaleah asked the young woman, "I don't understand any of this. Why am I being taken to all these dream realms? Why are things coming out of my dreams to attack me? Is this real, or is this just a strange dream?"

Marchosias looked at her compassionately and drew in a deep breath and tented her hands under her chin. She appeared to be looking for a place to begin. "I know this is all confusing, but yes, this is all real. You have a special talent for walking into other realms of reality, due to who and what you are."

Annaleah had heard this before from Satanael. What did they mean, who and what she was? She was just Annaleah Grace, no more, no less. She wasn't any more special than anyone else. The truth was, she was afraid. Both the Jorogumo and Satanael had told her war was coming, and Marchosias said she would fight beside her. Who was she to fight anyone in any manner, let alone in a war? She was just a normal southern girl, a little peculiar in her ways, sure, but certainly not a person worthy of such visitations.

Everything was so overwhelming, so confusing. Tears welled up in her, and she fought them back, determined to find out what was going on.

Marchosias allowed Annaleah a moment to gather herself, her head tilted with concern as she watched Annaleah. "It is much easier for those of us who dwell in these realities to communicate with you in Dream Time, as it is a special place in between your world and ours. That's why you are being pulled more and more into these dreams. Not only by those trying to help you, but also by those who wish you harm. I've come to show you something very important, something that might answer a few questions for you."

Annaleah held her head up high, trying to show both herself and Marchosias that indeed, she was stronger than she appeared. "I don't want to sound ungrateful for your help," she began, her he, "but I just want things to go back to the way they used to be."

Marchosias sighed. "Things are not always what they seem, Annaleah. I know you've felt different from others all of your life. As if you don't really belong here. Others felt it in you too, and feared you for it. Humans can be so cruel to those who aren't like them, who don't dress, act or believe as they do. Though they couldn't understand your power, they felt it. You have felt it too, and though it made you feel different in many ways, it has also led you to find out more about other worlds and to learning about the occult."

Annaleah's heart raced, but what Marchosias was saying made sense. When she was younger, she had felt like she was nothing like the other children, as if she had nothing in common with the other children. Now Marchosias was saying that this was in fact, true. It was a lot to wrap her head around, but things were finally starting to come together for her.

"It's time to stop being ashamed of who you are, of feeling ostracized for not being another faceless mask in a crowd of replicas." Marchosias said earnestly, walking a step closer to her. "There are no others like you, Annaleah. None. You are a one of a kind."

Marchosias paused as if to let this fact sink in before going on. "I know what you have been going through has been hard, but you must be strong. So much more is about to happen, and you must be prepared. Part of that preparation is knowing what is happening, and what has happened."

Annaleah was trying her best to keep up with Marchosias, all the while trying to sense her energies. What she put out was nothing like Satanael, there was no underlying threat and no sense of deceit. In fact, it felt as though she were trying to emit waves of gentle, calming energy, and for a moment Annaleah closed her eyes and let herself fall into it, to heal her frazzled nerves and settle her racing mind.

After a deep, calming breath, Annaleah opened her eyes and said, "What does that mean? Why am I one of a kind and what's really happening?"

Marchosias stepped closer to Annaleah, her dark eyes looking into her very soul. "Do you trust me?" Marchosias asked, her eyes burning.

Annaleah looked away, and her mind once again began to spin. Did she trust this woman creature? This was only the second time they had met, and the first time had been terrifying. Trusting anyone right now could turn out to be a mistake. Though Marchosias' energy was soft and soothing, she might very well be trying to hide something.

Fear crept into her heart, and she began to tremble slightly. She didn't want the winged girl before her to sense her fear, for she knew that no matter what, she was going to have to be a part of something much larger than herself. She was going to need to be strong. Marchosias promised to tell her everything, and stronger than the fear was her need to know.

Deciding to follow her gut instinct, she made her choice. "Yes." Annaleah answered softly, "I trust you."

"Close your eyes then. Let me show you."

As Annaleah closed her eyes, she felt Marchosias touch her gently on the left temple, and she was instantly flooded with vivid visions. She saw the creature Satanael, though he looked a bit different. His hair was a lighter shade of red, and did not flow about him as it had in the place where she had seen him last night. Instead it fell in loose, shining waves down his back. His eyes were a deep shade of amber, and did not hold the seductive danger she had seen before. His wings were a beautiful deep shade of red, but instead of being leathery and scaled, they were feathered and appeared as if the pinions were made of velvet.

"This is Satanael. I believe you have met him in his more sinister form," Marchosias said. "A very long time ago, he was the Creator's consort and lover. Though he was made by the Creator's hand, he felt as though he was equal to Her, because She had given him so much, and exalted him above any other angel. Indeed, Satanael was her very first creation. In time, he began to take Her generosity for granted, and to question it. His heart filled with narcissism and hubris. He began to think that because he was the first creation, he had a special power over even the Creator Herself. It is because the Creator loved him so that he was able to go so far. Her adoration and dedication to him ran deep and was utterly sincere. She let him create the first creatures on Earth, and this caused their first falling out. It was a great gift to him, you see, to create the first life to walk on the Earth she had so lovingly prepared. She wanted it to be a place of love, light and peace, but that which he made was savage and vicious and incapable of love in any form. At learning of the Creator's displeasure, Satanael became enraged with Her for not liking his creations. He felt his ability to create outweighed Hers."

As Marchosias spoke, Annaleah saw in her mind's vision what she knew were the dinosaurs, only they looked much more fierce and monstrous than those that were depicted in history books and museums. They looked as if they occupied some region of Hell seldom contemplated. Their eyes glowed with an infernal, hateful light. The flesh was loose and rotten, lumps of skin and meat falling from them as they moved, exposing the bone beneath. She saw them screaming in pain and fury, fighting with one another, not just for food and territory, but out of pain fueled hatred. Some fought in an attempt to end their own lives and the pain of walking day after day under a blistering sun which scalded their rotted flesh. Some fought out of insanity caused from the pain, but all of them fought. Annaleah felt tears of compassion for these terrible creatures fall down her cheeks.

"Satanael had no sense of empathy for the beings which he created." Marchosias explained. "Seeing them fight entertained him, and he encouraged their misery for his enjoyment. It fueled his growing sense of power. Though it hurt the Creator to reprimand him, reprimand him She did. Out of sympathy, she destroyed the monsters he had made. After a period of time, after the Earth had healed itself, the Creator formed mankind. Satanael was furious. Not only that she had killed his creations, but that She had made the first creatures Herself. She had taken back her gift and wounded his pride. He gathered other angels who he seduced with his power and beauty, and rose up against Her."

The scene shifted in Annaleah's mind, and she saw Satanael preaching to an enormous gathering of angels. Most wore armor and carried weapons, and listened to Satanael's battle speech with rapt attention.

"The Creator could have wiped Satanael out in the blink of Her eye if she had willed it so, but still, She loved Him above all others. Satanael was corrupted because he took this love for granted. When Satanael stopped being grateful for all that was given him, his heart began to change. Envy, pride, resentment, even hate grew there. Though he stood to destroy all She had ever made, the Creator still would not destroy him or Her other angels who had betrayed Her. The Creator, in the depths of her despairing heartache, withdrew from the battle. She said only that those who turned from Her would not be allowed back into Heaven, and that they would be transformed by their hate and betrayal. The race of angels known as the Ophanim stood guard at the gates of the Heavens, so that those who fell or were cast out could return no more to the Glory of their prior home. When the Ophanium had their stations, the Creator withdrew herself fully and mourned.

"And so the first war began. Brother fought brother and sister fought sister. Many fell, and many died. The Creator wept to see those she had created out of deep, pure adoration fighting with angels they had once loved and known as kindred. She wept for beings who were created to be immortal, and yet, because of the terror of betrayal, were dying instead."

Images Annaleah knew too well from her dreams came to her as Marchosias spoke. The sensations were as real to her as if she stood there amongst the battle. She smelled the coppery scent of hot blood freshly spilled, heard the strange and beautiful foreign words of angelic speech, saw the innumerable bloodied feathers falling from the sky, scorched or still aflame. Indigo eyes flashed with a light from inside them as the silver eyed ones began to ripple and distort, their forms changing into something altogether more terrifying, as a manifestation of their betrayal.

"This is why some of our kind, both of light and darkness, hate mankind," Marchosias explained. "They blame man for the first fight, the one where the majority of the angels fell, transforming them into impure, cursed creatures. They blame humans for the war, even though it was Satanael's rebellion and their joining in the betrayal that caused it. You must know too, that not all angels will be good to mankind, nor will all of the fallen be cruel. There are many, many shades of grey between the darkness and the light, which makes things much more difficult."

Annaleah's mind was spinning with all she was being told, and she struggled not to become overwhelmed. A lot of this was making sense to her now, a few holes that she had wondered about for so long being filled in for her.

No wonder the angels in her dream wanted to attack her, there she was in the middle of their war, hated and despised, their blame lying upon her kind's shoulders. She was lucky that she had awoken when she had, who knows what they would have done to her if she had not.

Marchosias' description of Satanael was spot on with what she had intuited about him, she had described him very well. So indeed, he had been trying to trick her! She was enormously relived that her mother and Bubo had come to her rescue. She wasn't entirely sure she could have fought off his seductive enchantments on her own.

Though being armed with these bits of knowledge was empowering, the knowledge was also extraordinarily terrifying. It was horrifying to think that she was going to be taking part in a war fought between the angels and the dark ones who had willingly fallen. Questions upon questions danced in her mind, swirling together until she couldn't focus on just one. They became a continuous stream of thought, and she couldn't grasp one to ask quickly enough before another raced in to replace it.

"There is so much to be told to you." Marchosias continued, "I do not wish to show you more than you can handle all at once. If this becomes too much for you, please tell me and we can continue this at another time. Just know this; war is imminent, and the more you know the better you will be prepared."

With her eyes still closed, but her mind's eyes open to a shifting scene of the vastness of the cosmos, Annaleah answered Marchosias. "I am ready to know more, please continue."

Annaleah's mind's eye shifted from the infinity of the cosmos to a battle scene. The face she focused her attention on was immediately recognizable as the Professor. It sent the sensation of a bolt of lightning, hitting her heart as if Thor himself had sent it to her directly.

"I believe you know this angel." Marchosias said. "You have met him here in this woodland clearing in something close to this form, though you know him best as the Professor. You sensed right away that he was something of an anomaly, and you knew there was power inside of him. He sensed the very same about you too, Annaleah. The two of you are not so different, as you will learn. What you are seeing is very important. It is something he does not know, but it is something he must come to know. It is imperative. His eviction from Heaven was a mistake. Because of this horrible mistake, he has sequestered himself away from our kind for a very long time, refusing to meet with us at almost every instance. He acts this way, not only with us, but within his role as a human among mankind. If he sees through you what I am about to show you, things will shift dramatically for the forces of light. Hope will revisit the hearts of the hopeless, souls ruined will be restored. I believe the very outcome of the war might be at stake."

As Marchosias spoke, Annaleah watched the beautiful angel she had seen before, only here he was more luminous, the light within him more alive and resonant. His eyes were a deep, resonating indigo instead of silver, telling her he had not yet fallen. Though he seemed intense and forebodingly broody, Annaleah still could not understand why he had fallen at all. Why would he choose to follow one like Satanael?

"He didn't choose to follow Satanael at all," Marchosias answered her, hearing her thoughts. "That is why he too, is one of a kind. The Ophanim had never had a battle before, and so they were new to their roles. Though this has never since happened, what occurred here is a travesty. I will speak no more and let you both see and hear this to you can better understand."

As soon as Marchosias finished speaking, Annaleah felt as if she had been immediately transferred into the scene, mere inches away from the angelic form of the Professor. He stood with another angel who was much taller. Though the Professor's wings were enormous and reached several feet over his head, the creature he stood with had a stature and wings many times his size. The power which emanated from this angel was almost a physical force; heady, strong and demanding attention.

"You cannot save them, Saraphael," the taller angel spoke, his piercing emerald green eyes glowing with ethereal light. Annaleah watched as tears spilled down the cheeks of the Professor, though he showed no shame in so openly weeping.

"I cannot stand by and watch them fall, Matatron!" the angel form of the Professor said. "I do not agree with what Satanael has done, and what is doing now. He is lying to these angels, doing something to their will and corrupting their minds. I cannot let them fall. He has poisoned them away from the truth; their doubt has made them reject the truth and take our home and all the love of the Creator for granted. Let me speak to them. I have to try!"

"My brother," Metatron said gently, his long white hair falling in loose cascading ringlets across his angular face, "If you leave Heaven, you too will be considered Fallen, regardless of your reason. Though your heart is pure and your spirit is brave, you will be locked from these gates and not permitted readmission."

More tears fell from the angelic Professor's eyes, but his expression remained resolute. "I know the Creator mourns, and though Her heart is broken, I have faith in Her. She will not let me down, once She learns of my reasons. I must do what I know in my heart is right."

Metatron hung his mighty head, tears now falling from his eyes, too. He feared that he would never see his brother angel again, at least, not in Heaven. He opened his arms and the full span of his snowy wings, and embraced his fellow angel, holding him tightly. Each knew that it might be the last time they saw the other.

"My brother," Metatron whispered into the angel called Seraphael's ear, "Go in peace and know that you have my support. I admire you greatly for doing what you feel is right. No other will do what you are about to attempt." In response, Seraphael kissed his brother's cheek, the love between the two palpable.

From over them came the scream of a wounded angel, its throat torn and bleeding fire. Seraphael reached out his arms to try to catch the falling, dying angel, and was ripped out of the gates of Heaven, never more to return.

Though he fell with the weight of the dying angel, still he tried all his angelic medicines on the fallen, dying creature. Though many angels are male, this one was female. Her indigo eyes were looking at him beseechingly as they turned from a deep purple blue to a cold sheen of silver.

"You have been lied to, sister," he whispered to her between healing incantations. She tried to speak, but her throat was still open, her inner light growing dim. "I ask of you to turn from Satanael. He is not who or what you think he is. He has turned you from the Creator. Come back with me and ask for forgiveness. I know you cannot speak; do you agree with me? Blink once for yes, twice for no." The angel in his arms blinked once, and tried to speak again. It proved too much for her however, and she shuddered in his arms before finally going still.

Seraphael threw his head back and wailed, the pain in his heart too much to bear. Though his descent had stopped as the angel he held had died, his transformation into a Fallen one had just begun. Many lives had already been lost, and those who had already fallen and were trying to invade Heaven paused for a moment. Never had they heard such a sound of torment before, nor known a sound of grief so raw. Though the Creator had chosen to mourn in privacy, the misery in the spirit of Seraphael could not bear to wait for its expression.

Seraphael, refusing to believe that he was no longer permitted into Heaven, flew back to its gates, still holding the dead angel in his arms, desperate for readmission. He tried to recite the opening words, but the gates refused to obey his commands. Furious, scared, his heart full of grief, Seraphael called to the Ophanim guarding the gates. With sadness in their hearts, they refused him entry.

"Please," Seraphael begged, "she repented before she died. Her spirit should be allowed to come back home! I have not pledged allegiance to Satanael, please, let us back in!" However, the Ophanim would not let them inside and turned from him.

The scene again began to shift in Annaleah's mind's eye, fading out slowly. She felt Marchosias withdraw from her mind.

"You see," Marchosias spoke, "He never really fell at all. He was the only angel who tried to save his brothers and sisters from falling, and was rejected from Heaven by a misunderstanding. His feeling of being betrayed is as great as Satanael's betrayal of the Creator. Now you know why he is bitter. Why he is a loner. Why he trusts no one. You, my dear, were sent here to fix that."

"How?" Annaleah asked, her heart breaking for the man she knew as the Professor.

Marchosias smiled at her warmly, "You Annaleah, are a gift…." As she spoke the last word, Marchosias closed her eyes and winced in pain. It passed quickly however, and the angelic looking woman straightened up at once and cleared her throat.

"I'm sorry, but that is all I can tell you for now. I am told that there is another of us who wishes to speak to you. I believe he will tell you the rest of the story better than I. Besides, you have a visitor, and you're also about to wake up. So for now, Annaleah, remember what you have been shown, and stay strong. There are many, many angels with you. Know we love you very much."

As Marchosias spoke the last few words, she began to fade. Annaleah began to climb the steps on the ladder of consciousness, but she could still see the anguish on the face of the Professor, and it burned its own unique form of pain into her heart. She vowed that if there was anything she could do to bring joy back to him, she would not stop until it was done.

Chapter Twenty-Four

Sweet Emotions

Saturday, August 13th

Annaleah has been in the hospital for several days now. My mind wonders to her constantly, though I try to maintain my routine in class. My students can tell I am distracted, and though most of them are mature enough to understand and act with empathy, there are a few who have taken to making this time even more of a Hell for me. If I had the strength they are used to and have come to respect, these creatures would recoil from me in fear instead of causing me even greater torment. It seems that the moment I've come to feel deep empathy, there must be a wretched few among them to tease it out of my grasp.

I am experiencing many new emotions since my visitation with Gabriel. Knowing that he has been with Annaleah for so long as her protector and that he sent me such an intense dream has had me doing a lot of thinking. I've known since I first saw her that she was different, but for an arch angel to get so closely involved is something I have not seen before. Who is this beautiful woman child? Why can I not stop thinking of her? Yes, she is different. I admit she is interesting to me, but this is the beginning of a new school year and I have many other things to occupy my thoughts and time. Yet, I return to her in my mind and even to her room as she rests. She has yet to awaken when I have visited her. Maybe it is a good thing.

I have held her hand as she slept, fascinated with the warmth of her flesh against mine. Her hand was so soft and small in my own. As I gazed upon our hands entwined, I felt a strange sensation over take me. The longer I looked at them, the more I became aware that just by holding her hand, my own hand became more beautiful. I am not sure if it was my eyes playing tricks on me, from stress and lack of sleep, or, if what

I saw was real. In her skin, and in my own, I saw the familiar arcs and flashes of luminosity, the telltale sign of angelic blood. Is she one of my kindred then? If so, why hadn't I ever seen her in the days I was still....

But I will not revisit there. Suffice to say, I have seen and felt things with Annaleah that seem to change who I am.

Who and what are you, Annaleah? Why does my heart beat like it shall escape my chest when I look at your face? Why do I long to taste your lips, to press my mouth over your cupid's bow and draw your very breath into my lungs? I ache to give you my heat, to see it blossom in your heart and spread its fire in your soul. Never have I felt like this for a human before. It is dangerous. Not only for fear of being betrayed again by someone who has the power to wound me, but because the love of humans has caused many wars. It is forbidden for my kind to love a human. Or so it has been said. Oh, if I could ask the Creator Herself, but no, it is not possible now....

This is another thought that has come to me as of late as well. Through many years of meditation and purposeful hardening of my spirit, I have moved past the betrayal I suffered so long ago. However, for some reason I'm unaware of, this very issue has been resurfacing in my mind. The pain has returned, but with it, as though to take the sharpest edge off of it, have come these new and intoxicating feelings for Annaleah.

Sometimes, when I visit her, I feel that I can feel her heart beating in my chest. As though each pulse is laced with something so profound and intimate it is beyond my ability to describe in words. Her youth, her supreme innocence, as well as the enigma of who she is, combines in her to produce one of the most extraordinary creatures I have ever seen.

Perhaps too, it what happened last night that has me in such a state of affairs. I was beside her bed, looking at her beautiful mouth, when her lips parted slightly and she exhaled a deep breath. I had been thinking about how poorly I had treated her, and of what I would say should she awaken to find me beside her. Her sharp exhalation brought me back to the present. The way her mouth opened ever so slightly reminded me of a woman who was expecting a kiss, and I wished then for her to awaken so that I might have the slightest chance of kissing her. Her sudden clasp on my hand in hers surprised me, but pleasantly so. It was no more than a quick squeeze, and then she let my hand go.

And then she said my name. She did not call me Professor, or Sir. In a loud whisper, as she let my hand go limp in her own, she said, "Sebastian." I think my heart, as well as my lungs, ceased working for a moment. I thought she knew I was with her, but I dismissed that thought as she went still again and fell back to her deepened dream state. I held her hand tightly, willing her to awaken, to say my name again.

It is rare for anyone to call me by anything but Professor in some form. Though the Chancellor does, on some occasions, call me Sebastian, it is never with any form of intimacy or deep affection. When Annaleah said my name, the emotion it carried was unmistakable. I wished so deeply then to know what she was dreaming, but just to know she dreamt of me…. Oh what that did to me!

I want to hear her say my name again, to see her lips part and feel her breath hot against me as my name forms on her lips. It is such a small thing, and yet so deeply personal. Why is it so intoxicating to me, I wonder, to be called by my first name? Perhaps it is partially because it happens so rarely. That she used this form instead of professor makes it much more cherished. She was calling to me as an equal, not as a teacher or a superior.

I leaned closer to her, hoping she would speak again in her sleep. Though I could have peered inside her dreams had I wished to do so strongly enough, I did not want to invade her privacy in any way. To mar her innocence in any manner would be unforgivable. I watched her eyes dart beneath her lids, a sure sign of dreaming. The closer I came to her, the more I smelled her scent. Honeysuckle.

There were too many emotions at once. From her scent, to her speaking my name. Suddenly, I had to get out of there, before I become overwhelmed.

As I turned to leave, one of our students walked into the room. I believe her name is Rachael. She looked a bit startled at seeing me in the room with Annaleah, but recovered quickly.

I hope she is not one for gossip; all I need is to have the ones who have been making the past few days a torment to know I have visited her again. Though I am sure a few teachers would love this little tidbit as well.

I will sign off for now. I am growing tired and need to retire for the night. Perhaps I shall see Annaleah in Dream Time, and maybe, just maybe, I can hear her say my name once more...

~SB~

Chapter Twenty-Five

Annaleah Awakens

As the sight of the forest clearing left Annaleah's vision and she began her ascent back into consciousness, she heard someone speaking to her from very far off. It was a voice she vaguely recalled, and though it sounded as if it were coming to her through thick gauze over many miles, she tried her best to remember whom it belonged to. Moving with a greater speed and awareness, she drifted towards to voice until it became clearer. With effort, Annaleah opened her eyes slightly and saw the yellow tinged lights of her hospital room and the faded white wall across from her bed. She tried to turn her head toward the speaker, but quickly became dizzy. A small moan escaped her lips, and she closed her eyes again.

"Whoa, hey, you're awake!" the voice said excitedly. "Hold on, let me get a nurse. I am so happy you're coming to. I have a lot to tell you!" Annaleah felt someone moving around her bed, and heard a buzzer as a button was pressed. A female's nasally voice responded, asking what they needed.

"Annaleah is awake. Just thought y'all would like to know." Recognition came to Annaleah then. It was Rachael! She smiled, and tried to open her eyes again. The grinning face of her new friend came into view, closer to her than she expected.

"There you are Annaleah. Don't try to move too much. I got the nurses for you. Maybe they can give you something to make you a bit more comfortable." Rachael beamed at her, then straightened up.

"Oh, I want to show you my jacket," she said, turning around. The black leather had long slash marks in it, appearing as if it had been made that way. It looked rather fashionable. "Bubo did this with her claws, but no worries, I love it. Doesn't it look fantastic?" Annaleah smiled at her friend, pleased to see her so happy.

Rachael posed in her jacket a few times before she stepped aside to let the staff that had entered the room do their jobs. Her short black pixie cut looked freshly trimmed and made her large kohl lined brown eyes appear even larger. Rachael took a seat beside Annaleah, as one nurse took her vital signs and another fed something from a syringe into an IV tube.

"How do you feel, dear?" the nurse taking her vitals asked.

Annaleah was happy to discover that her voice had returned, but her mouth still didn't seem to work quite right. Her words felt thick on her tongue. "Better, but a bit dizzy."

After some fussing and a promise to get some medication for her dizziness, the nurses left and closed the door behind them to give the two women some privacy.

"So, guess who just left a few minutes ago?" Rachael asked her, obviously bursting with the need to tell her. Annaleah knew who she wanted it to be, his pale, angular face coming to mind. If she tried, she could still smell his rain soaked leather, the memory of it both embarrassing her and flooding her with a heady, pleasant feeling. Had she really passed out in his arms?

"Tell me," Annaleah asked, a smile playing over her lips.

"I think you know, don't you? Your Uncle John says he's been here every day at some point to see about you. He never says much, but both your friend Seth and your Uncle John seem to think of him favorably. I think he has a thing for you, myself. I don't know how you managed it girl, but there have been many ladies before you pining for the Professor, and he has never once shown the slightest interest in any of them."

Annaleah felt a rush of girlish glee at hearing this. She tried to hide her pleasure from Rachael, but Rachael had already seen her reaction.

"Look at you blushing! You have the hots for the professor too, don't you?" Both of the young women giggled then, and Annaleah began to feel better, the dizziness abating.

"I can't say I blame you. He might be moody and snarky, but he is tall and handsome." Rachael titled her head and looked up toward the ceiling, placing her finger under her chin, as if she was deep in thought. "Kinda pale, but it looks great with his long black hair, don't you think?" She looked back at Annaleah and winked playfully. "So what did you do to get him so interested in you, besides passing out in his arms? Inquiring minds want to know."

Rachael's smile was full and genuine, and Annaleah felt the warmth of knowing she had a true friend glow in her heart. Letting her happy rush fade just a bit around the edges so that she could answer the question, Annaleah spoke truthfully. "I really don't know, Rachael. I'm embarrassed about it actually." Annaleah grabbed a bit of her long curly hair and wove it in and out of her fingers, trying to ignore the flush that she could feel growing in her cheeks. After a moment she looked up, hoping Rachael didn't see the discomfort in her eyes. "Can you tell me what happened? How long have I been here?"

Rachael's expression grew serious, and she sat up a bit straighter. "Well, I'm not really sure about everything, but apparently you were bitten by several poisonous spiders. You've had us all pretty worried about you, and that includes the doctors." Rachael's eyes were wide as she looked at Annaleah, driving home the fact of how seriously ill Annaleah had been. "No one knows what kind of spiders they were, and that's pretty freaky. From what I understand, it was hard to find the proper antivenin." Rachael leaned closer, her hands steepled, her eyes holding a sheen in them. Annaleah, you almost died." Her voice was almost a whisper. "You're very lucky to be here."

Annaleah looked at her friend, her heart skipping several beats. She wasn't sure she had heard Rachael correctly. When her heart began to beat once more, it did so at a furious pace. "I almost died?" She asked, her voice thick with awe.

Rachael nodded slowly, her eyes wide and somber. "You have someone up there in the Holy cosmos looking after you. When I heard about the spiders, I started to do some research. I decided to go the occult route since the doctors didn't know what type had bitten you. After doing a bit of work, I found a very interesting and obscure grimoire." Rachael paused to scoot the chair a bit closer to Annaleah's bed, glancing at the door as if to make sure they were alone.

"I read many things, from an Asian creature who travels in Dream Time, to a legend about the origins of spiders themselves. I thought you would like to hear the one about their origin, as owls come into it as well."

"Owls?' Annaleah asked, a bit confused. "What do owls and spiders have to do with each other?"

"Quite a bit actually," Rachael answered, her face blossoming into a smile. She rubbed her hands together, apparently anxious to share what she had learned. "You see, it is said that long ago, Satan was an angel named Satanael. After he fell he was called Satan, which has come to mean adversary or enemy. Anyway, supposedly the Goddess let him make the first living creatures on Earth, and he made terrible monsters. The Goddess destroyed them and it really pissed Satanael off. When the Goddess killed Satanael's creatures and replaced them with mankind, this led to war, and a third of the angels of Heaven fell with Satanael."

Annaleah looked at her friend curiously. Marchasias had just shared this information with her, and now Rachael was telling her the same thing. An uneasy feeling, uncomfortably close to fear, arose in her belly.

"Now, here is the interesting part," Rachael went on, unaware of Annaleah's discomfort. "Satanael was so angry about his creations being killed off that he made an entire species of a creature to snub the Goddess and satisfy his hurt ego. Guess what that was?"

Annaleah shuddered as she recalled the huge spiders dripping off the trees like a nightmare rain in her meeting with the Jorogumo. "Spiders?" she asked.

Rachael nodded. "Yes, spiders. And not just on Earth either. Satanael made special hybrids of them, half human and half spider creatures called--"

"The Jorogumo." Annaleah interrupted. The fear in her belly clawed its way into her chest, making her heart thunder. She tried to swallow but her mouth had gone dry.

Rachael blinked at her in surprise. "Yes. You know about the Jorogumo?"

"I'll tell you how at a later time, but yes, I do unfortunately. Please go on."

Rachael continued. "So anyway, there were all manner of spiders created. Insects to cover the earth and bring torment and even death to mankind, God's precious creation. Demons were made by crossing human's DNA with a spider's, and both were sent into Heaven to do warfare, and to destroy the Goddess's mankind on earth as well. Many angels became poisoned, and some were lost to the oblivion only angels endure. The Holy Angels went to the Goddess in despair, begging for help. She gave them permission to create one creature of their own. Any guess as to what this creature was?"

A gentle glow of peace overcame her fear as an image of Bubo and her mother came into Annaleah's mind. "Owls?" she guessed.

Rachael smiled and nodded once more. "Yeah, that's right. They created owls." Rachael paused looked at Annaleah, a smirk on her face, as if she had known Annaleah would guess correctly and was pleased she had done so. "Demons hate owls. This knowledge has been purposely repressed by the demons, who have tried to make owls look ominous and foreboding."

Annaleah shook her head, confused, and held her hand up for Rachael to stop for a moment. After gathering her thoughts, she asked, "Where did you find that? I teach the Occult and I've never heard that before."

Racahel tilted her head, a curious look on her face. She studied Annaleah for a few seconds, and seemed to be surprised that Annaleah had never heard of this before.

"Well, I looked it up in the school library's rare books section. It was in a leather bound grimoire that looked a million years old." Rachael continued to pierce her with a strange look in her eyes, as if she still couldn't believe Annaleah. didn't know this. "The title was in another language, and the script inside looked penned by hand. It was a spooky but beautiful book."

There was an uncomfortable pause before Rachael cleared her throat and continued.

"Anyhow, the demons made up stories to give owls a bad reputation so people would associate them with superstitions of death and bad luck. It couldn't be further from the truth. Not only did Athena the Goddess of art, wisdom and war tactics have an owl familiar, but the arch angel Gabriel is associated with them as well, being the angel of the night and of the moon. And so Annaleah, here is my question to you...."

Rachael looked at her friend with a merry twinkle in her eyes. "What dealings do you have with the angels? I mean, it makes sense now. Why else would an owl injure itself to come to you, and how on Earth would there be a spider in this part of the world, as of yet undiscovered, which came to you and almost killed you with its poison?"

Annaleah's mind went into overdrive, it was all coming together now. As she looked down at her hands to think about what Rachael had said, she could feel Rachael's dark brown eyes on her, as if Rachael were trying to pry apart her mind to see what she was thinking.

"Are you an angel?" Rachael asked. The energy between them grew heavier, as if the air had gone out from the room. Annaleah could hear her heart beat in the silence.

What if she was an angel? Satanael, Marchosias and her mother had all said that she was special. Not just special, but one of a kind. The notion was electrifying, exciting and terrifying all at once. Yet, what if those meetings were nothing more than very vivid dreams? She laughed nervously, not knowing what to say that would sound sane.

"I'm sorry, Rachael, I don't mean to be rude by laughing. I just can't imagine myself as an angel. I do love your story though; it makes a lot of sense." Annaleah was about to go on and tell her about her dreams, but all thoughts of doing so quickly vanished as Uncle John walked into the room, roses in hand. When he saw that Annaleah was awake, his face blossomed into an expression of pure happiness.

"Annaleah! Oh thank God you're awake!" Uncle John was at Annaleah's side at once, throwing his arms around her, roses and all. She returned his embrace, hugging him tightly.

"We thought we might lose you there, kiddo," Uncle John said as he let her go so he could set the roses on the side table.

"Rachael informed me of that," Annaleah said, shaking her head slightly in disbelief. "I'm still getting used to that news."

"Don't you ever do that to me again, young lady!" Uncle John scolded. At first, Annaleah thought he meant almost dying on him, but his face was too serious for it to be a joke. He meant hiding the fact that she had been bitten from him. Annaleah hung her head, not knowing what to say.

Rachael, sensing the tension in the room, cleared her throat. "Um, I have an essay due tomorrow, I should get going." She said as she rose from her chair. "I'm so glad you're feeling better, Annaleah. See you in class, okay?" She leaned over and hugged Annaleah gently. "I'm sure you will be out of here soon. See y'all. Nice to see you again too, Uncle John."

After the girls hugged and Rachael left, Uncle John looked once more at his niece. "I know I wasn't feeling well, but I would have insisted on you going to the hospital. I wouldn't have had to bring you myself, Seth could have brought you."

Not wanting to fight with her uncle, Annaleah said simply, "I'm sorry." She had been looking down at her hands at first, feeling ashamed for not doing just as he said, though she still felt that, in his state that night, alerting him would have been the wrong thing. When he didn't answer right away, she looked up into his eyes, which were just as green as hers. "Really Uncle John, I mean it. I'm sorry."

Uncle John nodded, looking intensely at her, and let out a long sigh. He grabbed her hand and gently kissed it.

"Don't ever leave me kiddo; you're all the family I have left." He cleared his throat, clearly uncomfortable with the level of emotion. Changing the subject, he pointed at a cluster of multicolored columbines in a light lilac colored vase. The bunch was tied together with an indigo ribbon.

"Guess who gave those to you?" he asked, a smile on his lips. Annaleah knew that look, he was about to tease her. She felt her face go hot again, but she smiled. She hadn't known the Professor had brought her flowers.

"He must really like you. He even remembered what kind of flower you were wearing in your hair the first day of class. He gets a couple brownie points in my book for that. And you made him out to sound so sinister."

Annaleah didn't respond, liking the life that teasing her had brought into her uncle's kind face. She was rather enjoying the emotions washing over her now. Knowing the Professor had been paying that much attention to her warmed her deeply.

"Do you like him, Annaleah?" Uncle John asked. She looked up at him, still smiling. She wanted to tell him that yes, indeed, she liked him quite a bit, but found she couldn't come outright and say the words. Instead, she nodded, still smiling contentedly.

"Good," he said, patting her hand. "You two would make pretty babies."

That surprised her. Annaleah had never heard him talk that way before. Her mouth opened in shock, her eyes wide. "Uncle John!"

He looked back at her, and seemed to mimic the shocked expression she was giving him, apparently to show her how silly she looked. They both laughed until tears came. After they had settled down a bit, Annaleah spoke softly, "Uncle John, I have a great favor to ask you."

"Anything, kiddo. What is it?"

"I want to ask you a question, and I want you to answer it. Not only to answer it, but to do so with sincere honesty."

She looked at her uncle, who stiffened up. His eyes looked both sad and frightened, as if he were being cornered.

"Annaleah, no, don't do this," he said quietly. She caught his eyes before he looked down at his feet. They held an old, glazed hurt in them.

The corners of his mouth had drawn out and twitched at the corners, as if he were trying not to cry.

Annaleah's stomach sank. Why was this so hard for him? She hated to see him hurting, but she had to know. It was important.

"Please, Uncle John." She said no more, but watched with a deepening ache in her heart as her uncle fought tears. She took his hands in her own and held them, both to strengthen her own resolve and to give comfort to him.

"Tell me about my father."

Uncle John nodded, a tear escaping from each eye. He squeezed her hands in return.

He looked at her, but Annaleah looked away, not able to bear the look of sorrow in her beloved uncle's eyes.

"I have been trying for your whole life to shelter you from this, Annaleah, but You're a grown woman now and you deserve to know. But don't say I didn't warn you."

Suddenly, she found herself wondering if asking had been such a good idea. Sometimes not knowing was better, for once you knew, there was no going back.

Too late now...

Chapter Twenty-Six

Uncle John's Difficult Confession

"I want you to know without the slightest modicum of doubt that I loved your mother," Uncle John began. His eyes had taken on the luminous, pale green glow that they both had when either of them cried, or were close to tears. Annaleah made herself look her uncle in the eye, out of respect and gratitude for his willingness to finally open up to her about something he had kept secret for so many years.

"Of course I know you loved her. Why would I doubt that?" Annaleah asked him sincerely.

Uncle John nodded. "Please remember that Annaleah, during this conversation." He bowed his head, eyes closed. She could see he was going inward for strength and the right words to say.

"Your mother was a very special woman. She loved life like no one else I have ever met. She was so happy. The smallest things would make her glow with joy. The first columbine of the spring, dancing barefoot in the rain, singing to the moon. She was always kind, always helping others, even at her own expense at times. But she did have her faults, Annaleah. Despite being one of the most innocent people I ever met, she was also.... one of the most ungrounded. The doctors said it was schizophrenia."

Annaleah felt as if she had had the wind knocked out of her, as if someone had kicked her hard in the chest. What had he just said? How could this be right?

"What? Are you serious?" She exclaimed incredulously, "Why didn't you tell me this before?"

Uncle John opened his eyes and looked at his niece, the green of his orbs now almost aflame as tears spilled freely down his cheeks.

"I am so, so sorry. It didn't seem fair to tell you about her disorder and take away the beautiful picture you had of your mother. She was a wonderful person, but she was, at times, very unstable."

Annaleah was silent, her head spinning. She listened to Uncle John through a veil of shock, trying not to let the distress at what she'd learned over take her senses. When a tear fell and landed on her hand, she looked at it curiously, unaware she had been crying.

"One morning, I found her outside, barefoot and in her nightgown. It wouldn't have mattered that much if it were spring or summer or winter even, had it been like most winters here in the south. But this particular year, it was a harsh winter. It had snowed the night before, at least a couple of inches. It took me a while to find her. I had to follow her footprints in the snow. They led from the house to the woods, to some clearing I had never seen before, nor since. I still can't figure that part out. When I found her, she lay crumpled in a pile, shuddering, half frozen in the snow. Though shivering and barely conscious, she was smiling. I threw my coat over her and carried her inside. Fearing hypothermia, I called 911. After they evaluated her at the hospital, they wanted to admit her to Castlebrook."

Annaleah covered her face with her hands, and tried unsuccessfully to hold her sobs back. Her heart broke bit by bit as she listened to what Uncle John's deep voice. It broke for herself, having been robbed of the beautiful picture she had always had of her mother. It broke for Uncle John, who'd had to keep this from her for so long in an effort to protect her. She thought about how hard it must have been for him to carry this painful secret, knowing how badly she had wanted to know the truth, and another wave of deep, aching sadness washed over her.

Of course it had broken for her mother too, for having to suffer a form of psychosis that must have confused her senses and expectations of reality. Annaleah knew too well what it was like to be different, to be misunderstood, to be feared for being different.

Annaleah thought of Castlebrook. It was the town's psychiatric ward. Everyone from the mildly troubled to the wildly disturbed were sent there; from wards of the state to the rich and pampered. Though it was a well-respected place, it wasn't somewhere anyone would want to find themselves.

"I didn't want to do it at first. I thought I could take care of her myself. After she was released from the emergency room, I brought her back home and tried to take care of her the best I could. She was sick with the flu, but bless her, she was still so happy. She said she had been talking to angels that night in the woods, and she believed it with all her heart and soul. Part of me believed her too. She had natural abilities as a healer, among other things.

"Then she disappeared a few weeks later, during another snow flurry. I found her wandering lost in the woods, barefoot again, and muttering to herself. Her feet were scratched and bleeding and she had cuts all over her, even a few deep gashes. When I tried to help her, she acted as if she didn't even see me. I allowed the hospital to transfer her to Castlebrook that night."

Annaleah listened to Uncle John, her breaths slow and steady, and her eyes wide as she tried not to let her sadness and disbelief overtake her. She trembled slightly as she stared at the floor. Unblinking, tears fell in large droplets down her cheeks.

id this mean she was mad, too? It made sense. She was at the age when the symptoms of Schizophrenia began to manifest. Were her dreams and visions a sign that she was losing touch with reality and slowly spiraling into a world of psychosis?

Annaleah squeezed her eyes shut and slowly shook her head from side to side, trying to deny the thought that she might be mentally ill. There were too many coincidences. Uncle John had mentioned the clearing in the woods. Did mental illness share the exact same facets of delusions? She didn't think so, so as she listened to Uncle John continue, she held this precious kernel of hope to her heart.

"A few days after she was admitted," Uncle John went on, "I got a call from her case worker at Castlebrook, asking me to meet with him. When I got to the meeting, they had her sedated. I couldn't even see her. They told me something that at the time I couldn't understand." Uncle John took a deep breath, his eyes wide. "Annaleah, they told me she was pregnant." He let out his deep breath, and a single tear made its way down his flushed cheek. He took his glasses off and wiped his eyes with a handkerchief before repositioning his glasses on his nose. Annaleah would have accused him of stalling for time had she not been so out of sorts herself.

"Though she had a good standing with most people nearby," Uncle John explained, "she didn't have any real friends. You know how it is to be different. To be judged, feared, even hated for what you are should you dare to deviate from the norm. You can understand my surprise when I found out she was with child." His eyes had taken on a deeper shade of green as they looked intently at her, his expression somber and serious. "The caseworker asked me if I knew who the father was, and I said I didn't. I asked him if Elise had told them who had gotten her pregnant, and they told me that she had insisted the father was an angel that she had met that night in the woods when I found her crumpled in the clearing." He shook his head, as if to clear it. "They wanted to find the father because they feared she had been assaulted." He returned his gaze to her, his eyes softened, sad. "They even put her through a polygraph test, which she passed. Your mother believed with all the conviction in her heart that your father was an angel."

Annaleah could see how farfetched this had appeared to Uncle John. It sounded pretty shocking to her as well, even after all that she had been through.

Annaleah reached over and grabbed her uncle's hand and squeezed it reassuringly, sad that this had been a burden he'd had to carry alone. Did he think the same thing was going on with her now? Did he fear for her mental health, fear that he would lose her too? She knew his heart was breaking, that letting go of the secret after so long must be taking a toll on him.

She took his hand and kissed it gently, her tears falling onto his hand.

Part of her believed in what her mother had said wholeheartedly, without question. Marchosias, Satanael and her mother had told her in Dream Time that she was one of a kind, unlike any other. Wouldn't it make sense then, that her mother hadn't been mad at all, and that she was indeed, the daughter of an angel? And what about the spiders? Could hallucinations follow you out of a delusion?

Wiping at her tears, Annaleah asked, "Do you think I'm crazy, Uncle John? Do you think maybe I should go to Castlebrook?"

Uncle John leaned forward, and looked her deeply in the eye. "No. Not ever." He squeezed her hand, the corners of his mouth still drawn out, twitching, as he fought with his own inner turmoil. "I want you to know that I never would have put you in Castlebrook. Taking care of you and watching you grow up has been the greatest joy of my life. I wouldn't take back a single second of it. You have changed me so much, helped me to grow, and because of you and who you are, I have had many sleepless nights myself, wondering if somehow, what your mother said was true."

Hearing this surprised Annaleah. Was he saying maybe she hadn't been mentally ill after all?

Confused, Annaleah looked down at her hand in Uncle John's, "wait, you said she had Schizophrenia, now you're saying maybe she didn't? Why? I don't understand."

Uncle John tilted his head, the look of sadness abating as the warm, sweet glow of love filled his eyes. "Because Annaleah, you are so special. You spoke your first words at six months, and were speaking in full sentences by the time you were a little over a year old." Uncle John leaned forward, looking her more deeply in the eye. "When you were born, they said you were born with a caul. I also know that being your mother's child had an effect on your talents; your ability to know certain things without being told, or your ability to see into a world others simply refuse to believe is there at all. That film over your eyes when you were born opened your inner eyes to a truth much deeper than most of us will ever know." He shook his head wistfully as he spoke, as if he too wished he could sense this wonderful inner truth he was talking to her about. "Perhaps it also has something to do with your inherent goodness and kindness. They say those born with a caul can defeat all manner of evils. I'm sure, being an occult expert, that you know that too. I'm not sure, however," he said, tilting his head as he spoke, "that you know you were not born with the normal blue of a newborn's eyes, but that your eyes have always been green. The doctors had never seen anything like it. Babies' eyes turn colors after a year or so, after they are exposed to light, but yours were always green." He shook his head once more, as if he were still trying to grasp what he was telling her. "There are so many things like that, honey, that make me think there might have been something to her claim. Then my rational mind takes over and tells me there is just simply no way that an angel could have fathered you. It has been an internal battle I have waged with myself, and one I never wished for you to endure."

Annaleah thought of her dreams, and of everything that had been happening to her in the last couple of weeks. What if what uncle John had told her was true to the point that it was more evidence that her dreams were real, a meeting place of sorts, a portal from this world to many others? What if being the daughter of an angel meant that she could attract these situations?

For a moment, Annaleah debated on whether or not to tell him about her dreams. It could put his mind at ease to know that she could really be half angel, and that her mother hadn't been lying. Maybe he would have some suggestions, or more information to tell her that he might still be holding back. He was her uncle after all, and he deserved to know.

As she looked at him, she noticed the dark circles under his eyes, the lines of worry creased into his expression, and the heaviness in which he held himself. He was exhausted, not just from his confession, but from worry over her health, and from the ill effects of his own health issues. He was trembling slightly, and seeing this made her heart break even more. Now was not the time.

Annaleah shook her head, her hair falling into her face and smearing the tears there. "You've been keeping this inside for so long. I'm so sorry," She whispered, and held her arms out to him, needing to hug him for her own comfort, and to reassure him that her love for him was still as strong as ever.

Annaleah felt her love for Uncle John flood through her as they held each other, and more tears came. She was confused and upset, but there was nothing that he could ever tell her that would make her love him less. He was so brave, so loving, to have done what he thought was the right thing to do, even though it must have hurt him every single day.

Before either of them could say anything more, a knock sounded at the door. Still hanging her head, Annaleah looked up through her mess of hair and tears, not caring what she looked like. She didn't feel like company.

Seth walked into the room, carrying an armload of books. When he saw the two of them, his face registered the intensity of the situation, and he began to back out of the room. "I'll just come back later, Annaleah, I am glad to see you awake though."

Uncle John got up, shaking his head. "No, please, let me leave. I think Annaleah needs you here now. I'll wait for you outside if you don't mind. I'm too tired to walk home tonight."

"Of course." Seth replied as Uncle John gave Annaleah a goodbye hug. She didn't want to let Uncle John go. He looked like he could use a break from the intensity of what had just transpired, so she didn't ask him to stay.

"Let me help you to the door Uncle John." Seth went to Uncle John's side and tried to put his arm under his for support.

Uncle John laughed and shook him off gently. "Thank you, Seth, but

I'll be alright. I'm just tired. I'll meet you outside." He smiled, looking ten years older than he had just a few days ago.

"See you later kiddo, I love you." Uncle John whispered in her ear. Annaleah told him that she loved him as well, holding back more tears. He looked so frail that she felt guilty for asking him to tell her about her father. It had clearly taken a lot out of him.

When he reached the door, he turned and blew her a kiss before he exited.

"What on Earth happened?" Seth asked, his blue eyes wide.

"Apparently," Annaleah began, wiping at her eyes, "My mother was a schizophrenic who thought she talked to angels. She was either crazy and thought that my father was an angel, or she really did have an angel for a lover, resulting in my birth."

Seth didn't speak for several moments. Instead, she heard him put down the books and saw him take a seat in the chair beside her.

After many moments, Seth said simply, "Annaleah." When he didn't say anything more, Annaleah looked at him, intent on asking him why he had nothing to say about something so deeply personal and intense.

As their eyes met, what Annaleah saw took her breath away. Instead of the blue she had known and loved for so long, she saw a piercing shade of indigo, radiant in his eyes. Arcs of light played in his skin, their colors electric and protean. He was smiling a peaceful, serene smile.

"Annaleah," he said again, his voice a thousand times more melodic than she had ever heard it before. "Your mother was not crazy, far from it. Don't be afraid. I know I look different from what you are used to, but it is time for you to know the truth."

Annaleah wasn't sure she could handle much more of the truth today.

"Your mother did indeed talk to angels." Seth told her simply. Annaleah found the energy emanating from him to be loving and wonderfully calming.

"How are you so sure Seth?" she asked.

"Because my sweet Annaleah," he said affectionately, "I know your father."

Chapter Twenty-Seven

Seth's Revelation

Annaleah's head still was spinning, despite the calming energy that emanated from Seth. Looking at her friend in his now deeply indigo eyes, she said, "How is that even possible, for you to know my father?"

Seth smiled warmly at her, the love he felt for her washing over her in waves, bathing her with a gentle, pacifying glow. Little by little, Annaleah felt her heart lighten and her nerves settle. Her heartbeat and breathing slowed their laborious rhythm, the pressures of her newfound knowledge easing as the beautiful energy continued to flow from Seth. Though she was still unsure what was actually occurring, she let herself be swept up in the gentle energy of relaxation that Seth was sending her.

After several moments, Seth asked, "Is that better?" When Annaleah nodded slowly, her eyes closed, he continued. "As you see, there is a little more to me than meets the eye. I'm also known by another name, one which I'm sure you are familiar with. We'll get to that. You asked about your father. I believe he would want to tell you himself. I will tell you this much; he too, like you and your Professor, is a one of a kind. He is not easy to contact in the human realm of physicality, and it will take a complex ritual in order to contact him. Though, once he senses your energy signature attached to his summoning, I am certain his arrival with be swift."

"So, what you're telling me then," Annaleah asked, her voice lower and a bit thick, as though she were slightly sedated, "is that my father is an angel?"

"Precisely," Seth answered, the luminosity beneath his skin growing brighter and more pronounced. His face shifted as well, the effect fluid and graceful. His features became sharper and more angled, as though he were transforming into something pixie like.

"So that makes me half angel and half human, right?"

"Something like that, but not quite. There have been many half human and half angels. Some of them were terrible, cruel creatures, but not all. You may know of one race from your studies, the Nephilim. Not all races of Halfling are terrible, though. As you're aware, there are several races of angels, just as there are many races of humans. Depending on the race of each parent, the Halfling can be beautiful, graceful and gentle, such as you, or terrible and cruel, such as the Nephilim. Of course, there are a thousand shades of grey in between the light and dark, though most seem to turn out by chance either one or the other."

Annaleah opened her eyes, more calm and relaxed even though the conversation was one of the most profound of her life. "Okay, so if I am not a "Halfling" as you call them, what exactly am I?"

"There is no real title for you my dear, as you are one of a kind. Most of the angels refer to you as The Otherling, " Seth answered. He continued to change in appearance, his hair now a lighter shade of blonde that cascaded down his shoulders.

"Everything I have come to know about myself and my life appears to be a lie." Annaleah whispered, her heart growing a bit heavy. Seth, apparently sensing her changing demeanor, seemed to intensify his soothing energy towards her. Annaleah accepted this gift gratefully, taking a few deep breaths to allow his energy calm her further.

"You have to be protected, at all costs. Your life is not a lie. Not everything you have come to know is false. I am still your friend. I always have been. Though you met me as Seth in the 5th grade, I have always been with you, since the time of your birth. Your arrival on this planet was carefully orchestrated, Annaleah. Though there have been things hidden from you, we have never lied to you. We all knew there would be a time when you would need to be told everything. We also knew that as soon as you knew these things, the darkness would come to find you as well. This part could not be helped. The Jorogumo has found you, as has Satanael. The time for you to know the fullness of your power is now. You must be prepared for what is to come, and that means knowing where you came from, and who you truly are. I know you are strong enough for this, even though it will be far from easy."

Annaleah looked at Seth with a sense of confusion and awe. "Tell me who you are Seth. Who are you really?"

In response, Seth stood up, now much taller in his new form than he was as Seth. His skin was pale and almost translucent, the arcs of light which sparked beneath it making him seem as though his entire being was aglow. Still emanating calming energy, he walked to her bedside and gently took her hand. At the contact of his flesh on hers, the love he felt for her overwhelmed her, and tears spilled down her cheeks.

"Don't be afraid," Seth whispered. Closing his eyes, he straightened up, still holding her hand between his. From behind his back, huge wings unfolded with an audible whoosh. Their silver blue feathers aglow with holy light, they seemed to be too huge to fit within the room. He encircled Annaleah within them, enfolding her with angelic love.

"I am the dream keeper, guardian at the watch tower to the West. I govern the element of water and emotions, and the moon is under my control and night time is my domain. I am the arch angel Gabriel."

Under the powerful calming emanations of Gabriel's love, Annaleah felt a blessed sense of control and awe. She smiled at her oldest friend, tears spilling from her eyes as she closed them again. Not knowing what to say, she sent her love back to the arch angel which held her hand so gently in his own.

"When I won the sacred duty to be your guardian, it was before you were even conceived." Seth's voice had changed, it was now deeper, and held the lilt of music within it. "I spoke to your father before he met with your mother in the woods, and swore to him my loyalty and protection. I have been with you ever since then. My love for you and duty to you has been the most precious honor I have ever had in my life." Seth leaned back a bit, smiling at her. "It was between Raphael and myself, to be your guardian. Though I, of course, won the honor, Raphael blessed you with the natural ability of healing before you were born. Your guardian had to be an archangel, Annaleah. Otherwise, in the company of another angel, your true form would have come out. You would have eventually transformed into your angelic state if you had stayed long enough around another angel. The archangels are the only ones strong enough to stave off your transformation. Given more time around Sebastian, you would have noticed the light within you coming forth. I am sure you have seen the telltale signs when you are around him. The three of us have been in the same room a few times now, and it took all of my strength and ability to hold your transformation at bay. Your Uncle John still does not know." Gabriel paused to look at Annaleah, his eyes full of gentility. "You are destined; you will come to find that out. Now however, you must draw on your innate healing ability. I will aid you as well. The warm, calming energy I have sent out to you has done more than just sooth your nerves, it had also helped to heal you. It is time for your release from this hospital."

"Good," Annaleah smiled. "I am ready to get out of this dreary place."

A thought flashed in her mind, her heart overcome with a bright, happy upwelling of hope.

"If you've healed me, then what about Uncle John?" She asked Seth, her heart still aglow.

"Now that you know the truth, it can be done. I would like for you to rest a bit more first, it can take a lot out of you." He smiled at her reassuringly, "For now, it is time for you to finally meet your father. He is requesting a formal audience with you, which means you need to call him forth in a circle. He says it might be a bit more difficult to do it this way, but he wants to meet with you outside of Dream Time. Besides," he said straightening up and folding his wings against his back. "You need to brush up on your invocation skills." Seth winked at her playfully.

Chapter Twenty-Eight

The Spaces in Between

After a brief time convincing the nurses and Annaleah's doctor that she was well enough to return home, she and Seth soon found themselves gathering up her few personal items prior to her discharge. Smiling through several endearing well wishes from the attending nurses and Uncle John himself, Seth led Annaleah out of the hospital and towards home.

"I still can't believe you, Seth, my oldest and dearest friend, are actually the arch angel Gabriel," Annaleah confessed, her green eyes wide with awe. "I mean, after all this time, shouldn't I have been able to tell that you were something special, something more than Seth, my old buddy? I'm an occult scholar for crying out loud!"

Seth smiled and reached across the seat to pat her hand reassuringly. "I understand how you could feel that way. Really though, if I wanted you to see me this way, then there is little choice on your part but to see me this way. That being said, I do have to exert some power and control in order for us both to be in human form around each other. It throws our vibrations off, to be clothed in what we refer to as "glamour." It's not our real form. It's just pretty illusions. The body you wear right now isn't your true form. It has been a constant effort to keep you as you are now, in order for you to fit in, but also for your protection. It's not something I'm doing as a power play, or to fool you, though I'm sure you know that."

Annaleah remained silent, digesting what Seth had told her, before she asked, "So, what is my true form then? What if I want to lose the glamour and see myself as I truly am? I have always felt different Seth, you know that, but to have it reaffirmed in such a dramatic way is a bit overwhelming."

"Of course it is," Seth assured her, watching the road ahead as he drove the short distance to her home. "A lot of what is about to occur is going to fit snugly into the category of overwhelming, but it can't be helped. Things are happening now Annaleah, and as mind boggling as they may be, you must be strong. There is much more to tell you. I think it's time for you to know your true form, though I imagine the dream I sent you has given you a good idea of that which you truly are. I have long known of your unease within your own body, and, as beautiful as it is, it is not your true form. You look a lot like your human mother, with her petite and graceful form. You resonate a lot with your father's power as well, and this is good. When we get to your house, let's be quick to prepare for the ritual. Your father wishes to bless you for the upcoming battles. I'll stand outside of the circle in my angelic form; this will help you to lose the glamour I have so long placed over you and to emerge as that which you truly are."

"As enthusiastic as I am about all of this, I haven't drawn a circle in a long time," Annaleah said quietly, "I'm not sure even where to do it, in a space that I consider sacred enough."

"No worries there, dear one; the clearing in the woods that appears in your dreams is more than just dream scenery. It actually does exist, though in a space that is made more out of dream materials than out of the real physical world that we're in now. Let me see if I can explain it a bit better." Seth grabbed Annaleah's hand and laced his fingers through hers loosely. "Let's say that our fingers represent the physical world, and the spaces in between our fingers and our hands is the esoteric, dream like world. They exist very close to each other, and in certain times, when the atmosphere or day of the moon or year is right, the gaps become more volatile and physical, until they overlap with the real world enough to be seen or felt. Holy days make them more solid, like Halloween or the Summer Solstice. Anyway, right now, the spaces in between are becoming more dense and vibrating at such a rate that the doorway can be opened. The clearing in the woods is truly there now, beyond the path, waiting for you to draw your circle there."

"That makes sense, in a way." Annaleah said, "I have had some very intense experiences there, but before all this happened, I never dreamed of the clearing."

"There was no need for you to. It existed before. This is where Uncle John found your mother after she and your father conceived you. Before that, it was a place of sacred rituals stretching back many millennia. You just happened to have it near your home, and, being who and what you are, it was only a matter of time before you stumbled across it, either in Dream Time or in reality. It just happens that you dreamed of it first. Now the portals are yawning, calling out to you. It is time for you to answer."

Seth finished speaking as he pulled in to the driveway of Annaleah and Uncle John's home, his handsome face smiling sweetly at his friend. "Are you ready to prepare yourself?" he asked.

Annaleah nodded, opening the car door as she replied, "Of course."

As Annaleah gathered her ritual items, Seth lit some candles and incense, trying to evoke the energy of magick and tranquility to her home as she prepared herself for ritual. She took her silver robe and dressing oils into the bathroom, where she would dress after her bath. When she emerged from the water, it would symbolize her washing away her earthly self, to re-emerge as her higher, more spiritual self. It also helped her to relax and focus her intent. She played relaxing music as she drew the water, taking deep breaths and doing her best to balance her chakras and open herself up. She imagined a bright white light encircling her as she stepped into the warm lavender and lilac scented water. The light warded off all the negative energies which she might have brought with her or attracted. She mentally cleansed herself of all stagnant energies and invoked the spirit of calm and the presence of light. As she bathed, she took deep, calming, meditative breaths and imagined, as she washed her flesh, that she was also washing all dirty ephemera away from her as well. Any doubts about what she was about to go through were being scourged from her spirit. All manner of spiritual impurity was symbolically washed away, to spiral down the drain with the remnants of her bath. When Annaleah stood dripping from her bath, she emerged pure, her innocence and integrity whole and intact. She was ready to be in the presence of the Holy and to invite it into a space that she would make sacred and safe for the invocation of her father.

Saying a healing, calming mantra in her mind to retain this state of peace and purity, Annaleah dressed in blessed oils before she slid the soft velvet of her silver robe over her head. Barefoot, she padded down the hall to the living room, where Seth sat waiting for her. He stood as she approached him, smiling appreciatively.

"You look beautiful. You resonate peace and tranquility, as well as spiritual purity. You are ready." Annaleah felt the magickal energy of her bath running through her. Reality seemed muted, a bit fuzzy around the edges as she smiled at Seth. He handed her a small basket filled with ritual items, and he carried a medium sized radio to play music. Annaleah had told him earlier that she wished to use music in order to build up what she called the "Calling Energy" to invoke her father. Drumming, commonly used for this purpose in many parts of the world, was used to enter a trance state and to build a platform of energy for the spirit being invoked to stand upon.

Wordlessly, they left her home and walked into the thick of the woods behind the house. The night air seemed heavier than usual, as if it were alive and waiting for the events to unfold. The chirping of cicadas and crickets seemed to have more meaning; the calls of the frogs and birds every now and again seemed to resonate even deeper with the sense of something phantasmagorical to come.

Seth led Annaleah effortlessly through the woods, honing in on the space where she would dance her invocation. Annaleah followed, allowing reverence for that which about to unfold to overflow in her heart and spirit, readying herself for the mystical.

After what seemed only a short while, the path opened to what was now a very familiar clearing in the woods. It thrummed with energy, its vibrations calling Annaleah forward. Bowing her head for a short prayer to her mother Goddess, Annaleah walked along the outside of the space which would be her circle, laying out beautifully carved stones of amethyst, tigers eye, blue chalcedony and malachite at the four calling corners, as well as various spices, herbs and colored candles. Seth watched her from safely outside the circle.

Annaleah stepped into the center of the circle, her head tilted upward. "I now cast this circle of protection; the space within it is sacred and holy. Only those that I call forth into it may come inside with me, and only the spirits of love and light may attend this ritual. As I will it, so mote it be!" Annaleah went clockwise around the circle, lighting incense and the candles, saying the sacred words and invoking each watcher at the towers of their directions. Once this was done, Seth turned on the music so she could dance forth her energies in order to summon her father. The first song was to build her own energies and confidence for energy weaving and invocations. For this purpose, Annaleah had chosen "The Hosts of Seraphim" by Dead Can Dance. It was a lilting song, and one that never ceased to send shivers of awe through her.

As she let the energy of the music flood through her, Annaleah let her connection to the melody inspire her movements and connect her spirit to the magick she was about to perform. Her movements felt guided by a spiritual hand, building the energy of divinity. As she danced, the air around her seemed to waver and shimmer, transforming the space into a sacred place.

As Annaleah continued to dance, Seth transformed himself into Gabriel. His transformation moved her, the warm glow of love beat forth from her heart and surged through her entire being. It was a beautiful transformation, the change happening in a fluid manner, as if he had done it a million times. It was his wings though, that were the most glorious. Shining silver blue, they outstretched in the air and caught the moonlight, which seemed to scintillate over each feather.

The energy continued to shift around Annaleah as she danced, her body seeming to leave invisible yet undulating energy trails behind her as she moved. When this song ended, the next one began. This was her "power song", the one that she would use to invoke the spirit of her father into the circle. It was of utmost importance that she chose one intimately bonded to her, and so she had chosen one that she held sacred in her heart. This song never failed to elevate her moods and to almost instantly transform her into a meditative state. As the beginning drumbeats sounded out, Annaleah shifted her dance and was enraptured by the music, her undulations drenched in moonlight and caressed by the shadows of the night.

She danced her invocation to "Severance" as played by Bauhaus. Peter Murphy's voice soon rang out, the poignancy of his timber, the depths of the words he sang piercing through Annaleah as she swayed and moved, her emotions overcome with the sense of true beauty itself, deep, raw and powerful. As she called forth the sacred energy to summon her father, she noticed the air change around her, charged and electric, and very, very cold. Chills ran through her body, prickling her flesh with good bumps. She smiled, her eyes closed as she lost herself to the sensations of her summoning dance, elated to be swaying under the moonlight. She felt her body change as she continued her ode to her father's spirit, her ballad to him. She saw her flesh pale and become close to translucent. Beneath her milky skin, arcs of light flashed, climbing slowly from her bent elbow to arc higher at her wrist, until her hand too was luminescent. She felt as though she was stretching out in the most gorgeously languid stretch, and she watched in a peaceful awe as her body grew longer, taller, and more graceful. And still she danced. She danced, and she changed. With one sway, her arms became longer and more slender even as they were more muscularly defined. Bending to the music, her back elongated and from her shoulders sprouted beautiful golden feathered wings. They fanned the air as she stood upright again, their height many feet over her head. Gabriel continued to watcher, his arms crossed and lips smiling. Annaleah fed, too, on his angelic energy, her eyes half closed in sacred rapture.

As the last notes of her Calling Song faded away, Annaleah lowered her head and bowed as a sign of respect to her father. As she did so, something quite extraordinary occurred…It began to snow! At first it was a light, gentle dusting just in the area where Annaleah stood in supplication. Then it began to snow everywhere. Big, fat flakes of snow fell from the sky, some so big they fell sideways. Annaleah looked up slowly. Feeling the coldness falling against her skin took her only slightly out of her meditative state. She turned to Gabriel, filled with awe. She smiled, her whole being suffused with love and pure joy. She tilted her head back and opened her enormous wings, letting the snow fall fully on her face.

Annaleah had never seen it snow before during a ritual, and certainly not in the heart of Georgia during the hottest month of the summer. She knew though, that it was a sign of the coming of her father. Snow was purifying, and for one as great as her father, she knew a bit of purification was needed. The snow would also serve as vibrational insulation from the energy of her powerful father.

The air in front of Annaleah began to waver, lines formed and shifted within themselves, as her father began to manifest. Annaleah watched as his form became solid. Before her stood what looked to be an ordinary man. He was of average height, with white hair that cascaded in ringlets down his back. His eyes were a luminous, piercing green, the color of her eyes after a crying spell. His presence did not startle her, but sent waves of gratitude and love through her being.

"Annaleah, my beautiful daughter," he said, his face wearing an expression of deep, fatherly love. "You must be wondering why I haven't come to you in my angelic form." His eyes were intense as they focused on her. "If I were to come as an angel, I am afraid that my energy would be too over whelming. Unlike my brothers and sisters, however, I do have a true human form, not one made of glamour. You too, my daughter, have a human form, though your true form is more angelic than human. Let me introduce myself. I have several names. In human form I am known as Enoch. In angelic form, I am known as Metatron."

Annaleah gasped, her hand fluttering up to her chest in surprise. Her father was the legendary angel Metatron? He was one of the most powerful angels in all of Heaven, the only one allowed to look upon the full countenance of the Goddess. To him the secrets of creation itself had been given, and many other wonders only the Goddess Herself knew. He was the scribe of The Book of Life, and recorded all of the deeds of mankind, and all that occurs in the Heavens.

Tears flowed down Annaleah's face as the reality began to sink into her mind and touch her soul. In all the wondering she had done in her youth about who her real father was, never in a million years would she have imagined her father to be an angel, let alone the most powerful one in Heaven. She thought of all the things that she had missed growing up, not having her father with her. Daddy daughter dances at school, or to check for monsters under her bed, or even just to hold her and whisper that he loved her. Uncle John was the closest thing she had to a father, and she loved him fiercely, but there had always been a deep aching emptiness that not having her real father in her life had left in her.

Wiping tears from her face with the back of her hand, Annaleah did her best to assimilate the knowledge she was given. Her heart was thundering in her chest so hard that her chest had begun to ache. She closed her eyes and took a slow, deep breath, willing herself to be calm.

"It had to be me to father you, in order to make you what you are." Metatron continued, his voice soft. "I was born a human, but I never died. I was taken to Heaven in a whirlwind and I was transformed into the angel Metatron. There are no others like me, who were born human, with human wants, needs and desires, human emotions and experiences. No other human has ever been transformed into an angel."

Her father's words resonated within her. The hammering of her heart slowed as she felt the same calming energy emanate from Metatron as she had felt from Gabriel earlier.

"My transition from human to angel was part of what is happening now. It was to prepare for the time when your conception would occur." His voice deepened. "You see, Annaleah, you are the child of an angel who was once human, and the daughter of one of the most pure women to walk this earth. Do not let the misunderstandings of others rob you of the beauty of the truth you know. Your mother was not crazy; your mother was exemplary in all ways. She was pure and innocent, and that is why I loved her."

Annaleah wanted to ask a million questions, but she didn't know if it would be bad form or disrespectful to do so. The man before her smiled, the snow falling onto him gently, melting slowly into his quite pink human skin.

"I know you have many questions, Annaleah. My time here is short however." He lowered his head slightly, an apologetic look in his eyes. "The energy of three angels together in this clearing is drawing the attention of the darker ones. So let me tell you what you must know for now."

Annaleah held her breath, willing the pulse of her blood to quiet in her ears. Time seemed to slow, and the air around her felt as if it had become denser. So many questions that had lain in her heart were about to be answered, the mysteries she had contemplated for so long were about to be solved, ending her cycle of spinning thoughts and pontifications. In the final moments of her wondering, she took a deep breath and let go of the burden that not knowing had caused her.

"You, my dear, were born of humanity so that you would know the workings, the joys and the sufferings that humans have. You were born of the angels so that one day, you might save them. Your Professor's fall was a terrible mistake, one the Creator has thought long and hard over. Her heart has been pained over it. You, my dear, are her gift to the angels and, more specifically, to the Professor, for her error in his falling"

A gift to the Professor? The thought that she had no free will in this lit a small fire of anger in her. She had always felt close to the Creator, and now she felt a bit betrayed.

So this was one of her main life's purposes? Tears welled up in her eyes, the pain and disappointment replaced by a deep depressing fog that rolled over her heart, pressing down on her chest, making it heavy with the sense of oppression. She felt as though she had been pierced with pain. To be handed like a trivial toy to a man she may or may not come to love, made her seem less valuable, less important somehow. Being a heavenly gift didn't seem so important to her. Had she no choice in it? For a moment she fought the urge to revolt against this, to push everyone involved away, to say she'd had enough. What if she hadn't liked the professor at all? What if he didn't like her? He had been menacing and hard to get close to, and he had seemed to see her as little more than an annoyance.

Though she did feel deeply connected to him in a way that was beyond any emotion she had ever felt before, she wondered what would happen if he wasn't attracted to her as well. Would she be punished? Would the Professor be punished? She was not a thing to be given away, she was a living, breathing creature.

As much as she wanted to ask these things, she swallowed her spinning emotions and willed herself to listen.

"You had to be human, not just angelic, as the realm into which Seraphael had fallen was that of the humans. You, my daughter, are not only his redemption, but the redemption of the angels who fell and who have bitterly regretted it, and who desperately want to ascend back into Heaven to be with the Creator."

Annaleah felt her eyes widen as her heat skipped a beat. To be a gift for the professor was one thing, but to be the redemption of the fallen was another. Even though she had been told who she was, she couldn't help but wonder, why her? What if she didn't want the role, or what if she failed? Though she had a lot of esoteric knowledge, she didn't feel prepared to do something so crucial to so many. How was she supposed to redeem the fallen? What would happen if she couldn't do it, would she become fallen too?

"There are those who will thwart your every effort," Metatron continued, a warning in his voice. "Some are not sad that they fell, but live to see hatred, death, pain and darkness overcome us all. This, my precious daughter, is why you are so special and why you must be protected. You are truly one of a kind."

As he spoke, Annaleah continued to feel a million emotions raging within her. Was what he was saying true? Was she really the salvation of the angels? Was that even possible?

"It is possible," her father said, reading her thoughts, "though I have no time left to explain to you how or why it is. Just know you are loved, and there are many of us with you, though you cannot see us. Your very existence is the result of thousands of years of love; your heart beats for righting wrongs done long ago." Metatron straightened up to his full height. "I only have a short time left. Come to me Annaleah." He said her name gently, sweetly, as if saying it was a sacred prayer of reverence.

Though she was overwhelmed, she went to him. She felt as much love for him as he was radiating toward her.

As they embraced, Metatron kissed her on the hands, for in her angelic form she was too tall for him to kiss her cheeks.

"I bless your hands, child, that they would know strength when you need them most. and gentility when you think there is need for none."

And then he was gone...as If he had never stood before her, in the blink of an eye, leaving only swirling snowflakes and the imprint of booted feet.

Chapter Twenty-Nine

Sebastian's Nightmare

Sunday, August 15th

It is one of my favorite times now, the early hours of morning when the sky is still heavy with inky darkness. It is neither truly morning nor night, but some magical place in between, the time when the mystical happens. The world looks more beautiful to my eyes, more mysterious, full of secrets waiting to be discovered. I wish that I was able to sit in appreciative contemplation of this sacred time, but alas, it's nothing peaceful that has brought me to write in my journal. I have awoken from a horrific dream, and though not much truly disturbs me, here I sit shaking with the residual dread I held within this dream.

It began in the place where Gabriel had sent me when he gifted me with the dream of an angelic Annaleah. It looked to be empty, but the energy of it was alive and thrumming. I smelled wax and incense, and though there was no circle there, the energy of one recently having been drawn was strongly evident. And, quite strangely, it was snowing. The moonlight reflected in silver blue against the falling flakes, some of which were almost as large as my hand. Though most dreams are laced with the fanciful and devoid of common sense, I knew that snow falling here was not commonplace. I knew it was still summer, and so the symbolism was not lost on me. Something pure had been here, something innocent and even Holy. Just what it was, escaped me.

I allowed myself some time to appreciate this scene; to draw the scent of well-made amber incense into my lungs and to feel the chill of the air against my flesh as the snow fell gently. The wind blew softly and lifted my hair; this too, I paused to enjoy. I listened, but there was no sound save for the exhalation of my own breath and the trees creaking as they moved in the moonlit snowfall. I sensed her then, or at least her energy. Annaleah had been here, and not that long ago. I went to one knee, pressing my hand to the snowy ground. Here her bare feet had touched, I thought. It was she who had drawn the circle. Was it also she who had made it snow? Curious.

From behind me came a clicking sound, at first so faint that I chose to ignore it. I continued to press my palm against the ground, but now I felt something different. Something which was coming to destroy the beauty of whatever it was Annaleah had done here. It shook deep within the earth as it made its foul way to the surface. Something almost as old as myself was coming, hot with anger and hatred, ready for blood, pain, and utter destruction. The purity of Annaleah's deed, and the innocence of her energy's signature had torn the fabric of the in between worlds, making a portal. Though she had closed her circle well, the lingering energy of whatever she had done served as a beacon to the darker ones. And now, they were coming.

As the clicking behind me grew louder and more insistent, I turned. The moonlight seemed reluctant to shed its beautiful glow on whatever it was that made this hateful noise, leaving only a deep stain of shadow that resonated with the energy of filth and sickness. In the deepness of this shadow, it seemed as though there was only an abyss, with no forest or trees behind it, but a tear in reality which was an ugly, black wound. From this wound the clicking noise grew. Before I registered the sound as insectile, hundreds of black, shiny spots with many legs poured forth all at once. It was as if the abyss before me had given birth to fear, as several dozen spiders of varying sizes burst forth, legs moving in a way I have always seen as alien. My Goddess, the Creator, would never have created something which seemed to live solely for inflicting the pangs of adrenaline laced fear into those it came across. The terrible clicking sound was that of thousands of legs moving against shiny black carapaces, all advancing toward me. These creatures were what had hurt Annaleah; there was no question of it. This angered me deeply, and I used this to my benefit. This many spiders could only mean one thing. Something evil was coming.

They continued to pour forth from the blackness that the moonlight could not touch, but, where Annaleah had drawn her circle, they would not enter. Soon, I stood in a circle of no more than ten feet's width, the ground beyond it alive with eight legged evil. Though these vermin were repulsive and formed a great threat to my well-being, I knew the greater danger was not from them. Something else was coming. These little harbingers were nothing more than a message that their master was on the way.

"Show yourself, Nephila! I know it is you beyond the blackness, what do you want?" I demanded. In response, the spiders moved aside in front of me, making a pathway from the black abyss to the circle where I stood. I heard her laughter; the mad spider queen was amused and feeling certain of herself. Her demented cackles seemed to come at first from behind me, then to my left, and then above me, echoing off of the trees and off of empty space.

"Seraphael..." she whispered my angelic name, as though she was speaking directly into the cup of my ear. I turned at once to where I thought she must be standing, knowing she would not be there, but turning still. More laughter. Amused, lunatic laughter.

"Enough games, Jorogumo!" I said, angry at being treated in such a disrespectful manner. "Show yourself and face me, or leave me like the coward you are. Is that it, Nephila, are you afraid of me?" After I spoke, I felt the stillness. The spiderlings ceased moving their multitude of legs and stilled the hard shells of their bodies. From the abyss, I heard a frustrated cry of anger at my insult, and watched as the darkness grew. As it stretched, it seemed as though it truly was a wound, stealing the life force and energy of the scenery around it in order to expand, injecting disease and filth where once only beauty and peace had been. Nearby trees wilted and died, turning to ash before being swallowed by the undulating growth of the blackness.

From the darkness of the abyss she called to me, "Seraphael, your pride is foolish. Perhaps tonight I shall devour you and feed you to my babies." I saw the tip of one of her legs then, yellow and black and shiny, with several small tufts of hair at the end of her foot. Another foot followed it, until I could see her horrific form. She was in her half human, half spider form. From the waist up, she was beautiful, even though quite mad. Her long black hair, from which several strands were loose, was tied into an elaborate knot on the top of her head. Her dark eyes were heavily lined in black kohl, and her lips were the color of blood. She wore a gold and black kimono over her top half, which had torn and lost its elegance when she had transformed her lower body into its arachnid form. Her lower form was that of a giant spider, hard and shiny, mostly black with some yellow markings.

She looked upon me with eyes of maniacal hunger, ready to pounce on me and fight to the death. I wondered briefly what I had done to incur her wrath. She continued to look at me wordlessly as she made her way from the black wound in the forest to the path made by her spiderlings, to the edge of the circle in which I stood.

"Ahh, yes, even the great Seraphael knows I am beautiful. I can see it in your eyes, fallen one. I could let you have me. Oh yes. I could take you to places of ecstasy even you could not imagine. Surely you must have wondered what it was like to be with a female? I could teach you." She licked her lips at me in what she must have thought of as a seductive way, but it reminded me of a vampire licking blood off its victim, and I shuddered. She saw this and drew herself up quickly, as if she would strike me should I dare step too close.

"You are a fool Seraphael, a FOOL!" she spat, insulted. "If it weren't for that bitchling Annaleah, I could have you as I want you!" Her eyes flashed red with the intensity of her anger. Feeling the wrath of their queen, the spiderlings around her began to make an odd, chittering sound, as if they were shivering in the snow.

"Don't speak her name. She is of light and purity and you are of darkness and filth. Your vile lips will never be worthy to utter her name." I meant every word I spoke.

The Jorogumo walked as close to where the circle had been drawn as she dared, pacing around its perimeter. She seemed unperturbed by my latest insult. After a few moments of silence, she said, "There are others more handsome than you, Seraphael. More mysterious and powerful. You must not realize to whom you speak. I have powers of my own, you see. I was blessed by the fallen who made me, and hailed me as the queen of their shadow creatures. I could make you suffer greatly, Seraphael, is that what you want?" She turned to look me in the eye as she spoke my name, and I was not quick enough to look away before she had entered my mind. She fought me with visions she had implanted within me, an ability that our kind, good or evil, have both been endowed with. For a moment I was taken from this dream to a nightmare within a dream...

She showed me Annaleah sleeping, a scuttling mass of spiders covering her unconscious form, weaving silver-white strands over her body to encase her in a tomb of silk. They worked quickly, injecting

venom into her as they spun their threads over her, making a gift for
their mother and queen. The Jorogumo advanced from the shadows
beyond, in her full and terrible spider form, giant and monstrous. She
towered over Annaleah briefly, flexing her enormous jaws in anticipation
of the killing bite. Venom ran the length of her mandibles, dripping
onto Annaleah and burning her flesh.

I struggled against the invasive visions, throwing her out of my
mind with the force of my will. I was fueled by anger at her invasion,
and for the harm she meant to one I now held dear. My anger was raw
and intense, and for a moment I thought the scream the Jorogumo let
out was from the pain inflicted from being violently torn from my mind.
As I recovered from her tormenting vision, I heard the hooting and
screeching of a parliament of owls, followed by the insectoid panicking
of many arachnid bodies moving all at once.

When I opened my eyes, I saw an owl dive bombing the Jorogumo,
and thought of the owl that had smashed into my classroom window. It
was, indeed, a great horned owl, puffed up and feral looking. It snapped at
Nephila, tearing a slice of flesh from her cheek with its curved beak. The
spider queen screamed and spoke in Japanese, nothing I recognized, but
I am assuming it was a curse of some sort. From the trees many more
owls appeared, and not just horned owls, but many species. I saw barn
owls, snowy owls, screech owls, and many others, all working together
to attack the Jorogumo and her colony of spiderlings.

As owls carried off and devoured the spiders, the Jorogumo looked
at me with one of the most intense expressions of pure wrath and
hatred that I have ever seen. She held her hand to her bleeding cheek
and made an odd, chittering sound to what remained of her cluster of
spiders. They retreated at once, a mass of black all headed back to the
gaping abyss from which they had emerged.

Nephila backed up to retreat into the abyss. Pride would not let her
turn her back to me, and so she stared at me as she headed to the wound
of shadows, following her babies. Before she made her withdrawal, she
threw her head back and with a vile sound, brought up a mouthful of
spittle and venom. This she spat at me, but it didn't go very far. In her
heightened emotional state, she must have forgotten about the circle's
energy still around me. The venom filled spittle bounced off of the
protective field and landed on the Jorogumo, further infuriating her. I
couldn't help but laugh at the expression she wore as the venom hit her

wounded cheek; it was a mix of pain, surprise and scorn. With insult added to injury she turned around and fled for the abyss, carelessly stepping on several of her spiderlings in the process.

I bowed my head in a moment of thankful prayer. I had come to this dreamscape unarmed. I knew the presence of my kindred were with me. I paused too to send thanks to Annaleah, and to ask for her further protection. I wondered if she had any idea that her powerful circle had served as my protection, or if my brothers and sisters of the Light had simply held its power in check, knowing I would wander here in Dream Time. I sent my gratitude too, to the owls, for coming to my assistance when I needed them.

As I lifted my head from prayer, a great horned owl landed at my feet. In its beak it held the slice of flesh it had torn from Nephila's cheek. It dropped this at my feet and looked back up at me. As its large golden eyes looked into mine, I heard its thoughts.

"We have helped you because Annaleah is also very dear to us. We know how special you are growing to her, and how you have come to feel for her. Protect her, for she needs you as you will need her." The owl's voice was that of a soft spoken woman.

I nodded my assent, and said, "I promise." In response, the owl bowed her great head in respect before she opened her enormous wings for flight. After she had taken off, the rest of the owls rose from the trees around me and flew into the night, leaving me alone as the snow continued to fall.

I awoke thankful, but disturbed. I know this will not be the last time I see the Jorogumo, or her nasty little cluster of spiderlings. Next time, she will be more prepared. She knows it is not for myself that I am afraid, but for she who has captured my heart and breathed life back into my soul....

I have vowed to more than just myself, that I will protect her. I am not sure what her part will play in the grand scheme of things to come; though I know it is a role of the utmost importance. It is more because of what she has done for me that I will protect her. This is probably selfish of me.

I do know none shall harm her. I would let my spirit burn in oblivion before I let that happen. I think the Jorogumo is planning on that...

~ SB ~

Chapter Thirty

And So It Begins

Monday morning, Annaleah felt well enough to return to her position at the University, much to the distress of both Uncle John and Seth. As far as Uncle John was concerned, she was still in the recovery process and needed more time to convalesce. Seth wanted her to prepare for the coming confrontation that he emphasized was imminent.

"These beings," Annaleah said, "they wish to take not only my life from me, but my way of life and my enjoyment of it. If I were to hole up here and shake with fear, wouldn't they win? Would they not see me as weak and ready to be devoured? Let them see me going on with my life; let them see that I am not afraid of them. Besides, I'd really like to see the Professor."

Seth looked at her with a mix of empathy and dismay. "I understand where you are coming from, but there is real reason for you to be afraid. The creatures that are after you aren't playing." The look in his eyes was intense, and brimmed with warning. "They wish to kill not only you and all whom you hold dear, but ultimately to wipe out humanity itself. Though the latter is a lofty and unlikely scenario, I use it to let you know the severity of the situation."

Annaleah frowned, shocked at this situation. She had to fight for all of humanity's sake? She didn't know the first thing about fighting, though she had always thought that should she be in a close up fight with anyone, she'd for the eyes to buy her some time to get away. How on earth was she supposed to fight something not of this world?

Though she knew she had little choice, and that it was an honor to be chosen to be the Goddess's weapon of choice, her head swam with thoughts that came so fast that she barely had time to register each one. Part of her wanted thing to go back to the way they had been before.

Taking a deep breath, she listened to Seth. "They don't wish for the redemption of those that fell. They adore chaos and hatred; they thrive off of confusion and pain." Seth's eyes narrowed, and he drew out the word thrive for emphasis. "Though you have learned a lot of what is taking place, of who and what you truly are, you still have not been trained or prepared for what is to come. I understand that you want to go on with life as you know it, but the simple fact is that it might change, and for the worse." A worried look crossed his face, one mixed with sympathy and love. "Should you not be able to fight, or at least be aware of the enemy, then I am afraid the results might be disastrous. Please, think not only of yourself, but of those who will ultimately have their fate decided by your actions."

Annaleah dropped her head into her hands completely overwhelmed and on the verge of tears. She hadn't chosen this fate, and though she was greatly afraid, she knew the fate of many depended on what she did. Just one day, she concluded. Just let her have one last day of normality. "Then just give me today. Let me go to the University and see the Professor; let me see Rachael and let the students know I am alright. Give me the illusion that things are normal."

"I am afraid that might not be the best course to take at this time, Annaleah. Though I am very thankful that you are better, letting the faculty think you need a few more days at home might be in your best interest. You are in no danger of losing your job, the Professor and the Chancellor have your position secured. Should you return to your job and then take more time off, it will seem eccentric at best. I only ask that you take a few more days off, and let me prepare you."

Annaleah lifted her head, knowing what she must do, but disliking it greatly.

"I understand that you want to see the Professor and Rachael as well, but they could very easily come here to see you. Let me at least school you in basic self-defense. I will do everything in my power to make sure you are protected and that you never need to fight, but just in case you do, I want you to know how to handle yourself." Seth paused and looked Annaleah in the eye.

After a heavy sigh of defeat, Annaleah uncrossed her arms and sat heavily on the couch. "Alright, but after a few lessons or training or whatever it is you have in mind, I would really like to see the Professor." She smiled and looked away. "I have no idea what I will say to him, though."

"If you're worried about whether he likes you or not, don't be worried, I can attest to the fact with utmost certainty that not only does he like you, but he has vowed to protect you. I actually think he might be falling in love with you."

Annaleah's mood changed instantly, her heart leaping in her chest. For several seconds, she couldn't breathe, let alone form a coherent thought in her mind.

She watched as Seth flashed her a knowing smile, his eyes twinkling.

"Really?" was all that she could say for the moment.

Seth took her hand in his and gave it a gentle squeeze. "Yes, really. I know you remember the dream you had in the woods when you kissed him. Well," he paused to lean closer. His entire face smiled, from his lips to the twinkling in his eyes. "I gave him the same dream."

Annaleah gasped, knowing that it meant the dream was in a sense, very real. It had actually happened. That meant that their passionate kiss was real, too, and that the professor really did have feelings for her. There had been an intense, powerful connection between them.

"Which means that yes, you really did kiss the professor. For him, it was the turning point in how he saw you," he said, cocking an eyebrow and leaning toward her, "Though I gave you both the same dream, the decision for the two of you to kiss was your own. I only wanted for the two of you to see each other as you truly are, in your true forms. I wanted you two to eventually form a bond, but that seems to have happened of its own accord." Seth smiled at Annaleah, his eyes still twinkling.

Annaleah was enrapt, hanging on every word he said, her heart beating thunderously. The attraction she felt for Sebastian was at times overwhelming, and though she knew now that he had deep feelings for her too, she wondered if he felt his attraction as deeply as she did. The kiss had not only been one of passion, but one that seemed to awaken within her a burning fire that consumed her. When she was in his arms, her mouth pressed to his lips, she felt as if her soul was aglow, and that every atom of her being was infused with the perfect light of pure love.

Seth had said that he had sent the dream, and in a way that knowledge diminished the purity of it. In a way, he had manipulated them both by pushing them together, which was very disappointing, and a flicker of anger flashed in her heart. He had said that their kiss was not of his doing, which was a relief. Perhaps there was a bit of their own free will involved.

"Though he had been attracted to you from the beginning, he fought it fiercely, taking it out on you in petty ways. I knew that had to change." Seth continued. "I had to draw out his attraction to you and deepen it to the point that he would protect you. I went to him as Gabriel, and we had an important conversation."

Seth took her other hand in his, so that he was holding both of her hands in his.

"I promise you, he wants to see you just as badly as you want to see him, but for now, we need to train you."

"I am all yours." Annaleah said, trying to be more serious.

Seth sat back into the couch, looking thoughtful. "Okay, am I correct to assume that you have a ward up on the house?" he asked her.

Annaleah felt a bit worried and answered, "I haven't put one up in a while; I have been a bit.... preoccupied."

"Alright, after a brief lesson, you and I need to put the ward back up. It shouldn't take long. I think the first thing you need to know is defense against thought invasion. Both angels of the darkness and of the light are able to do it. The Dark Ones use it for unethical reasons, to intimidate and try to weaken their opponent, or to coerce them toward their own goal. I think you might have seen this in action when you met Satanael. Though you don't necessarily have to be looking into their eyes for this to happen, direct eye contact does make it much easier to do and the effects are more powerful." Seth paused to look Annaleah in the eyes. "The saying that the eyes are the window to the soul is truer than most people know." Seth's expression changed, softer now, but still intense. "The eyes have power unto themselves. The angels of light use this to their benefit for communication. At times, there are simply no words to convey what must be told, so visions are given to share what is so important that words cannot be trusted. I believe you have seen this in action too, with Marchosias. You, as the offspring of an angel and a human, have this ability. I ask that you use it wisely. Before I teach you how to use it yourself, I am going to teach you how to defend yourself from a low level psychic thought attack. So far, so good?"

"Yes," Annaleah said simply.

"Alright, in just a moment I am going to send you a thought, and I want you to try to resist me. When you feel the thought getting a bit uncomfortable, I want you to imagine yourself in a room. It's a small room is and your safe place. Paint the walls as dark black as you can imagine perfect darkness to be. Shut out all light, so that you are hidden. This is called black boxing. You will become invisible and difficult to infiltrate. Should a more powerful entity come to you and still be able to penetrate your black box, I want you to imagine the black box around you encased in brick. Make the bricks as real as possible and try to see them in as much detail as you can in your mind's eye. This should make it almost impossible to break into your mind. There is one last level left, should all else fail. This is to attack the one invading you. You must be strong for it, stronger than the one who is able to penetrate your mind. It might be painful for the both of you, however, you must assert your will power. You must be sure of yourself, and forceful." Seth paused, looking mildly disturbed.

Annaleah was about to ask him what was wrong, when a sudden gust of wind seemed to rock the very house itself, followed by the steady drumming of rain. Seth went silent and seemed to be concentrating quite hard.

"Something isn't right," he said. "The west wind feels wrong...."

Seth's words were cut off by a blood curdling scream coming from upstairs. Annaleah's heart dropped in her chest and her blood froze in her veins. Both she and Seth raced upstairs, following the source of the scream to Uncle John's room. There in his room stood a small, hideous creature. It looked like a terrible version of a dark elf, only more brutal and sinister. Its skin was sallow and mottled, the shade varying in degrees of pale grey and blue, as if it were made of mold and rot. It was very thin; the bones beneath its blotchy skin protruding and making it appear as though its skeleton was trying to break through its fragile skin. The ears were long and pointed at the top, tufts of hair topping each one. The small, beady eyes gleamed with abhorrence at both Seth and Annaleah. But it was the hands and claws which terrified Annaleah the most, for the bony fingers ended in long, sharp claws which dripped with blood.

From behind this creature came a gurgling noise, and Annaleah saw to her horror that Uncle John was lying on the floor, a pool of blood slowly spreading around him.

"Uncle John!" Annealed screamed, her heart flooding with fear and panic. She moved toward him, but the creature blocked her advance, hissing and drawing its bloodied hand up threateningly, as if to strike her.

From behind Annaleah a bright light flashed, pulsating for a moment until it became strong and steady. The energy of the room changed at once, as if it were being purified. The being let out a shriek and covered its eyes, smearing blood on its face as it did so.

Annaleah knew that her friend had transformed from Seth the human into Gabriel the archangel. In doing so, she felt herself begin to change. Pulses of luminosity flashed like lightning under her skin. All of this barely registered beyond the grief crushing her heart within her chest.

"Demon Abuchubae, servant to the demon king of the moon, hear me call your name and thusly bind you," Gabriel called out in a forceful voice. "Demon Abuchubae, minion of the west wind, I cast you out in the name of the Holy ones, by the words of the mighty Creator, I rebuke you! You must obey me, for with the knowledge of your name I gain power and control over you. I cast you out by the Goddess and Creator, by the archangel Michael, whoever defends us in battle. Go now or you shall be cast to the fiery pit of Hell, or destroyed by me outright!" Though Gabriel's voice was stern and authoritative, it was also beautifully lyrical. It resonated in the room sending a shimmering vibration through the air, a scintillating energy of absolute power.

The demon Abuchubae tried to cover its ears and eyes both at once, and, failing to do either effectively, ran on all fours towards the window. Reaching its means of escape, it turned, and in a voice that sounded like a high pitched hiss said, "I will go, for I have done what I came to do." It let out one last hiss, then turned back to the window and broke through the glass, leaping to the ground below.

Gabriel went to the window to make certain the demon had gone, watching as it ran away. His heart was heavy with sorrow, knowing the situation with Uncle John was dire. He was still alive, but for how much longer was uncertain. Annaleah was kneeling beside him, holding his hand with one hand with her other against his chest, trying to apply pressure where the wound had been inflicted. She was sobbing uncontrollably, tears running down her cheeks and dripping onto the floor to mingle with the blood.

The war had begun

Chapter Thirty-One

Love Is Everything

Annaleah turned to Gabriel, her eyes red and raw with tears of grief. "Do something, please!!" She begged, sobbing. After she spoke, she tilted her head back and wailed, a cry so rife with pain and loss that Gabriel was sure the Goddess herself heard it, and shed a tear for the ferocity of agony Annaleah felt.

After the heartbreaking cry ended, the silence, punctuated only by the drumming of rain on the roof, seemed to reinforce the direness of the situation. Gabriel could see Annaleah's chest moving up and down with sobs, but no sound came out. Seeing Uncle John so near death affected him deeply. Here was a man who had raised not only his closest human companion, but who also had not once turned Gabriel away, never knowing that he was more than what he seemed.

After taking a moment to compose himself, Gabriel knelt at Annaleah's side, looking deep into her eyes. Though Gabriel was immense in his angelic form, neither he nor Annaleah found his size to inhibit their eye lock. Annaleah herself had already begun to transform. Her green eyes were tinged with gold and her blonde hair shone like the sun.

"You can heal him, Annaleah. He has not yet crossed over to the other side, though he is very close." Annaleah looked to Seth, trying to read his expression, but couldn't see it through her tears.

"I know the turmoil that is in your heart, but in order to bring him back, you must do as I say. Can you do that?" Annaleah nodded, and tried hard to calm her raging grief enough to follow his directions. Her uncle's life depended on it. 'Your father blessed your hands for battle, but you can use them to heal as well. This healing is a battle of sorts, a fight against death itself. You must act fast before death wins." Seth's voice sounded desperate and stricken, though his words were clear and precise. "Place your hands over his wounds, and think of the happiest memories that you have with Uncle John. Feel the love that flows between you both, and fill yourself with it. Send this love from your soul, from your heart, down through your arms and into your hands.

Send the love to Uncle John with the intent to heal him." Seth sighed deeply, and placed his hand on her shoulder. "You can do it, Annaleah, but you must do it now."

Closing her tear filled eyes, Annaleah did as she was asked. She placed both hands over the torn, bleeding flesh of her uncle, and began with her first memories of him. She saw in her mind's eye Uncle John in his younger days, his hair less gray and somewhat thicker. His face was rounder, and the small lines around his eyes and mouth were yet to show. In her memory, they were at Daytona Beach, and she thought she was around six years old. Uncle John wore hunter green swimming shorts and flip-flops, a spot of bright white sunscreen dotting his nose. She remembered teasing him about it, and that he had laughed with her. Tears continued to flow from beneath her closed eyes as the love swelled within her heart. She smiled through her pain as she recalled how he had given her his own ice cream that day, after she had dropped hers in the sand. She didn't even have time to cry for its loss before he had handed her his treat. "It's OK, kiddo," he had told her, smiling, "I wasn't really in the mood for ice cream anyway." As she remembered, her heart began to grow with her special love for him, which she let blossom until it filled her completely. The warmth of her love glowed within her, and she felt a very real, pleasant heat undulating from her heart.

"That's it, Annaleah." Gabriel encouraged her. "Keep going."

Now they were in the ocean, Uncle John holding her up above the waves, telling her she was the prettiest fairy mermaid he had ever seen. "Fairy mermaids are very rare," he had said, looking quite serious. "You are so beautiful and sweet, I think they just might make you their queen." Annaleah had thrown her arms around him then, hugging him tightly. Before she let him go, she had whispered in his ear, "I love you, Uncle John." He had kissed her cheek softly and hugged her back, before telling her with a sweet smile that he loved her very much.

Annaleah was brought out of her reverie when Uncle John began to make sharp, strangled choking noises. Her eyes flew open, panic lacing her heartbeats as she watched him cough up blood. The light of her healing began to fade, and she looked at Gabriel in alarm. She had not expected any movement or noises from her uncle, and seeing the light fade as she took her focus off healing him frightened her.

"Don't worry; sometimes healing can be painful," Gabriel reassured her, "Keep going. You will know when it is time to stop."

Annaleah closed her eyes once more, placed her focus back on her memories and healing, and concentrated. Chasing her fear away was not an easy task, but knowing her uncle's life was quite literally in her hands gave her strength and willpower. In moments she found another precious memory. It had been her first day of second grade, and she was excited to tell Uncle John about it when she got home. "What was your favorite part?" he had asked her. "We had chocolate marshmallow crisps in our lunch today and they were so good! I knew you would just love them, so I brought you one home." She reached into her book bag where she had stored it and carefully unwrapped it from its cellophane wrapper. With her eyes full of love and expectation, she offered it up to Uncle John, who took it reverently. He placed a bit in his mouth and a look of pleasure came over his face. "This is amazing, Annaleah! I am so grateful that you thought of me and wanted to bring some home for me." Then, he had scooped her up into his arms and hugged her tightly. Annaleah had been so proud of that moment that whenever the school had served the treat for dessert, she bought an extra one to bring home. He always made such a fuss over it, and over her. It was just another of many examples of the loving bond they had shared between them.

The next memory came quickly. Annaleah recalled rushing home from school in tears. She had a huge crush on a boy named Tommy King, one of the most popular boys in middle school. She knew she was seen as an awkward girl by most, strange in her ways. She had been somewhat of an outcast even then, preferring to follow her own heart rather than succumb to the trends and demands of others. She had often been ostracized, but, try as she might to fit in, she just couldn't be comfortable conforming to the ways that others seemed to fall into so easily. She had talked to Uncle John about Tommy before, telling him how handsome he was with his light brown hair and deep brown eyes, and the smattering of freckles across his nose. Uncle John had encouraged her to ask him to the school dance, though Annaleah was certain he would say no. Not only had he said no, he had stood up in the lunchroom and openly mocked her in front of half the school, saying she was weird and too tiny to be able to dance with anyway. They had laughed and pointed, and someone even threw some food at her. She had run out of the school, not caring that she was going to get into more trouble than she had ever been in her life for leaving school grounds. The hurt in her heart was something that only Uncle John could fix.

She had run home in tears, hoping that today was his day off of work, as going to the hospital was out of the question. Luckily, he had been home, reading one of his crime novels, sitting in one of the white wing backed chairs, with his feet propped up on the cream colored ottoman. She ran to him and he simply held her, letting her cry for several minutes before gently prying her away and looking her in the eyes.

"What happened?" He had asked, his warm eyes full of concern.

"I knew he would say no. But he didn't have to make fun of me. He called me weird and too tiny to dance with. He made them all laugh at me. I can't ever go back there!" She fell against his chest and began to cry again.

"Annaleah, I want you to listen to me," Uncle John had said, pulling her away from him again so that they could look one another in the eye. "A very long time ago, your mother once said something that stuck with me. She was a lot like you, different from most people, but to me, she was different in the most wonderful ways. What made her seem odd and even untouchable to some, only made her seem more precious and rare to me. Do you want to know what she said?" Annaleah had nodded her head.

"There had been some strange weather going on, lots of rain and even a small snow flurry in late summer. People talked about your mother as if she had something to do with it, knowing she was not a Christian like most in this area, but a witch. I was walking home with her after buying a few groceries one day, and one rather well-to-do towns person saw us. She turned and pointed at Elise, and proclaimed loudly to everyone else on the street, "It's because of this strange woman who will not go to church that the rain keeps falling. It is because of this heathen that there was snow in the middle of summer! What do you have to say for yourself, witch!?

"Your mother was not about to be talked down to, Annaleah. She was a gentle woman, but also proud. She looked right at this pompous woman, squared her shoulders and said, "I would rather sit alone in the light of my own truth, than to sit with a thousand others in the darkness of conformity." Do you know what that means?" Uncle John asked.

Annaleah had looked at her uncle blankly, not really sure if she knew or not.

"It means, my dear," he told her, stoking her hair softly, "that the world is full of people trying to be just like everyone else in order to fit in and be accepted. By doing this, they ignore what it is in themselves that makes them unique and special." His eyes held a far off, sad look as he spoke. "Sometimes they try to erase themselves in order to be what society expects them to be. They do this so much, that that they lose themselves altogether and don't even know how to act without someone else telling them how." He shook his head, and his glasses slid down his nose. "The world is full of carbon copies. Don't be one, Annaleah. Even if you have to struggle to remain who you are, it is the most precious gift that you can give yourself." Pushing his glasses up to their rightful place on his face, he looked deeply at her. "If you fight to be true to yourself, one day, you will find out just how special you are. There is someone out there who will love you for who you are strong enough to be. Don't rob your future husband of the love of his life. This Tommy person is a fool. Don't let him rob you of the jewel that you are, the rare and precious person that no one else can be."

A small whimper interrupted Annaleah's memory, and, at first she thought it might be something within her recollection. Coming out of her vision and opening her eyes, she saw that her hands and arms were glowing with white light. Looking further, she saw that her beloved uncle had stopped bleeding, and though still unconscious, was no longer in the clutches of death.

Overjoyed, Annaleah moved her hands from where his wounds had been and softly placed her head on his chest. When she heard his heart beating steadily, she let out a breath she had not been aware she was holding.

Gabriel's eyes glistened with tears as they held her gaze with intensity. "You see Annaleah," he said from beside her, his voice soft and reverent, "Love is the strongest energy in the universe. It has the power to heal the most grievous wounds; the ability to fight death and rekindle life itself. Love can heal what nothing else can. It is with love, Annaleah, that we will win this war."

Exhausted, but more thankful than she had ever been in her life, Annaleah held her hand out to Gabriel, with her head still upon her uncle's now healed chest.

Gabriel smiled and took her hand.

"We will win, Gabriel. Thanks to you, and thanks to Uncle John, I know that we can."

Chapter Thirty-Two

Enter Michael

"Things are going to start happening quickly now, Annaleah," Gabriel said softly. "The Dark Ones, as well as the ones who walk in the light, will be able to pick up on the energy you sent out to heal your uncle. The dreams of the war in Heaven that you have had all of your life will give you a good idea of what to expect. Though you may have believed that your part in this war would be to wield a sword and slay the enemy yourself, this will be far from your main goal. Should it come to that, we all want you to be able to defend yourself, and so you will be armed. However, your main purpose, sweet Annaleah, is to call the fallen to repent. You also have another very important mission, but for now, redemption is your main objective."

Annaleah's brow creased, her heart full of worry. "How am I supposed to do that, Gabriel? Don't they already know that they can be saved? Why am I so important?"

"I don't have the time to answer that question for you, I'm afraid. Uncle John is out of the woods, but still needs medical attention. I'll take him to the hospital in my human form. You'll have the divine protection of our brothers and sisters of the light, so I don't want you to feel alone. You will be protected. I'll return once your uncle has been admitted."

Once more standing to the full enormity of his height, Gabriel seemed to fill the entire room with light, wings and purity. From his luminous robes he withdrew a gilded trumpet, both simple and elegant. Placing it to his lips, he played one long, blaring note. The sound was somber and deep, reverberating through the room, through the walls, through every atom of Annaleah's being. Her intuition told her that this was undoubtedly his calling to his angelic brothers and sisters that the war had begun.

Annaleah's golden wings unfurled from her back, seeming to fill what space that Gabriel's wings did not occupy. She felt the electric arcs of light pulsate from beneath her skin, and with a quick glance she saw how her skin, like his, was alabaster and flawless. Her transformation from human to angel was complete.

"I'm frightened," she confessed. "What if I fail? I haven't trained. I should have let you teach me more, instead of being troubled by the mundane issues in my life."

"Now is not the time for self-doubt," Gabriel said tenderly. "Your role was well thought out by the Goddess Herself. Your destiny is unfolding, sweet Otherling. It's okay to be afraid; it will keep you on your toes." He began to transform back into his human form as he spoke. His wings folded against his back, his hair growing shorter as his body seemed to change effortlessly back into her best friend.

Now in human form, Seth turned to the window and looked out expectantly. The rain had stopped. The moon and stars had reclaimed their place and shared their light as if nothing was out of the ordinary.

"The Light Ones are coming, but so are the ones of Darkness. Michael will give you a sword, but I don't think you will have to use it."

A sword, she thought, panic prickling in her heart? She had never held a sword in her life, how was she supposed to defend herself with one? What if the demons took it from her and used it on her? Going further into her fear, Annaleah tried to imagine what the demons she was about to fight would look like. She had seen the Jorogumo and the demon that had attacked Uncle John, but all her other knowledge of her enemy had been gleaned from books. She felt woefully underprepared. What would happen if she was unable to defend herself? What if she lost a loved one in battle?

Gabriel had told her there was no time for self-doubt, but it was hard to heed these words. With great effort, she swallowed as many of her concerns as she could, knowing that it was time to fulfill her destiny. With a deep sigh, she smiled, trying to build as much courage as she could.

She watched as Seth bent down and effortlessly lifted Uncle John into his arms. To see him do so was a bit strange to Annaleah, even knowing he was an angel in human form. Seth's body simply did not look as if it had the strength to lift Uncle John with such ease.

Reaching the doorway, Seth turned before leaving to look at her. "Be strong, and know that I believe in you." He flashed her a smile before carrying Uncle John out the door.

Now alone in the room, Annaleah stood, her heart thundering. From beside the window she saw a small sphere of deep indigo light flicker into existence and begin to expand. The beautiful light undulated and began to form the shape of a large man with wings even larger than her own. The light grew denser until a glorious angel stood before her, his light so bright that it was hard to make out any of his features. His energy was powerful, and the light was so intense that everything in the room took on an indigo tone. Annaleah, feeling this angel's importance and energy signature, bowed her head and knelt before him in reverence.

"Do not kneel before me, Annaleah." The voice was melodic and deeply masculine. Though he spoke plainly, his voice was so beautiful that it sounded to Annaleah as if he were singing. "All adoration and acclaim should be saved for the Creator Herself. Rise and face me as your equal."

Annaleah looked up and saw that the angel had lessened the brilliance of his light, so as not to bewilder her with his presence. His long wavy hair was a deep shade that reminded her of the midnight sky, as were his eyes. Though most of the angels Annaleah had seen had delicate elven or pixie like features, the angel before her was different. He looked as if he were built for war, with defined musculature and pronounced masculinity. His jawline was square, his arms bulged as if he had been weight-lifting for eternity. He smiled at her benevolently, as she took in his physique.

"I am the archangel Michael. It is my pleasure to meet you, Annaleah." He held out his large hand to her in a most human gesture of meeting. With quiet awe, Annaleah took his hand and shook it, looking into his deep, beautiful eyes.

"I am honored to meet you, Michael. I only wish it were under better circumstances," Annaleah said, her voice only a little louder than a whisper. She watched as one corner of his mouth curled up into a smile.

"Likewise. Though this is our first formal meeting, I have been with you and your uncle for quite some time now. We have no time to reminisce, however. There is a portal opened, and the Dark Ones are using it to cross over to your world. For as long as humanity has walked the Earth, there have been dark entities living among you that have been cursed and Hellbound. They use these portals as ways to evade their prison and walk on the Earth. Ever since the Jorogumo was able to find you in your Dream Time, she has been hard at work expanding on the portal.

"I have been instructed to give you a weapon. Though you have not been taught how to use it, should the need arise you will find, intrinsically, the knowledge already there. Do not fear the sword, but respect it. We will be guarding you so that you can do that which you must do."

He held out his arms to each side, and a light began to glow in each. In his left hand the light became a long, slim bladed sword, and in his right, a simple belt and sheath. He handed these to Annaleah, who somehow knew exactly how to put the belted sheath around her and place her sword within it. After she had done so, she looked again at Michael, confusion in her golden eyes.

"Come to me and I will take you at once to the clearing in the woods. I can feel that they are already breaking through from there. It was once a sacred place, but now I fear, because of them, it has been profaned."

Michael opened his tremendous wings, beckoning Annaleah to him. Annaleah hesitated, still overwhelmed by meeting one of the most well-known angels of all time. He looked at her, compassion in his dark eyes.

"Do not underestimate yourself. I know it has only been a short time that you have been aware of who and what you are, but your Holiness is written in your DNA. Your spirit is that of an angel, one of us. Though there are many races and classes of angels, we are all holy and divine creatures. You were made for this, Annaleah. If anything, it is I who should be in awe of you. Now please, come. We must go."

Annaleah took in what he had said and nodded wordlessly before crossing the short distance between them and pressing herself against him. He embraced her gently, enfolding her in his arms, and then encircling her in his beautiful wings. He bent down and whispered in her ear.

"Now hold onto me tightly. This may be disconcerting for you. We are going to teleport ourselves there. Think of it like traveling in Dreamtime; often there is no recollection of how you got from one place to another, but suddenly, you find yourself there." Michael paused for a moment to let Annaleah take in what he had said.

"Are you ready?"

"I think so." As soon as she said this, Annaleah felt an intense force pulling at her, as if every atom of her being were being vacuumed and pulled. Thankfully, it only lasted a moment before she found herself on the path that led to the clearing.

There in the clearing, was where she thought Hell itself must be.

The forces of Heaven and the Hordes of Hell were already at war.

Chapter Thirty-Three

The War

Michael was right; the place no longer resembled anything remotely holy. Many of the trees had been broken in half, some scorched, others uprooted and tossed aside to make room for battle. Though the path to the clearing still existed, the clearing itself was now a bald patch of wounded earth, expanding in every direction. The red clay, so famous in Georgia, was now red with spilled blood, from both those who fought for the light and those who fought against it. Feathers littered the ground and floated in the air, tinged with blood or half on fire. Reptilian scales glittered like confetti falling from the sky, catching what light there was from the stars as they fell to the earth below.

And then there were the creatures that fought on the torn and bloodied earth. Though the Light Ones were Holy, looking at them as they engaged in war was fearsome. The expressions they wore showed the intended annihilation of their enemies. Their lips, which normally smiled with love, were drawn tight over teeth that flashed like the blades they wielded. Indigo eyes were wide and wild as they concentrated on the death of the Dark Ones. Bloodied wounds marred the beauty of most of them, their great, feathered wings torn or even broken; their snow white flesh split and weeping blood. Some spoke in their ancient angelic tongue, words which sounded forbidden to the ears of those not indoctrinated. The sound of blades hitting flesh, bone and metal was punctuated by screams and battle cries.

The Dark Ones varied tremendously in their forms, but were all horrific to look upon. Most of them had wings that Annaleah thought must have once been beautiful like the angels of light, but were now transformed as a mark of their transgression against the Creator. Some had wings filled with scales and others had wings like leather. All of them had faces filled with hatred, their eyes flashing with infernal fury. Annaleah saw most had some type of horns as well; some twisted and curled, others long and straight. They made bestial sounds as they fought the angels of Light, screams and howls the likes of which she had never heard, even in her dreams. A few of the larger demons seemed to shift their features as a battle tactic, meant to terrify and confuse their opponent. She watched as one tore at the earth with its clawed feet, kicking the dirt backwards as if it were a bull about to charge.

The air smelled of ozone, torn earth, scorched skin and the metallic tang of blood. It held the undercurrent of fear and tensions long kept, so electric that it seemed to pulse through Annaleah. The scent of smoldering sulpher crawled through these odors, slithering through them as though the malodor itself had violent intentions.

More Holy ones arrived from the sky, some falling haphazardly as they engaged in a struggle with the beings that had once been their brothers and sisters. From below, in the ravaged soil, still more demons emerged, dirt smeared and crazed, thirsty for blood. Infernal fire bathed them as they broke free of their prison, climbing over one another in their lust for war. Some even turned on each other as they struggled toward the solid ground above.

All of these beings filled Annaleah with terror so intense, so raw, that for a moment, she contemplated running. The moment passed quickly when she saw Marchosias engaged in battle with a demon that looked as if it were winning. It held one of Marchosias' ebony wings out to her side, intent on breaking it off of her body. Annaleah, finding her courage, was about to run into the heart of the battle to defend the fallen angel that had become her friend.

"No," Michael said into her mind, knowing that the sounds of screaming and war cries were too loud to be heard any other way. "You are far too important to be running into the midst of this war! Marchosias knows what she is doing, let her fight."

Frustrated, Annaleah turned to look Michael in the eye, speaking to him in her thoughts. "Then why am I here? What is the point of the sword and even bringing me to this place if I am not to fight? I can't just stand by and let her get slain by that terrible creature!"

Suddenly, the fighting shifted. Heads of both the Dark Ones and those of the Light turned to look at Annaleah, as if they had heard her speak aloud. She watched as one of the angels of Light used this distraction to land a killing blow to a demon that resembled a pig and human splicing experiment gone horribly wrong. With one swift blow, its bloody head went rolling across the scarred ground.

Several of the Dark Ones, enraged, charged at Annaleah, one of them running at her on all fours. She raised her sword and prepared herself for their descent upon her. Gracefully dodging one wolfish demon, Annaleah heard its yelp of agony as Michael swiftly ended its life behind her.

As another abomination sped towards her, with one fluid move, she buried her sword to the hilt in its chest. She locked her eyes with the creature's sickly yellow ones before pulling her weapon free of its scarred, mottled chest.

The next Dark One was soon upon her, and this one had no weapon. Its mouth was an open gash filled with long, sharp teeth that curved backwards towards its throat. The orange eyes were wide set and large, like pools of vile filth lit with loathing for anything with a modicum of decency in its soul. The rotting skin it wore did not seem to be its own, as if it had been carved off of a corpse and hung loosely over its bones. It was ragged and slashed in many places with dried blood clotted in filthy blotches. The battle cry it emitted as it charged at Annaleah sounded like both the scream of a woman being tortured and a deep, animalistic guttural growl.

Had Annaleah not been emboldened by the adrenaline of her kill, the sound would have turned her blood to ice within her veins. As the demon ran at her, its mouth opened obscenely wide. It held one of its elongated and disjointed arms out to the side, the fingers of the large, meaty hand spread out to display long, razor sharp claws.

Annaleah stood her ground, surprised by the strength of her resolve. Not knowing what she would do until the moment of the struggle was upon her, she found the strength to have faith in the Creator. It was immediate and absolute, and filled her like a prayer. As the demon hurled itself through the air at her, she whispered three simple words to the Creator. "I trust you."

In the instant before the Dark One was directly over her, Annaleah dropped to one knee, thrusting her sword upwards with all of her strength. The demon, instead off falling on her as it had intended, was effectively disemboweled by its own momentum. Blood spilled from the killing wound and splashed over Annaleah, marking her as a warrior. The demon fell to her left, on the ground, the light of life gone forever from its evil eyes.

As Annaleah sighed a breath of pure gratitude for her survival, a familiar chittering sound began to weave its way towards her through the sounds of chaos and war. A chill ran through her, and a sense of dread, knowing what it was that made the noise. Suddenly, the ground seemed as if it had come alive, swarming with innumerable hard black shiny bodies. Hundreds of spiders crawled up her robes so quickly that her heart rose to her throat, making it hard to scream or even breathe. She jumped to her feet, dropping her sword to brush the hateful insects off of her.

"Very impressive, Annaleah," said a patronizing voice.

As panic laced her blood with an icy grip, Annaleah knew the voice belonged to one of the vilest creatures she had ever come across. There before her stood Nephila, demon queen of the Jorogumo.

Chapter Thirty-Four

The War Rages On

Annaleah felt needles of despair pierce her heart as it became more difficult to brush the spiders off of her. Her arms were growing heavier and less flexible, her thoughts muddied and fuzzy. She realized with a profound despondency that she had once again been bitten by the poisonous children of the Jorogumo. She looked upon Nephlia, thinking to herself that she didn't even feel the bites.

The Jorogumo laughed, a high pitch screech of lunacy, her kohl lined eyes wide and maniacal. She held Annaleah's gaze with her own as she advanced slowly, in her half spider and half woman form.

"You wouldn't have felt my babies bite you this time, Annaleah," Nephila spoke, coming closer. "The only ones allowed to bite you are the smaller ones. Too bad for you the smaller of them are the most poisonous." She threw back her head and cackled, opening her arms as she did so. On the ends of her fingers were what looked like elongated, sharp metal claws.

"Do you like them?" the Jorogumo asked, once more appearing to have looked within Annaleah's mind. She held her hands out for her to see. "I had them specially made. These are no ordinary nail guards, dear. They are made to rip flesh and sever limbs. They are rather pretty aren't they?" Nephila paused for a moment to admire them, then looked Annaleah coldly in the eye. "They will look even prettier eviscerating you."

Annaleah looked for her dropped sword to defend herself, willing strength back into her poisoned body. Now she found she couldn't even lift her arms. Her breath was heavy in her lungs and took effort to draw in. A tiny spider ran across her face and disappeared into her long hair, sending waves of revulsion through her, but she could do nothing to remove it. Her eyes still cooperated, however, and she looked helplessly at the Jorogumo as she breached the final distance between them.

"Oh now, Annaleah, why such despair?" taunted the spider demoness. "Oh, I bet I know. You are about to die and there is no one here to help you. No Gabriel, no Marchosias, no Michael and no... what do you call him in his human form, Professor?"

Annaleah hadn't thought of that before, but now she did wonder where her friends were. She wanted to tell Nephila that this was a war after all, that had the spider queen not thrown such a low blow and poisoned her like this, she would have been able to fight her without having the help of her friends.

Nephila cocked her head, as if to hear what Annaleah was trying to say. "What's that, dear? Cat got your tongue?" More crazed laughter followed, further filling her soul with sorrow. Nephila was now right in front of her, smiling in victory. She ran the blunt end of one of the nail guards down Annaleah's cheek, wiping away a tear that she was unaware she had shed.

"Goodbye, Otherling. I can't say it's been nice knowing you." The Jorogumo raised her arm high over and behind her head in a blow meant to kill. Her fingers were spread wide, and Annaleah couldn't help but look at the gleaming metal nail guards which seconds from now would be tearing her flesh apart.

Annaleah, knowing she was about to die, thought of the Professor, and how she wished she could at least kiss his lips just once. In one final burst of hope, she tried once more to force her body to move, but was rewarded with only searing pain for her efforts.

"I'm sorry Sebastian," she said to him in her mind, the anguish of never seeing him again more raw than the fact that she was about to lose her life.

"Oh don't worry about Sebastian," the Jorogumo told her, hand paused in the air, "I plan to kill him too. You can reunite in the after world."

Her hand came down in an arc, and Annaleah, resigned to her fate, cried one last tear.

Suddenly, from the right, a large white creature leapt from the shadows and attached itself to the throat of the Jorogumo. Annaleah realized she had seen this beast before. The horrendous creature that

Satanael had called Tantibus held Nephila's throat in its jaws. Blood poured out around its pale mouth as it shook her. The surprise and alarm in the dying demoness' eyes was almost enough to elicit pity from Annaleah. Almost.

As the nightmare creature worked its jaws to sever Nephila's head from her neck, it arched its scorpion like tail and stung her repeatedly. The huge, torn wings of the white, scaled beast opened and closed in the air, fighting for leverage. Finally, with a growl of determination, Tantibus shook his mighty jaws and severed the head of the demon spider queen. The empty eyes stared in horror at nothing now, the mouth frozen in a silent scream. The head spouted a dark scarlet liquid as it rolled over the war ravaged ground before being crushed under the giant cloven hoof of a demon engaged in battle. Tantibus, still in killing mode, fell upon the Jorogumo's body, attacking her where she had fallen.

Instantly, the spiders swarming over Annaleah turned to ash and began to blow away in the winds of the war.

"Crazy bitch," Annaleah heard a masculine voice say as her consciousness began to fade. "I told her to stay away from you."

Annaleah, blinking her eyes an attempt to remain conscious, struggled to turn her head to see who had spoken.

"Did you forget me so soon, Annaleah?" Into her field of sight stepped Satanael, his long red hair flowing out as if it were engaged in an aquatic dance.

Annaleah, her strength now gone, didn't even try to answer. She felt herself begin to fall as the poison overtook her body. Satanael moved quickly and caught her in his arms. He lifted her easily, and began to carry her off to the path that led to the clearing.

Through heavy eyes, Annaleah looked up into a face which looked handsome, even though she knew the creature which held her was the embodiment of evil itself.

"Well now, Annaleah, it isn't every day that one gets saved by the devil himself, now is it?"

As the last remnants of consciousness slipped from her, she heard him laughing.

Chapter Thirty-Five

The Battle in the Woods

Satanael carried Annaleah down the path, whispering words under his breath to undo the poison the Jorogumo's children had injected into her. His words were an incantation, leaving his lips as a dark mist and disappearing into Annaleah's pale skin. He entered her mind as he spoke, knowing that even if she had been trained against a thought attack, she would be helpless to evict him from her mind in her current state.

Satanael, now a safe distance from the site of the war, turned off of the path and moved into the woods. He carried Annaleah until he found an area large enough to lay her down, and gently placed her on the grass. He spread himself out over her, close but not touching her. He wanted enough of the venom to leave her system so that she was still incapacitated, but no longer in the throes of death. His dark incantation ended, the tail of the dark mist leaving his lips with the last syllable. He watched with amusement as it snaked its way through the air and disappeared into her skin. His great scarlet wings opened over her, as if he were attempting to shield her.

He bent over her, only a few inches from her ear. "Now Annaleah, my pretty one, we are going to erase some of your memories and replace them with ones I will plant there myself." His crimson eyes swept over her, drinking in her sweetly innocent and paralyzed form. He carefully stroked her cheek with the pad of his index finger, taking care not to slice her with his with his long, glass like fingernails. She moved slightly at his touch, and he smiled when her lips opened and she began to breathe freely and easily once more. "You are far too beautiful and far too valuable for me to let you die."

Satanael allowed himself to look upon her for a moment longer, enjoying the surge of lust and hedonistic want that came with indulging himself in her beauty. He watched the swell of her breasts as they rose and fell with each breath she took, his eyes now rimmed in yellow around the scarlet irises, changing as his mood did. He lowered his face to just above her chest and closed his eyes. His nostrils flared as he breathed her scent in, a low growl of appreciation rumbling in the back of his throat.

The heat of desire aflame in his veins, he whispered to her again. "There will be time to make you forget Sebastian. In time you will know and desire only me. You will rule by my side, as my queen, never knowing what it was you were born to do. You will have power beyond measure, and the light you breathe now will be the same one you fight to eradicate. I will teach you to love the darkness until it is the only thing you crave.'

Satanael traced the curve from her ear down her jaw, over her throat to her jugular vein. He felt the pulse of life there, and bent his head to kiss her there.

A powerful voice rang from behind him. "Get your vile hands off of her!" Startled by the interruption, Satanael, baring his fangs in an effort to warn whoever had disturbed him, turned to see who had spoken.

Seraphael, shimmering in luminous arcs of dark blue and silver, stepped from the path which led to the sacred clearing. His long ebony hair flowed out behind him in the wind, making him look regal and righteous.

His enormous wings were folded tightly to his back, glowing a beautiful silver blue, as if they were made of moonlight and shimmering snow. In each hand he gripped a long and deadly sword.

Satanael closed his lips around his fangs and smiled, as if he were happy to see Seraphael. "Seraphael, brother, so good to see you," he purred. "It's been... Well, it's been too long, hasn't it?" His words were sickly sweet, dripping with poison.

"You are not my brother." Seraphael told him, his voice sharp and full of anger. "Step away from her now."

"We were brothers once, Seraphael. We sang glory to the Creator. We spun stars together through the Heavens, chased comets and danced before the Throne of the Goddess." Satanael gestured to the sky, his eyes following his hand as it arced upwards. "We can be brothers again, Seraphael." He said, lowering his hand and looking at the angelic form of the professor. "We can share her. Brothers share, don't they? I haven't hurt her. Look at her." The Devil's gaze fell to the unconscious form of Annaleah, who appeared to be sleeping peacefully. "I have even tried to help her. I spoke ancient words over her to help draw the poison out of her body. Come, look at her beauty and see it is unmarred. We could take her together, Seraphael. She would never know. You cannot tell me you don't desire her. No one but you and I will ever know."

Seraphael walked swiftly towards Satanael, raising his swords. "This is your final warning, Satanael, get away from her!"

Satanael rose slowly, his eyes locked on his enemy. Abandoning his charm, he let his hatred for anything that had any light within it overcome him. The red returned to his eyes and shone with the fire of intense fury. He took a small step away from Annaleah, spreading his wings out to their full span in an effort to distract Seraphael as he charged him.

Seraphael's swords began to glow, bathing his beautiful face in a soft light, as he got closer to Satanael. His silver eyes locked to his enemy, strength and will flooding through him.

Satanael began to change as he advanced, his handsome face contorting and morphing into something repulsive and monstrous. His skin darkened to a deep red, as if it had been burned and charred. Two great, shiny black horns, immense in their size, began to grow from his temples, curving upwards sharply. Black spines sprouted from his charred flesh in random places. His ears grew thin and pointed, stretching upwards. Thick black fur sprouted forth from his waist down, and his legs curved backwards at the knee. His feet, their color lost somewhere between dark red and black, became giant cloven hooves. From his tailbone emerged the tail of a great dragon, tipped with a scorpion's stinger. Only his wings, the leather skin and hard scales, remained unchanged, and unfolded in the night.

Seraphael gritted his teeth, adrenaline surging through his blood. Each of his swords glowed more deeply with a holy light, as if responding to his preparation to fight. For the first time since he fell, he could feel the light of the Goddess Herself surrounding him.

With a clash of teeth, claws, horns and swords, Seraphael met Satanael. He heard the hate filled war cry of his enemy through his own screams of battle. It was guttural and fueled with hatred. Within the guttural cry echoed the firmaments of Satanael's dark soul; the glory he held for the evil that he had become and the hatred he held for the Light.

Satanael lunged forward and raked Seraphael's chest with his claws, opening four long wounds. Burning pain radiated across Seraphael's chest. Shocked, Seraphael fell back, giving Satanael the advantage. Satanael used his weight to force Seraphael to the ground, falling onto his chest.

Looking up into the face of his enemy, Seraphael refused to let his spirits fall. He had faith in himself and in the Goddess, which he could still feel around him. Anger flooded through him. He struggled, a scream of frustration let loose from his lips as he knew he was pinned. He looked up into the grossly grinning maw of Satanael, a growl of rage forming deep in his throat.

"You should have shared her, Seraphael," the evil one taunted, spittle dripping from the corners of his mouth. As the spittle landed on Seraphael's cheek, Satanael wedged his knee into his enemy's chest, causing the pain to blossom in a burning fire across his body. "I thought greed was for my kind, but you have proven me wrong. Now, you will die, and I will have her all to myself. Over, and over." Satanael, his yellow teeth like daggers in his mouth, closed his eyes and laughed.

Seraphael, fueled by the obscenities Satanael spoke against Annaleah, used his rage as his strength. He shook with rage as he thought of the Devil defiling the woman he loved, the woman he would die to protect. Images flashed in his mind of Satanael pressed over her, and he shook his head, growling in an effort to dislodge the hateful images from his mind. He let the outrage sustain him, he let it light in his blood and start a fire, burning in his blood an energy of righteousness. This outrage was what he needed to fight off the fiend atop him, and he was thankful for it.

Still holding onto his swords, Seraphael fought to raise his arms, his hot anger now turned into a mighty surge of will and strength. It was a white hot boiling within him, blinding his senses to all that was around him, scouring away his pain and weakness until all that he knew was rage. Adrenaline coursed through him, and with a cry of fierce determination, he threw the weight of Satanael off balance, freeing his arms fully. As he arced his arms upwards, he dismembered each of Satanael's outstretched wings, sending them falling off to each side.

Satanael, his eyes wide protruding circles of shock, leapt off of Seraphael, and tried to flap his now severed wings. Satanael stumbled, cursing profusely, his expression empty, his eyes blank. He howled in agony and rage, blood spewing from the gaping wounds in his shoulders, dousing the trees around him with filth. The trees turned black and burned where the blood hit the bark. Before long, they would die of disease and rot.

Satanael screamed, and Seraphael knew that he must be enraged at the loss of his wings. The larger the wings, the more status you had in the ranks of the Dark Ones. Now that they were no longer there, Seraphael wondered how Satanael's rank in Hell would be affected.

"Tantibus!!!" Satanael screamed, trying to pick up his bloody, severed wings. Had Seraphael not been wounded himself, he would have stood and finished Satanael off once and for all. He looked at his chest and the blood pulsing freely there. He was in no shape to go chasing after the devil and his steed.

Tantibus came from the path, kicking up earth and knocking over small trees as he raced to his master. Seraphael watched as his enemy prepared for retreat.

"I will come back for you, traitor. You and your little bitch will pay dearly for what you have done. You are a fallen one, and you shall be destroyed as such!" Tantibus lowered himself and allowed his master to mount him, then raised himself once more, the master now atop his steed.

Tantibus, carrying Satanael away to be healed, burst out of the woods and onto the path, screaming his terrible cry into the night.

Seraphael brought his hand to his chest, and through teeth clenched in pain, whispered ancient words of light to stop the flow of blood. After a few moments, the blood stopped flowing so freely, and he felt some strength returning.

It was time to go to Annaleah.

Chapter Thirty-Six

Seraphael's Sacrifice

Seraphael tried to sit up, but despite the healing incantation, he was still weak. Although knowing that a few more moments of reciting the ancient words would help restore his strength, it was time he did not want to waste away from Annaleah.

Satanael had said something about the Jorogumo's children having bitten her once again, and this seared his heart deeply with sorrow and fear. Time was of the essence now. He had almost lost her once before, and could not bear to lose her again.

With a mighty groan of pain and determination, he rolled from his back onto his stomach. He dropped his swords in the grass and crawled as quickly as he could towards Annaleah's side, grabbing handfuls of long grass and weeds to pull himself forward. He ignored the pain, his eyes locked on the unconscious woman who had now become the most important part of his life.

Still fighting the pain to move forward, he didn't even try to stifle his tears. How could he have let her come to an end such as this? He had vowed to protect her, and yet there she lay, unconscious and near death. He had failed himself. Worse, he had failed her.

With the thought of his failure being a dishonor to Annaleah, the pain in his soul became too much. Tears threatened to obscure his view, but he let them flow freely, hoping they would cleanse him of his sin. There in the grass lay a Halfling like no other. Half woman, half angel. She had awoken in him a tenderness, a spark of hope that he had not known was still alive in him. He had thought it had died millennia ago when he was evicted from Heaven. The memory of his betrayal was something that had wounded him for an eternity, and yet, the thought of losing the woman who had borne in him a hope he never thought he could feel again was much more painful. After the Creator had left him and allowed for no explanation, the only defense he'd had was to harden himself against all of life. He still had left enough decency inside not to let the Darkness overcome him; still held enough of the light in his soul to keep the pain of the treachery from turning into hatred. He had used isolation, self-importance and knowledge as a weapon and as his defense, treasuring his solitude above all else. He had never let anyone get close to him, and had never been tempted.

Annaleah had changed all of that; her mere presence had shown him that his ability to feel love was not lost. His heart raced when he thought of her and he felt a longing to touch her gently, and to hold her in his arms. This had led to the opening of other great things within him and he felt again the kiss of hope for his redemption and for a normal life among the humans. It was something that he had not only never dared to think possible, it was something he had deemed a silly and useless waste of time; a thing mortals turned to in order to feel closer to something just outside their reach.

As he crawled closer to Annaleah, he thought too of Gabriel, and of how he wished he could thank him. Had it not been for the dream Gabriel had sent him, he may have never let himself feel as he felt now. "If I live," he promised himself, "I will thank you, my brother soul. I vow this to you."

With a last mighty heave, Seraphael reached Annaleah's side. He looked down at her beautiful, supine form, his heart breaking. Though he could see her chest rising and falling with slow inhalations of breath, he could tell from the slowed movements of the pale and weak arcs of light beneath her skin that she was in great danger from the poison lingering in her veins. She was alive, though only barely.

Seraphael forced himself to his knees, ignoring the pain, so that he could look upon her more closely. Her waist length golden curls fanned out around her in the grass, framing her like a halo. The fire of purity still shone from within it, only much weaker than he had seen it in the dream Gabriel had sent him. He had never seen her out of Dream Time in her angelic form, and she was more than beautiful, she was divine. He longed to touch her, to somehow heal and awaken her, to hold her in his arms and never let her go. He found himself wondering briefly if things would work the way they did in fairy tales. If he kissed her with nothing but love, would she awaken and be healed? He realized that, though he was burning to kiss her, he would not mar her purity by kissing her while she was unaware.

Through the haze of his despair and the agony of his fear of losing her, one clear thought came to him like a breath of fresh, sunlit air, clear and perfectly formed. He could call to the Creator, and beg Her to heal Annaleah. He knew that the Goddess was not one who would engage in war Herself, leaving the trivialities of battle to those who fought within the darkness or the light. Though She had caused him the greatest pain he had ever endured, he was willing to risk Her refusal of him. She might not hear him, and even if She did, there was every chance She wouldn't answer. Why would She? He was a fallen one now, cast from the throne of Heaven to the hateful earth below, to suffer among the humans as if he were one of them.

Another perfectly formed thought entered his mind, as though sent to him with merciful intentions. He could call to the Goddess by Her sacred, holy name. It was forbidden to all to speak it, except under the most dire of circumstances. To speak Her true name in any way that She might deem unworthy was to risk immediate and irrevocable damnation.

Seraphael found the thought filled him with hope, and the prospect of an eternity in Hell as one of the damned did not faze him. To lose Annaleah was worse than the threat of Hell. To lose her was to lose everything.

He gathered as much strength as he could muster, and lifted Annaleah in his arms. As her head fell softly against his shoulder, his heart filled with adoration for her. Outstretching his wings, he began to pray for the first time since before his fall. "Forgive me, Oh Goddess, for calling your perfect and holy true name. I come to you out of love, and out of desperation. I hold in my arms a Halfling which I have come to love. I would sacrifice myself to the tortures of Hell itself should you choose to heal her. Forgive me, Goddess, if I incur your wrath." He wept, his chest heaving as he struggled to speak. "I ask only that you save her." Seraphael trembled with the weakness of his injury, yet he still held his beloved up to the heavens, prepared to give his very soul should she be spared.

Lifting his head and opening his silver eyes, Seraphael readied himself. He treasured the feeling of Annaleah in his arms, knowing that he may never hold her again.

"My sweet Annaleah, forgive me if I fail you. If I do, I pray that Gabriel will let you know why I did what I felt I must do."

He knew what death was to an angel, an absolute nothingness, a ceasing to be, unless the Illuminare happened to be close by to collect the last spark of her soul, in a hope of resurrecting her later.

With the last breath of strength in his lungs, Seraphael said the Goddess's name before collapsing into the grass, Annaleah still held tightly in his arms.

Chapter Thirty-Seven

The Goddess

Seraphael, falling slowly backwards to the red Georgia earth, saw the intense white light that was the harbinger of the Goddess' arrival. As it pulsed through the trees, he knew the Creator had heard him. It was as though time had stopped when the last syllable of the Goddess' one true and holy name had been uttered. The powerful effects of speaking Her secret name slowed everything down and, for a moment, bathed the world in a haze of pure, dazzling light. It was a luminous blazing pulse that fanned out until it covered everything all at once, as if it emanated from the center of the earth and shot out in all directions, holding itself in the world long enough to burn off all that was unholy and impure.

Seraphael felt disoriented, as if his descent to the ground took hours. Every movement seemed to take a great concerted effort, as though he were moving through setting concrete. Closing his eyes against the blinding light sent out before the coming of the Goddess, to purify the land for Her arrival. She was too holy to stand upon a land so ravaged and battle torn; the scars of the emotions it held too brutal for Her to withstand in her sacrosanct purity.

The screams of the unholy filled Seraphael's ears, their death cries filling the sky and hammering into the earth. Still he continued his descent, Annaleah pressed tightly against his chest in an attempt to protect her from harm. Caught in the spell of time unraveling itself to burn the impurities away, he felt compassion for those that died. Not only his brothers and sisters of the Light, but for those who had turned from the light and hardened themselves so that all goodness was lost to them. There was no hope left for those who rejoiced in evil and celebrated suffering. In his mind he saw the faces of those who were once in Heaven with him, chanting the holy name of the Goddess and holding the universe itself together with the recitations of precious words. He remembered how Satanael had used his wit and charm to gain power in their minds, turning many away from the Goddess. He was quite convincing with his lies and his empty promises, and many had believed him. He had caused a great number to lose their way, and, in doing so, lose their place in Heaven. Some walked among mankind, forever regretful of what they had done and hoping for a chance of redemption by helping the humans. Others were loyal only to Satanael, still enamored by his guile and lies. They believed that one day the Creator would be overthrown and the world, as well as humanity, would be rid of the light, free for them to reign over and debauch as they chose.

It was the last of these creatures that still screamed their deaths into the night. Seraphael knew that he had caused their deaths by calling to the Goddess. She would not come to any place where there were any of the Damned. The pulse of blinding light, by the intense power of its purity, would kill them all and effectively end the war. The ramifications for calling Her were many. It was an unfair and unethical war tactic, and he knew he would be judged for it, not just by the Creator, but by the Damned as well. He would certainly be remembered for it, and hated by those who had escaped the purification by returning to Hell before the burning light was sent, or by those who had not yet emerged to fight. The death toll for the enemy would be innumerable, and for the Dark fiends, there was no return from death. For them it was oblivion. The deaths of the damned were irrevocable. There were no Illuminare for them.

When Seraphael finally met the ground, the air rushed out of his lungs from the impact. He saw one of the mysterious Illuminare as it floated slowly past him. It was made up of both darkness and light in an odd but beautiful combination. Its form held to that of an angel, but was featureless, as though it were midnight sky in the shape of a large winged man, with lightning coursing through it in random places. This small sect of angels, once belonging to the order of Thrones, had willingly transformed themselves into guardians of the angels of Light who had been slain in battle. They were only seen when there was a Great War between the Light and the Darkness; their purpose to capture the last spark of light and life from a dying angel. They drew this last breath out of those who had fallen in battle and saved it within a sacred vessel so that the angel would not fade into oblivion. It was their hope that someday these last remnants of angels would be brought back to life and glory and returned to Heaven once more. Angels, not having souls like humans, could not return to Heaven after they died. If their last breath was not captured by the Illuminare, they were lost forever, as if they had never existed at all.

The searing pulse of light was now gone, and the night was devoid of sound. The quiet ran so deep that Seraphael found himself wondering if the Light had killed the Holy angels as well. Straining to hear something, anything, his heart beat fiercely, the blood of his wounds now flowing freely.

He looked down at Annaleah, praying that she still breathed. The arcs of light beneath her skin grew weaker and the golden luminescence of her hair was now all but gone. He saw, to his horror, several Illuminare unweave themselves from the shadows, coming closer with their sacred earthen pots.

"No!" he cried out at them, "You cannot have her. She can't die. Not here, not like this." He clutched Annaleah and laid upon his back, facing the sky. His vision of the stars was obscured as the Illuminare came closer, waiting for Annaleah's last breath and spark of light.

And then he felt Her. At once his lungs filled with sweet, fresh air and his wounds were no longer a tapestry of blood and pain. A gentle yet powerful luminosity was building in front of him, driving the Illuminare back a safe distance. Seraphael felt love surrounding him, and the return of hope washed over him. The undulating light blossomed out like the petals of a flower until it described the beauty and form of the Mother of All That Is. Seraphael knew his strength and health had been returned to him, but was afraid to look at Her, not knowing if She was angry for having been summoned into the middle of a war.

"You may go elsewhere, dear Illuminare, for you will not be needed here quite yet," She said softly. The beauty and calm in her voice broke Seraphael's heart, and he wept for the beauty of it and for the pain of having been so long separated from Her.

"My most beloved Seraphael, do not be afraid to look upon me. I promise no harm will come to you." Her voice was filled with love, it was musical and sweet, and when She spoke flowers began to bloom in the earth around Her. The soil, the trees and the life that had lived there began to heal as She stood among them.

Seraphael lifted his head with humble reverence and looked upon the Goddess, his heart feeling as if it were shattered and healed both at once. The light that emanated from Her was scintillating and protean, the colors washing into themselves and flowing from green to blue to silver, then to rose, white, gold and purple, all weaving in and out of Her form of light. She was tall and thin, and looked as though She would be fragile if she were physical and not ephemeral. Her cheekbones were sharply defined, her chin thin and pointed. Her ears were like that of a fairy, and in them she wore scrolled silver bands that curved around the pointed tips. Her eyes were pools of shining indigo light, beautifully framed with long lashes and dreamily lowered lids. Her robes too, were made of the protean light, as was the twisted wooden staff she held and the silver floral crown that she wore on top of her head. Her hair flowed long around her, dancing in the wind as if it held a happy song within it that only it could hear. It flowed down and around Her form, fanning out on the ground around Her feet, twirling languidly.

"I have so much I wish to say to you, Seraphael," She said, her voice both beautiful and full of remorse. "I am sorry for what you have been through and all that you have been made to endure. I have been waiting for you to call to me." She stepped forward a step, her head tilted as she looked deeply into Seraphael's eyes. "I would have come the first time you spoke to me, by my true name or otherwise. I waited on your invitation. I am a lady, you see. I will not come unless I am invited." A smiled curled on her ephemeral lips, the light within her form now pulsing with colors, all of them filled with divine love.

"You have every reason to be angry with me," She continued, "I owe you so much. There is more that I want to tell you and I wish I could stand here with you longer, but I am afraid I cannot. I cannot leave the throne of Heaven for too long for fear that our enemies will storm Heaven and try to overthrow it in my absence. Though it is still guarded by the Ophanim, I must return quickly. My presence here changes a lot of things, as you know."

Seraphael, his soul aflame with a myriad of palpable emotions, let his tears spill down his face. He struggled for words. Her radiance and beauty was overwhelming. It had been an eternity since he had been in Her presence. With loving compassion, the Creator glided over to him, her head cocked sweetly to one side, her hair still moving in a fluid dance. As she moved, more flowers bloomed, in colors Seraphael had never seen before. The fragrance they injected into the air was sweet, heady and wonderfully intoxicating. The Goddess' hair flowed out behind her as she moved, as if it moved in a dream. With a long, thin finger made up of Her glorious kaleidoscope of lights, she softly wiped a tear from Seraphael's face with such love and compassion that he was utterly overwhelmed with feeling.

"Give her to me, Seraphael," She whispered, looking deeply into his eyes. Seraphael stood, using his wings for balance, and looked back into the purity of Her gaze. He looked too at Annaleah, his soul filled with love for the woman who had changed his life so much.

Seraphael gently held Annaleah out to the Creator. As the Goddess gathered Annaleah to her bosom, and Annaleah's head came to rest peacefully against Her, the Goddess' hair spread out around her and began to transform into glorious, light filled wings. Long strands wove together to form pinions of light, tresses blossomed upwards and out until the Goddess, holding Annaleah, was surrounded by a pair of the largest, most stunning wings Seraphael had ever seen. They shone with light from within, like that which made up the Goddess' essence, protean and changing. The light began to flow through Annaleah, reigniting the arcs of luminosity in her skin and rekindling the golden glow in her hair. As the Goddess held her like a sleeping child, the life that had once threatened to leave Annaleah forever began to flow back into her once again.

Seraphael fell to one knee, his gratitude and reverence overpowering his senses. His lips that had once so long ago spoke elaborate prayers and recited complex rituals now spoke only two words over and over. "Thank you, thank you, thank you."

With a sharp inhalation of breath, life filled Annaleah once more, the threat of death now gone. Opening her eyes, she looked up into the face of the Goddess, and felt for the first time the true power of Her peace, purity and divine love.

"Welcome back, Annaleah." The Goddess said, placing her gently on her feet once more. Annaleah felt hot tears moisten her cheeks as the depth of the Goddess' love flowed out around Her. It echoed in her heart, sending pulsing heartbeats filled with gratitude to reverberate within her.

Having healed Annaleah, the Goddess' wings fell from their expansive stretch in the sky and once more became Her hair. It continued to drift slowly around her, as if it had never stopped undulating to some fanciful, dreamy tune.

"There is still a lot for you to do. You have no time for Death," The Goddess said, "I am very proud of you, Annaleah." She smiled serenely, her eyes taking on an even deeper shade of indigo. "There is much I wish I could say to you. But, my time here is at an end." She bowed Her beautiful head slightly. "I honor you both, and your love for one another. It was your love for your uncle, Annaleah, that saved him, as it was Seraphael's love for you and his willingness to sacrifice himself that saved you. Cherish each other, for it is love, always love, which is the most powerful force in the Universe."

As the Goddess spoke, her light began to draw into itself and her form grew smaller as She withdrew her energy and presence from them. The couple watched as the light diminished, until with a bright blink, it was gone.

"Annaleah," Seraphael whispered, his voice thick with emotion.

She turned to him, her heart thundering with awe and adoration. She stood, taking in his beautiful angelic form, basking in his splendor. She held his gaze with her own, walking to him slowly before throwing her arms around him and collapsing into his arms.

She knew in his angelic form he was called Seraphael and in her time with him she had only called him the Professor, but she didn't feel these names to be right on her lips. As she laid her head on his chest and heard the steady beating of his heart, she called him by the name that felt the most right in her heart.

"Sebastian," she said, enflamed in the energy of perfect calm and peace that he exuded toward her. With the uttering of his human name, it felt as if she had claimed him.

Chapter Thirty-Eight

Revelations

Annaleah listened enraptured to the strong beating of Sebastian's heart as she pressed herself against his chest. A wellspring of love burst forth from her soul and washed over her completely, making her shiver. He held her tighter, and she listened as words of gratitude for her life escaped his lips.

She looked up at him, taking in his angelic form. He gazed into her eyes tenderly, a smile curving on his lips. She reached up, holding his face on each side with gentle devotion, her eyes never leaving his. As she held his face in her hands, she noticed his eyes had changed. They were no longer silver, but a deep, glorious shade of indigo. Having been healed and blessed by the Goddess Herself, he was no longer a "fallen" angel. He had been redeemed.

Sebastian, deepening the intensity of their connection, lowered his face towards Annaleah and said, "Say my name again." His voice was low and breathy. "Say my human name." He paused to run his finger slowly down her cheek. She felt his heart thundering against her, matching the fire in her own heart as her eyes closed in enjoyment of his touch. A sigh escaped her mouth, and Sebastian ran the pad of his thumb over her parted lips. She relished the delicious trembling that ran through her.

"Sebastian," she whispered breathily. Annaleah slowly opened her eyes, starving to lose herself in the impressive and beautiful depths of his midnight eyes. Her lips were hot and moist, awaiting a kiss. She had never hungered for anything in her life more than she craved the feel of his mouth over her own.

They continued to look deeply into one another's eyes, seized by an emotion neither had ever experienced before. It was as if their bodies and souls were over powered with an energy that overwhelmed them, surging up from their hearts and pulsing throughout their bodies. The adoration they felt for one another fueled this emotional scintillation, and emanated from their hearts as their very souls merged in a burning inferno of potent emotions that surged and grew until the emotions were a glorious pyre; a myriad of undulating feelings. Holding each other, they became aglow with the power of their merging that bonded them together as twin flames, one soul within two bodies.

"I knew you were different the moment I met you," Sebastian whispered into her ear, still holding her close. "I never should have treated you as cruelly as I did."

Annaleah kissed him on each cheek and said, "Please don't be sorry. I know where you were coming from now. I would go through everything again, a million times. To be in your arms is worth fighting a thousand wars."

With her heart beating quickly, filled with love and a desperate yearning, Annaleah watched as Sebastian lowered his head and prepared to kiss her.

"There you two are! We have been looking for you both for quite a while now. Thank the Goddess you are both safe." Gabriel emerged from the woods to their left, followed by Michael and Marchosias. Their kiss interrupted, they turned to Gabriel. Disappointment flooded through Annaleah, but she smiled warmly at Gabriel.

"Oh, sorry guys. There will be time for that later." Gabriel winked at them, his eyes twinkling merrily. "I am assuming it was one of you who called the Goddess," he said, nodding his head towards Seraphael. "Smart move. It could have gone wrong, but we're glad that you were brave enough to do it. Michael got separated from Annaleah after he killed one of the demons that had charged her." He looked towards Michael. "I just got here after admitting Uncle John to the hospital. From what I gather, there were many more damned than holy fighting. There was some sort of struggle and the angels of Light were having trouble coming through to the clearing. It is over for now, but I am afraid there might be a retaliation from the damned at some not so far off date."

"It was worth it," Sebastian replied, holding Annaleah close. "Even knowing the repercussions. Annaleah was close to death; the Jorogumo had poisoned her. Satanael had taken her and was about to have his way with her when I arrived. I was injured and weak, and had little choice but to call to the Creator. I knew it meant that I could have been damned for it, if my cause had been deemed as unworthy. I was willing to be one of the damned, if it meant saving Annaleah. I could not bear to lose her again."

Gabriel was at their side almost instantly, worry in his face. Michael and Marchosias were right behind him, concern in their expressions as well.

"You almost died? Satanael was with you too? I'm so glad you are okay." Gabriel threw his angelic arms around Annaleah. Breaking her embrace with Sebastian, she returned his hug, happy to see her friend again.

"There is something I must say to you, Gabriel," Sebastian said. He placed his hand on Gabriel's shoulder and looked him in the eye for emphasis. "Thank you. A million times my brother, I thank you," He paused, trying to get control of his emotions. "I know as the angel of dreams, that it was you who sent me the beautiful dream of Annaleah. If it weren't for that dream, I am not sure who or where I would be today, or what side of the war I would have gone to. Yet, because of you, and the dream of seeing her in the clearing, I knew that she was special. Why else would the Dream Keeper come to me with a dream after so many centuries of silence between us?"

"You are quite welcome, brother," Gabriel answered. "I have wanted to come to you again for years, but I didn't know how I would be received." Gabriel looked at them both and smiled. "You and Annaleah are destined for one another. The dream was my way of showing you both that you belonged together, and of thawing you, Seraphael. You see, you never truly fell. The Goddess has wanted you back in Heaven for a very long time, but you had hardened yourself against Her, and against love itself. It was almost impossible to get through to you."

Sebastian looked at Gabriel, his eyes taking on a hardened sheen. "What do you mean I never fell? You were there when it happened. I tried to save an angel from falling and.... You know what happened! How can you tell me that I never fell? You know what I have gone through, the agony I have endured." Sebastian's eyes were shimmering with disbelief and confusion, his brows knitted together. "It made me into what I had become for so very long." His expression changed to sadness and anger, hurt pressed into the creases in his face. "How can you deny I fell, after all of this?" He spread his arms out, indicating the war.

Gabriel hung his head. "I do not deny what you have gone through, Seraphael." Stepping back, Gabriel looked at Annaleah, encouraging her to speak. "Annaleah, it is time to let him know the truth."

Seraphael turned to her, his eyes looking bewildered and troubled. "Annaleah? What's going on?" She went to him, compassion and love glowing within her. She thought of what she wanted to say to him, and found that words were not enough.

"Do you trust me, Sebastian?" she asked. His face softened.

"Yes, Annaleah I trust you." His voice was low and subdued.

"Then come to me, and let me show you what really happened." Seraphael stood in front of Annaleah and closed his eyes. She touched him softly on the temple, closing her eyes as well. She entered his mind with her thoughts and showed him the scene Marchosias had shown her not so long ago. She gave him the image of her father, Metatron, his long snowy white hair flowing out into the deepness of the cosmos. She brought him back to the moment when Metatron warned him not to go to the aid of the female angel who had fallen.

Sebastian flinched, but didn't break his contact with her. Seeing Metatron after an untold age was shocking and unexpected, and he had to stifle a cry of surprise.

It was as if it were yesterday, seeing Metatron's youthful face and long flowing hair, against a backdrop of the Universe itself. He could feel the concern and pleading in his friend's eyes and it stung him, the pain as intense as a physical wound.

The scene played again as he watched the angel he had tried to save fall and burn, her ashes scattered into the night by a war torn wind.

Tears threatened Sebastian now, and the lump in his throat was difficult to swallow back. What was she trying to tell him with all this, he had gone through it all before, why show it to him again?

The scene shifted and now he saw the Goddess. She was standing at the gates of Heaven, weeping for his loss. The sight of this all but broke his heart, and flooded him with the need to go to Her and comfort Her.

"*It was the first conflict in all of time,*" Annaleah told him with the voice of her mind. "*The Goddess had not prepared for Satanael's betrayal, and she was deeply hurt by it. She was deep in mourning, and unable to deal with the loss of her lover as well as your loss. A lot of Holy angels died in battle, and she felt each loss deeply. She felt that She had failed in so much, and She went into a period of solitude to learn from what she saw as her flaws and errors.*"

In this time Heaven was governed by the Archangels."

Sebastian could see all of this clearly in his mind as Annaleah spoke to him. The saw the Goddess' deep indigo eyes filled with tears, her withdrawal into a deep cave in the secret parts of Heaven. He saw the angels govern in her leave, protecting Her and Heaven itself with their very lives.

"Your eviction from Heaven has been a terrible mistake she has regretted since it happened."

"What?' Sebastian replied. *"A mistake? All of this time? Why wasn't I told? Why didn't someone try to do something?'* His voice sounded heavy and pained as he spoke within her mind.

"I don't know the answer to that, but I will ask you, if someone had come to you with this message, would you have listened? Would you have believed?' Annaleah wanted to hold him, to comfort him. She felt his pain and it wounded her, too.

"I don't know,' he answered truthfully. *"I was hurt and angry for such a long time. I cannot say I would have listened to anyone."*

"Then listen to me now, Sebastian," Annaleah implored him. *"She never meant to lose you. Perhaps this is why she came to you so willingly when you called to Her. Perhaps this is why, sweet angel Seraphael, your eyes are no longer silver. They are indigo, my precious one. You were never truly one of the fallen, but by calling to Her with only love in your heart, she had a chance to make things right. If you truly wished it, you could enter back into Heaven right now, and be with Her."*

Annaleah knew her words must have roused Sebastian, and she wondered if he sensed her fear that she would lose him to the Goddess. Seraphael broke the mind lock and opened his eyes. Feeling him leave her, Annaleah opened her eyes as well, and looked deeply into Sebastian's.

"It is true I have wished for nothing more than to never have fallen," Sebastian confessed to Annaleah. "To be in Her grace and company." Hearing him say this sent a hollow pang of pain into Annaleah's heart. She feared that he would, indeed, leave her for the glory of Heaven he had so longed for. She knew she would let him go with no grudge against him, if it would make him happy. If it would bring him joy, she would gladly watch him go and rejoice in knowing he would finally know peace. However, this did not mean she wouldn't cry for months afterwards.

Sebastian placed a finger tenderly under her chin, gazing with adoration into her eyes. "There is no reason to fear my leaving you,

Annaleah. There is no longer a place in my life without you in it. I have felt things for you that I never knew I was capable of feeling." He smiled down at her, his eyes shimmering. "The thought of losing you is more than I can bear. I will always be on the side of the Light, and no one will ever take the place of the Goddess. You, however, sweet Annaleah, have brought me what no one and nothing on this earth or in Heaven could ever have done." He paused, his Adam's apple working in his throat. "You have brought me hope. You have brought me peace when I was resigned to living with animosity for the rest of time. You have changed me and there is no going back. There is no me without you."

A sweet flood of relief washed over Annaleah, and love blossomed inside her. From within her chest, a beautiful golden light began to glow. It pulsed and undulated, growing strong and bright as love blossomed strong and steady within her.

Gabriel, Marchosias and Michael walked to her, each placing a hand on her with reverence.

"Annaleah Nicole Grace," Michael spoke in his deep, masculine voice, "Daughter of Elise Leeann Grace and the Arch angel Metatron, Halfling and one and only true Otherling, it is time. Those who fell but did not turn to the Darkness will see your light. It is a beacon, and is something that they have hoped for since the moment they fell from grace. It is to the love you have in your heart that they will come. It is time to redeem the fallen."

Chapter Thirty-Nine

Satanael's Last Stand

Seraphael let out a cry of pained remorse and alarm at seeing how the clearing in the woods had been desecrated. Everywhere, except for the blessed spot where the Goddess had stood, blood soaked the earth with feathers, scales and all manner of severed flesh scattered within the blood. Some trees had been uprooted and tossed aside, others broken in half. The soil steamed in places, as if trying to scour itself from the terror that had occurred here moments ago.

Annaleah took Seraphael's hand, squeezing it gently. "We can sanctify this place again; plant new trees and rededicate it as a Holy place."

Seraphael's mind spun, his heart sinking as he took in what he saw. The damned had been burned to ash, and where the wind had not blown the ashes away, detailed outlines of their bodies told of their anguished deaths. It looked as if an artist had lovingly carved each detail of wing, horn and claw into the ash, purposely trying to evoke a sense of terror and empathy from any who looked upon the expressions on the faces of the damned. Seraphael walked past a body of ash that had its hand over its eyes, the mouth contorted in pain, shock and death. He stopped and bent to look at it, wondering if it was one he had known once long ago, before the Fall took place.

As he examined the details of the dead unholy being, he took in the mix of scales and feather in its wing, he reached out to touch it. His curiosity turned to horror as the place where he softly placed his finger caved in. From this spot, the ash around it began to fall, until the entire body was no more, having been rendered to a pile of gray dust upon the broken earth.

Michael placed a hand on his shoulder. "It was their choice to follow the Darkness, Seraphael. Don't feel too badly for what they went through. War is never a pretty thing. Come, let's move on. Though this place has been destroyed, it is still accessible. Those who want redemption will come."

Seraphael, still feeling the pain of what had happened here and knowing his calling of the Goddess had caused it, stood and tried to forget what he had seen. The emotions coursing through him were new to him. Having hardened himself to all feeling eons ago, the onslaught set his mind and heart ablaze.

Annaleah took his hand again, and asked her friends, "What do I do now?"

Before Gabriel could answer her, the ground began to rumble and shake as though the earth beneath their feet had begun to growl low in its throat. As the ground shook harder, Annaleah fell to the red Georgia earth, stunned.

"What's happening?" she asked, her eyes wide with fright. Instead of answering her, Gabriel, Seraphael, Michael and Marchosias flanked her with swords drawn as guardians. The air was charged with electricity, heavy with dread and foreboding.

A deep, haughty laugh rang out seemingly from everywhere at once. Its mocking tone was instantly recognizable as Satanael.

Now his voice seemed to come from behind a tree that bore long claw marks, "Did you really think you could get rid of me that easily?" His words echoed in the sky, followed by more laughter.

"Did you think I would retreat without another word, Seraphael? Do you truly think yourself so great a threat to me?"

His voice now seemed to come from the vicinity of a large, blood soaked stone. "You will pay for what you have done to me, all of you. Calling in the Goddess was an unfair tactic that even I would not have stooped so low to do. You must have really been terrified, "Professor." Laughter rang out from what seemed to be the whole sky, raining down with scornful mockery upon those assembled below.

From all places at once, Satanael announced, "Prepare to die."

The rumbling beneath them grew, forcing those who stood guard over Annaleah to brace themselves or fall. The earth began to open, a small hole at first, quickly caving in on itself to open into a larger wound within the earth. Sulfuric steam belched forth from it, the stench powerful, carrying within it deadly intent. From the great depths below this terrible opening, a scream of rage issued forth, chilling Annaleah's blood with its raw, palpable hatred. The vibrations in the earth and the growling continued to rise until, from this terrible opening, a figure emerged that was more terrifying and repulsive than anything she had ever seen.

Its clawed hand, with slick webbing between the long, dark fingers, tore for purchase at the earth. Its arms were covered in coarse black hairs that looked like tufts of fur. The head was that of a black goat with red eyes that glowed within their sockets. The horns were a dark red and curved away from its head, the tops singed black and dripping blood. The barrel chest was well defined with muscles, the taut skin over it a deep burning red from which small, sharp bony plates protruded. The legs bent backward at the knee and were also covered in the thick black fur. They ended in two great hooves that scalded the earth beneath them, sending stinking smoke into the air. On its shoulders were the remains of once glorious wings. They were soaked in blood and showed the beginning stages of decomposition, the skin black with rot and filth. Veins and sinews showed through the numerous crude stitches that appeared to hold the wings onto its shoulders.

Gabriel, the guardian closest to the opening within the earth and the monstrosity that was emerging out of it, said, "It's Satanael, in his Baphomet form!"

Seraphael's resolve strengthened, both swords drawn and ready for use in his strong hands. Satanael was capable of shape shifting into many forms, and he saved that of Baphomet for when he wanted to strike the most terror into the hearts of his enemies.

As soon as he was born from the stinking hole in the earth, Satanael launched himself at Gabriel, the guardian closest to him. He raised his clawed hand and aimed at Gabriel's heart. With one swift blow of his sword, Gabriel sliced several inches off of Satanael's claw, sending pieces of it flying into the darkness. Unperturbed, Satanael grabbed at Gabriel's throat, both hands reaching their mark.

Seraphael, unwilling to leave his protective position near Annaleah, felt helpless to defend Gabriel.

Annaleah felt her body tremble with a righteous rage. Her blood coursed hot in her veins as her heart pumped adrenaline with the force of thunder into her flexed muscles. Seeing the only friend she had ever come to trust and love in such a vulnerable position transformed her into something she had never known she was capable of being. It was time to be a warrior, to fight with something far more powerful than forged steel and sharpened blade. She stood and called to Satanael.

"Let him go and fight me!" Annaleah cried, her fists clenched at her sides. Her three friends turned to her, shock and terror bright in their eyes. Satanael released Gabriel's throat and tossed him to the ground. He looked her right in the eyes, but she had already black boxed her mind. He tried to enter her thoughts, but found no entrance.

Gabriel stood quickly, sword drawn, and moved to stand in front of Annaleah. Satanael turned to him and spat with vehemence, "You must honor her request! I have let you go; if she wishes to fight me, let her fight! You heard her. None of you will interfere."

Seraphael charged at him with his swords, a war cry escaping his lips. Satanael grabbed each sword, the blades slicing deeply into his flesh. He lifted the blades, impervious to the pain and blood pouring from his wounds, and threw Seraphael several meters away. With his eyes on fire within their sockets and blazing a deep red, he turned, growling at Marchosias, who had struck him with her swords in the Achilles tendon. He balled his hand into a fist and struck her hard in the face, spitting on her when she fell to the ground.

"ENOUGH!" cried Annaleah, before Michael could launch his attack on Satanael. Michael turned to her, his sword held high in the air, ready to slay their enemy.

"Let me fight him! How many of you have to die to protect me?' She looked at them, hoping the look of ferocity was enough to convince them. "Please, trust me Michael. Take Seraphael and the others a safe distance and let me fight him."

Annaleah remembered what both Gabriel and the Goddess had told her about the power of real, raw, unfiltered love. She had seen it heal her uncle right before her eyes. Perhaps it wasn't brute force that would win this war. Maybe, just maybe, it was love.

Satanael tilted his head back and laughed, a taunting, cruel laugh of victory. "Do as she says, Michael, and I might spare you all from death everlasting. I don't see the Illuminare here now. There will be no chance of being born again for your lot tonight. Only a deep, dark oblivion if you stand in my way. She wants to fight me, let her fight."

With great sadness, Michael lowered his head and his weapon. Satanael rubbed his hands together in delight, a wicked smile on his lips.

Annaleah saw Gabriel restraining Seraphael, who called out her name with tangible desperation. Hearing the pain in his voice as he repeated the word "no" over and over again, her heart ached.

"Stand and face me, Satanael." she demanded. Satanael gave her an incredulous look, followed by one of mock fear.

"Oh no, woe is me," he said, placing his bleeding hands on his cheeks, "here I am all alone to face the Otherling, whatever shall I do?"

Annaleah, ignoring him, closed her golden eyes and let her heart flood with love for Seraphael. Becoming lost to her adoration, she let the rapture of her devotion to him blossom into a beautiful glow within her soul that washed over her spirit and ignited her entire being. As she did so, she felt an intense, tingling heat that spread like little lines of lightning under her skin. Pleasantly surprised by the powerful sensation, she opened her eyes for a brief moment and saw that these pulses of light became like lightning bolts dancing just under her skin, building up in their intensity, growing more luminous and forceful with their light.

Satanael clicked his tongue, amused. "So that is your tactic, to blind me with beauty? I already thought you beautiful, Annaleah. If you wanted me, you should have simply said so." His tone was still filled with mockery. Satanael, filled with pride and self-assurance, made no effort to attack her, his hubris allowing him plenty of time to taunt her.

A peaceful gratitude filed Annaleah, mixing with the power of love within her, and she closed her eyes once more to go back within.

How perfect, she thought, that he wouldn't even think to strike out at her, so sure was he that what she was doing couldn't harm him.

Annaleah felt the love for her friend Seth course through her being. She relived the first time she'd met him in the fifth grade. He had been her only friend and had stood by her when none of her other peers would. She saw his youthful face, dimpled and smiling, his blue eyes warm with returned friendship. She thought of the countless secrets told, the laughter they had shared, and the bond that held them together to the ends of the earth. As she concentrated, she felt the arcs of light merge together, snaking their way into each other until her entire body began to buzz and emanate a dazzling golden white light that she could see through the thin layer of her closed lids.

His mocking tone now gone, Satanael asked, "What is it that you are doing, Annaleah? Whatever it is, it won't work. Pitiful and pathetic really, to think that you could conquer me with such an insubstantial effort."

Annaleah, feeling the power of love surging through her, was at peace. With complete trust in the Goddess, she prayed for assistance. With the voice of her mind and heart she prayed in silence, "Help me, Oh Goddess, and fill me with the love you had for Satanael before he fell. Let it course through me with the height of its power, and fill me with its intensity."

As soon as the last word of her intention was formed in her mind, Annaleah burst into golden flames, which, though they sprang from her, neither consumed or burned her. She was infused with an emotion so forceful and overpowering that she was amazed she was able to stand in the midst of it. Images burst into her mind, their strength instantly fortifying and devastating all at once.

Annaleah saw the great and beautiful face of the Goddess, the protean lights shifting in passion for Satanael. She saw the handsome angel he had been before he'd fallen. He was holding the Goddess tightly in the blissful action of devoted love.

From a distant place, she heard Satanael screaming, angry and confused as the golden light from her fire leapt from her blazing form and ignited him. The fire of love had become very unfamiliar to him. It was nothing like the flames of Hell, and it wounded him deeply.

"What are you doing? Stop it at once, you filthy bitch!" His words were like the memory of a dream that happened long ago. They reached her as if they had been spoken from a far off place, but they no longer mattered. More visions came to her, of sonnets Satanael had written for the Goddess, ones only the high archangel of music could write. She saw him working hard, with tenderness to guide a legion of angels to sing in full chorus of his love to the Creator.

Annaleah heard his anger turn to anguish. The hot poison under his words was gone, replaced instantly with tangible anguish. The cry he unleashed from the place where he had once kept his soul hung in the air between them, heavy and somber. His cry was that of a wounded animal, and it echoed his pain into the sky.

Annaleah opened her eyes and watched as he did his best to recover himself. He drew his breath in through sharply pointed teeth in order to puff up his chest in an effort to appear larger and more ferocious. He knew her battle tactic now, and she could see the hatred for her in his eyes.

With obvious rage and all flickering of amusement gone from his eyes, Satanael threw himself at her. He was rewarded for his effort by bursting into flames and bouncing off of her, leaving her unharmed.

Screaming in agony, he unleashed a myriad of curses that she had never heard before. Unaffected, Annaleah stood her ground, still enveloped with the Holy fire of burning love.

As Satanael screamed and rolled on the ground in torment, a great bolt of lightning tore across the sky, followed by a resounding clap of thunder. Looking up, Annaleah saw that a host of Ophanim had ridden on the lightning bolt and were descending from the heavens, each holding a great and heavy length of chain blessed by the Goddess Herself.

Unable to put out the flames, Satanael's cries of pain turned again to that of hatred and anger. He stood, prepared to retreat into the gaping maw of the earth from which he had come. When he reached its entrance, the Ophanim blocked his entry, spreading out their enormous wings to bar his way. Infuriated, Satanael screamed profanities and lunacies and tried to force himself through the Ophanim. Annaleah watched as they threw their chains around him, binding him within their lengths.

"Satanael," a voice Annaleah did not recognize spoke, "for crimes innumerable against the Goddess and all of mankind, you are hereby sentenced to serve a thousand years chained to the bottom of the Euphrates river." After this simple statement, the host of Ophanim pulled the chains, eliciting another cry of rage and pain from their prisoner. Annaleah watched the great gouge in the earth begin to seal itself, taking with it the stench of sin and sulfur as they ascended into the sky, Satanael still ablaze with the light of pure love.

With the terrible hole gone, and Satanael banished with the ascending Ophanim, Annaleah, her body still inflamed, looked for her friends. They walked toward her, swords abandoned now that victory had been achieved. In their eyes she saw a weary myriad of heavy emotions. A fresh wave of flames washed over her, and flickered their light into the darkness. These Holy flames summoned forth the ones who had been hiding, waiting for the chance to come to her for redemption.

It was finally time to redeem the Fallen.

Chapter Forty

Redemption

From all around her they came, some creeping out of the shadows while others manifested themselves out of thin air. Still others came on wing, landing softly upon the damaged earth. Annaleah's fire had gained in strength, its golden light shining out several feet from her luminous body, dancing and flickering in a glorious light show. Though many of the Fallen were coming, they all stood at the edge of the light, seeming hesitant and unsure of how to proceed.

"Do not fear me, nor the love which will redeem you to your rightful places in the Heavens. Come to me, and know the Goddess once more." Annaleah's voice rang through the clearing, and calmed the troubled hearts of those who had forsaken themselves.

The first Fallen, her head down in both respect and shame, approached Annaleah. Her silver eyes glistened with tears as she moved toward the Otherling. One wing was folded against her back, while the other was held out at an angle, bleeding, clearly broken in the battle. Red clay and blood dirtied her otherwise beautiful robes. Her long brown hair clung to her face in places, held there with dried blood and tears.

"I stand before you, Otherling whose name is Annaleah, and before the Goddess Herself," the Fallen said. "I wish to confess my sin of siding with those who fought against the Goddess during the Original Fall. All these countless years I've held onto the fact that I never fought on the side of the Dark Ones in wars against the Light. My heart is full of suffering, but has never been open to the darkness of true evil. With all my being, I repent and ask for redemption." After she had spoken, the Fallen closed her eyes, waiting on the response of the Otherling.

Annaleah held out her hand to the Fallen before her, and said, "Vassaga, Fallen angel of the Heavens, your repentance has been accepted. Stand with me in the light and love of the Goddess and be redeemed." As the Fallen angel took Annaleah's hand, the fire that enveloped the Otherling leapt onto the Fallen, encasing her form with the brilliant fire. It consumed her and healed her, the broken wing stopped bleeding and straightened. Now, held out against the sky, the full span of both her wings glistened with the same powerful fire that shone from Annaleah.

As the light grew in both intensity and size, the ground under Annaleah's and Vassaga's feet began to change. The light touched the ground where it had been scarred and torn, and healed the terror it had undergone in battle. The great gouges inflicted in the soil sealed over, hiding the angelic and demonic blood that had spilled onto it once and for all. Emerald green grass sprouted forth from the dirt and beautiful flowers bloomed within the leafy blades in a myriad of vivid colors. The flowers, with their blossoms, hid the stench of war and death with a sweetly enticing perfume. The night was now alive with the transformation of the clearing back into the Holy site it had once been.

The light continued to radiate in beautiful, undulating waves from Annaleah, flowing over and encompassing the Fallen angel Vassaga. Annaleah, acting as a conduit for the Goddess' love, channeled the memory of Vassaga's creation to her, sending with the vision the emotions laden therein. Both Annaleah and Vassaga witnessed the moment the Goddess had formed love and light into the angel that became Vassaga. Together, they saw the look of raptured concentration as the Creator sculpted light into wings, hair, eyes, and a face. When the form pleased her, the Goddess blew a breath through the being's nose, and life burst forth from the angel. The newly born Vassaga, after taking her first breath, began to sing an impassioned hymn to the Goddess. As the vision of the birth took place, all sin was removed from the Fallen, and she was born again in the Light clean and whole, all wrongdoing forgiven.

Annaleah knew that Vassaga was finally ready for her reunion with the Goddess as Vassaga withdrew her blazing hand from Annaleah's. Vassaga, beating her wings against the deep cobalt of the sky, rose into the Heavens, spiraling upwards, singing in Enochian of her love for the Goddess, and how she awaited the euphoria of finally seeing Her face again.

Annaleah could feel the communal courage and hope that surged through the Fallen at seeing one of their own redeemed. It was a joyous thrumming that permeated the air and reverberated their sentiments in her heart.

They all tried to come towards her at once. Annaleah knew that in Her infinite wisdom, the Goddess had prepared for the onslaught of the Fallen all converging towards her. Each was met in their own private clearing in the woods, having their own sacred and private audience with the Goddess and Annaleah. Though many gathered around her at once, it seemed effortless to hear their claims and purge them of their long held sins. As each Fallen came close enough to be touched by the radiance of the Holy fire, Annaleah could feel the power of the Goddess helping her to guide each one out of the shadows that had lingered in their souls. She had always loved and trusted the creator, but she was left all but breathless by the beautiful way in which the Goddess came to meet each of her now redeemed children. That was the omnipresent glory and power of the Goddess, to be able to address each one privately and personally, all at once.

From all around the clearing, thousands upon thousands of multi colored lights rose into the sky and ascended until their brilliance could be seen no more.

Michael turned to Marchosias, placing his hand on her shoulder. "Why don't you join them, Marchosias? I know the Goddess will be overjoyed to see you in the Heavens again. She has spoken of you with a great fondness and aching in her spirit."

Marchosias nodded. "Yes," she said, smiling. "I think it is time to go home. See you there." She brought two fingertips to her forehead, and gave her friends a parting salute before walking towards the convergence of the Fallen. It wasn't long before she too, rose into the sky in a swirling of protean, shimmering light.

Annaleah smiled at her friends, feeling their eyes upon her as she moved through the throng of Fallen that had finally grown thinner. The ascending lights of the redeemed were fewer and fewer in the sky. When the last lingering lights could no longer be seen, Gabriel, Seraphael and Michael made their way across the clearing to her.

Smiling serenely, Annaleah felt a glow in her soul that was full of a gentle, yet beautifully powerful love and peace. The luminescence and adoration of the Goddess blazed within her, making her feel all the more beautiful.

"The Illuminare are coming," she said simply, a peaceful smile on her lips. As soon as she spoke this, several forms made their way into the clearing. They were darker than the night that surrounded them and appeared to be made of condensed shadows so deep and dark that no light from outside would shine through their solid forms. Within this impenetrable darkness, sparked bolts of light like powerful lightning and sporadic flashing arcs of illumination, as though fireflies were alive within them. They held the shape of angels, but did not move like them. Instead, they flowed with ethereal, ghost like grace, seeming to have no feet. One glided around Annaleah, circling around her and then ascending into the sky before descending again and making its way to her once more. They seemed to be dancing almost, a strange ballet of mysterious spiritual importance.

Annaleah, still inflamed with the spirit of the Goddess, opened her arms in welcome to the enigmatic Illuminare. In return, their dance slowed, and several glided over the ground and hovered before her. The nearest reached its hand inside its chest, not stopping until most of the arm had disappeared inside its inky depths. A few seconds later it withdrew its arm, and within its hand it held an earthen pot the size of a large human fist. This it handed to Annaleah. Annaleah took it with great reverence. Many more Illuminare followed suit, placing their sacred vessels at her feet before withdrawing a few meters away.

"I speak to the sparks of life within these pots," Annaleah said, her voice soft with gentility and full of the power of creation. "I speak to the last breaths of life captured by the sacred Illuminare. To the angels who fought for the Light and gave the ultimate sacrifice, I speak to you. All is not lost, for nothing ever truly dies. For all you have done, I thank you. For the pain, for the battle you so bravely fought, I thank you. For waiting endlessly within these earthen pots for the time that you might once again have a form and ascend to your home in the Heavens, I thank you. With the supreme blessing of the Mother of All That Is, the holy and pure Goddess of creation, I summon you forth, back into the forms which you knew when you were angels."

At once, the lids over the sacred pots lifted up as if on their own, a deep indigo light radiating from inside each vessel. Throwing back her head and closing her eyes, Annaleah opened her arms wide. From the center of her body a mighty pulse of illumination burst forth, a powerful luminescent surge that pulsed a full 360 degrees around her in a circle of pure, radiant light. As the pulse mixed with the indigo light within each vessel, the light within the pots transformed into the forms of the angels that had breathed their last breath of life into the waiting hands of the Illuminare. As they stretched their wings against the horizon, a melodic chanting filled the air. Before taking off to the Heavens, thousands of angels filled the first breath of their lungs with a song of loving gratitude. Many a wing opened and closed to mark cadence with the holy hymn they sang, white feathers floating across the sky and dancing on the wind.

It was a hymn of love and the utmost devotion, in the native Enochian tongue of the angels. Annaleah found herself joining in, somehow knowing intuitively the words they sang. She was moved to tears by the outpouring of love all around her. The air seemed to vibrate with poignancy, as though it too, was trying to chant this holy hymn of devotion.

As the newly reborn angels of Light stood together in the open field chanting, Annaleah turned to her friends. "Will you please accompany them back to their places in Heaven? The Goddess is very pleased with you and has requested an audience with each of you."

Smiling and nodding their consent, Annaleah watched as the three angels prepared to take flight. She caught Seraphael's arm before he could leave her. "Not you," she said breathily, her lids lowered. "I have other plans for you."

As Michael and Gabriel arose into the sky, Seraphael took Annaleah in his arms, relishing the feel of her soft skin against his own.

Other plans indeed, he thought smiling broadly.

Chapter Forty-One

At Last

Sebastian and Annaleah, after returning to their human forms, arrived together at the Professor's quarters. She was still glistening with the afterglow of having channeled the Goddess, and Sebastian couldn't keep his newly indigo eyes off of her. As they approached his door, he paused to reach out slowly and stroke her hair. Soft golden light began to glow where he touched her, her tresses illuminating his slender fingers.

"You are so gloriously beautiful, Annaleah," he purred, his voice low and thick with desire. She smiled at him, a rose tint rising in her cheeks. When she looked at him, her heart felt as though it were beating starlight instead of blood, warming her chest with the intensity of passions flowing therein.

"You know Professor," Annaleah teased, smiling coyly. "The last time I came here it wasn't such a pleasant situation for me."

"Well then," he said, twisting the key in the lock and opening the door wide, "let me make it up to you." He put his arms around her waist and swept her into his arms, carrying her into his chambers. Annaleah briefly saw the sitting room where she had conversed with him not so long ago, and felt a residual chill crawl its way up her spine. If Sebastian had felt her shiver, he made no mention of it. He carried her through the sitting room and through the door to his bedroom. Long scarlet curtains hung over the windows, a beautiful contrast to the walls covered in black and silver scrolled wallpaper. She had a few seconds to take in the ebony of the velveteen blanket on his bed before she was gently placed on top of it.

Sebastian began to speak to her in the Enochian tongue, which strangely, like the hymn sung by the revived angels in the clearing, she found herself easily able to understand. The words felt as if they were pouring themselves over her, captivating her with enticing, hypnotic pleasure. As he touched her intimately with his words, her skin felt as if it were inflamed, burning her with sweet sensuality. It was his hymn to her. His voice low and enticing, his accent quickening her heart as it mixed with the words he spoke to form a ballad of magnetic allure.

"Aai biab blior aao daphaht amma. Aoivea alar aalo adoian chirlan dooaip dosig. Emna eors eophan eol."

The language of the angels dripped like enchanted honey from his lips, seducing her body, mind and soul. After each word was spoken, Annaleah translated to herself the meaning of them, speaking them aloud softly in English. Hearing them again in her native tongue sent waves of entranced bliss throughout her body, igniting her spirit with burning passion.

"You are my comfort amongst the unspeakable and the cursed," she said breathily, "The stars that have settled in thy face rejoiceth in the name of this night. Here in this bed, a thousand lamentations I shall make you."

He continued in the eloquent tongue, arcs of light flashing underneath both of their skins. He sat on the bed beside her, tracing the space between her parted lips with the pad of this index finger. She closed her eyes and took the tip of his finger gently into her mouth for a brief moment. When she released his finger, he continued to trace the lines of her flesh; her cheeks, her jawline, her throat.

"No love has been born in any heart greater than that which lives in mine," she continued, her voice low. As Sebastian was about to continue seducing her with his Encocian words, she opened her eyes and looked at him with urgent longing.

"Oh Sebastian, shut up and kiss me already!" she said, not able to wait a moment longer.

Sebastian sensed her need and obeyed. He leaned slowly towards her, his midnight black hair trailing over her cheek as he relished the look of desire in her eyes.

When Sebastian pressed his lips to Annaleah's, everything around him ceased to exist. All that was real was his mouth hot and moist against hers, sending him into waves of ecstatic bliss. All pretense of composure was gone as he knew they had both lost themselves fully to the fervor that consumed them. As they fell into each other's arms, the light of their pure love sent arcs of radiance throughout their bodies, which leapt from one to the other, joining them in spirit as one.

When their bodies finally met and made them one being in body, mind and soul, the arcs of light flashing within them burst into flames inside them, setting them both on fire with the holy purity of Heaven blessed love. Here and there the flames flared like lightning, curving through the air and crackling with power. One such bolt even knocked over a vase of columbines on Sebastian's dresser, though he barely noticed.

After their passions were spent, Sebastian lay in his bed, the afterglow of their lovemaking washing peacefully over him. Holding Annaleah in his arms, listening to her breathing, he was truly, deeply happy for the first time he could recall. Though he had been on this earth for centuries, he had not really lived until he had met the woman who had now fallen into a peaceful sleep against him. He had been empty without even being aware of it, hardening his heart against anything that might have given him pleasure or comfort. She had been worth waiting for and every one of his troubles seemed insubstantial when compared to the peace and meaning she brought with her into his life.

Sebastian, elated and happily exhausted, leaned forward and kissed her gently on the forehead before settling back down next to her. Though he was countless centuries old, he knew, because of her, his life had only just begun.

Epilogue

Several months later

Uncle John sat at the kitchen table talking animatedly with Rachael and Seth. Annaleah watched contentedly as they poured through wedding books and bridal magazines, oohing over a particularly glamorous gown and discussing the best wedding colors to bring out the emerald of Annaleah's eyes. She had decided to let them make most of the plans and wedding preparations, as her wedding gift to them, only allowing for herself the final say in the choice of the gown.

Annaleah smiled, her heart full and content watching her loved ones prepare for the day she would walk down the aisle to become Sebastian's wife. Her mind wandered as she looked upon the happy face of her uncle. Seeing Uncle John so happy and healthy never ceased to make her heart overflow with gratitude. The glow of life that flowed through him now was something she had missed dearly these last few years of his illness. Watching him happily describe his version of the perfect wedding was almost enough to make her challenge her memories of him ever being ill at all. Almost.

As her love for Uncle John warmed her heart with gratitude that he was alive and well enough to enjoy this day with her, her thoughts went back to the day he had returned home from the hospital. She smiled as the memory made her heart grow warmer still.

In her mind's eye, she saw his green eyes wide with astonishment as he confided to her that he had seen an angel who had looked just like her. Though he had no clear recollection of the demon that had tried to kill him, the dream he'd had while he was near death was still vivid in his mind.

"I was in a very dark place. I didn't know which way to turn," he had confided to her, his eyes wide and gleaming with the memory as he recalled his dream. "I was frightened, cold and in pain. I wondered if I was dying, and if so, what my fate was going to be. I began to pray. Then, there the angel was, wearing your face to comfort me. She glowed with a radiant golden light, holding her arms wide to me, her wings open to the sky as if to block out the darkness, pain and fear. She told me not to be afraid, and to come to her. When I embraced her, I felt her light flowing through me. Every part of me was bathed in it, every cell illuminated."

He paused to remove his glasses and wipe at his eyes as he shared his experience with Annaleah. "I could feel my wounds healing from whatever it was that had attacked me. The warm waves of light purified me. I felt love like I have never felt. I knew that it was this beautiful, pure love that healed me. I knew that when I regained consciousness again, I was going to be healed of cancer too." His eyes looked dreamy and far away as he spoke, his voice trembling. "I was diagnosed with cancer so long ago, and I had been fighting it for so long, but I knew in that moment, every cell of sickness in me had been healed. I felt the love destroy it. I felt an inner wisdom telling me that I was meant to live. I was so happy, so grateful." He looked upwards, towards the heavens, his eyes sparkling as he recalled the experience. "I have never known such peace and joy." His eyes gained a little more focus and he went on. "I have faith now, stronger than any faith I have ever known. Seeing this angel was one of the most real things I have ever experienced, even if it was a dream. And Annaleah," he looked her in the eye, his eyes glowing the tell-tale green that only happened when he cried or was overcome with the intensity of his emotions. "I believe your mother now. I don't think I would have been visited by an angel had she not known angels herself. I think she was a blessed woman who few understood. I am lucky to have had her as a sister. I am further blessed to have you as a niece."

Annaleah had come close to telling Uncle John everything then; to explaining that it was indeed her who had come to him and healed his wounds, erasing his cancer with the light of her love. She held him instead, a gentle voice telling her that some things were best left unsaid and some mysteries were more magical if they retained their wonder.

A knock at the door brought Annaleah back to the present moment. She rose to welcome Sebastian, who was smiling happily. Rachael looked up from turning pages in a bridal magazine, her eyes twinkling.

"I swear, you still blush every time you see him, Annaleah," Rachael teased. Annaleah's blush deepened. Seeing Sebastian made her recall the wonderful things they had experienced together in his bedroom the night before, but she wasn't about to tell her maid of honor that was why she was blushing.

"I cherish that flush of color," Sebastian said, putting his arm around her waist and kissing her on the cheek. He bent to whisper in her ear. "I know why you are blushing." He smiled when the heat in her cheeks deepened even further.

After regaining her composure, Annaleah saw her friends were all staring at her with huge smiles plastered on their faces.

"If ever there was a match made in Heaven," Uncle John said, his green eyes crinkled at the corners, "Then I believe you two must be it."

As Annaleah and Sebastian made their way out the door for another romantic evening, she was almost certain they were thinking the same thing.

"If only you knew the half of it," she heard Seth say as he reached over and grabbed Rachael's hand.

After the door closed behind them, Sebastian looked at her, and Annaleah saw true happiness in his expression.

"If only indeed," she said, and kissed him with the promise of more passion to come.

The End

About the author

Heather lives in LaGrange, Georgia, with her husband, Billy, and her daughter, Makaylah, along with their four cats. Raised in a military family, Heather has been to most of the 48 continental states, as well as having lived for a brief time in Bloxham, England.

Heather is an avid crafter, with a passion for painting glass to resemble stained glass, and a knack for making jewelry. Her passion remains in writing, with Makaylah always helping her to come up with ideas.

Coming soon from Heather M. Walker

The Reclaiming of Charlotte Moss

Black Velvet Seductions

Latest titles from Black Velvet Seductions

Their Lady Gloriana by Starla Kaye
Cowboys in Charge by Starla Kaye
Holly's Big Bad Santa by Starla Kaye
Her Cowboy's Way by Starla Kaye
The Love She Wants by Mila Winters
Punished by Richard Savage, Nadia Nautalia & Starla Kaye
Accidental Affair by Leslie McKelvey
Right Place, Right Time by Leslie McKelvey
Her Sister's Keeper by Leslie McKelvey
Playing for Keeps by Glenda Horsfall
Playing By His Rules by Glenda Horsfall
Sympathy Dance by Sue McConnell
The White Spider of Savignac by V. L. Smith
The Stir of Echo by Susan Gabriel
Rally Fever by Crea Jones
Behind The Clouds by Jan Selbourne
Trusting Love Again by Starla Kaye
Runaway Heart by Leslie McKelvey
First Submission - Anthology

See more of our titles at
www.blackvelvetseductions.com

Our titles are available from:
Amazon
Smashwords
LuLu
Nook
and other retailers

Find Black Velvet Seductions on Facebook
And follow BVS Books on Twitter